TERROR SCRIBES

T0315682

EDITED BY
ADAM LOWE
&
CHRIS KELSO

Published by
Dog Horn Publishing
45 Monk Ings, Birstall, Batley WF17 9HU
United Kingdom
doghornpublishing.com

Edited by
Adam Lowe
& Chris Kelso

with help from
The Terror Scribes community

Typesetting by
Adam Lowe

Cover by
Marianna Stelmach
vuzel.deviantart.com

UK Distribution: **Central Books**
99 Wallis Road, London, E9 5LN, United Kingdom
orders@centralbooks.com
Phone:+44 (0) 845 458 9911
Fax: +44 (0) 845 458 9912

Overseas (Non-UK) Distribution: **Lulu Press, Inc**
3101 Hillsborough Street
Raleigh, NC 27607
Phone # +1 919 459 5858
Fax # +1 919 459 5867
purchaseorder@lulu.com

TERROR
SCRIBES

INTRODUCTION

from Adam Lowe

My own forays into horror have been patchy. I've always written work that could be considered transgressive and gory. I used to write a lot of horror, in fact. But I've always felt most comfortable flitting between the genres like a cyborg butterfly with a mouth full of narcotic offal.

I attended my first Terror Scribes meeting in 2009. At the time, my novella *Troglodyte Rose* had just been published by a local publisher of young writers: Cadaverine Publications. It certainly had horrific elements. It was inspired by film noir, cyberpunk, B-movies, the kind of science fiction-horror of *Alien*, and lots of roleplaying games (although whereas my friends always preferred *Vampire: The Masquerade* and *Mage: The Ascension*, I always preferred *Wraith: The Oblivion* and *Kult*). I've always been fascinated, I guess, by the intersections between the grotesque and the beautiful. The aesthetics of horror, you might say. Clive Barker's sado-masochistic horror in *Hellraiser* appeals to me, for example, with its chains and leather and beautifully disgusting angels of wrath.

The monstrous has always fascinated me. I like to confront the terrifying. But still, I was scared about that initial meeting in Bradford. I had never been in a room with that many horror writers before. How monstrous would they be? Would they snarl and bite? Would they carry skulls and write with quills? Would they sign their autographs in blood?

I anticipated nerves (an unrealistic fear, those who know me might say), and wondered whether I would be welcomed into this circle of writers. I wondered if there would be room at the table.

And there was.

What I remember from that first meeting was how laidback it all was. There was no hierarchy. This clearly wasn't a society or an association. It certainly wasn't a guild or a union either. It was just a gathering of friends—some of them old friends, and some of them, like me, new.

Sometime later, Sue Phillips indicated she wanted to step away from her role as group admin for the online hub of the Terror Scribes on Facebook. Something of a social media whore myself, and never a man to say no, I enthusiastically jumped at the challenge. This, as my friends will tell you, is one of my most endearing traits. It is also, I'm well aware, my biggest weakness. Because no sooner had I been promoted to an admin on the group than I suggested I compile a Terror Scribes anthology. Forget that I also had to finish my own novel (the full-length version of that same novella I carried with me those three years ago in Bradford), that I am co-writing another, that I *still* haven't finished my gore-fest musical *Nero High School Slaughterhouse*, and that I also had a publishing schedule so packed I'd been working pretty much every day since 2008 . . . No, I was excited. I wanted to publish a Terror Scribes book. I wanted to see all these wonderful writers of the grim and macabre in all their perfect bound glory. And then, you see, we'd have an excuse to throw a party. (Parties being another thing I'm famous for that also occasionally manifest as a flaw.)

Then there came another suggestion: perhaps we could bring the book to Alt.Fiction for a 'soft launch'? Well, I mean, I do like a challenge after all. And I wanted an excuse to party, didn't I? Didn't I? All I needed was a co-editor as young and eager as I was. In stepped Chris Kelso, and the race began.

So it was that I battled the gnashing hordes of the Impending Deadline Army, and slogged away through the dead of the night. So it was that I became estranged to my friends and howled insults at the computer monitor as InDesign CS3 thwarted my evil plans. So it was that I made lots of semi-hysterical posts on Facebook, fully expecting my own collapse from exhaustion and madness. And yet, to those who bore witness to this spectacle (which is, I'm afraid, a pretty regular thing whenever a deadline approaches), one thing was clear: I loved it. Perhaps I'm a masochist. Perhaps that's the real reason I'm drawn to the horrific. But whatever. I have. I've enjoyed every moment of exquisite suffering to put together this book in what was an amazingly compressed period of time.

So here it is. Hopefully in time for Alt.Fiction. And what delights me most is that I get to re-read all these deliciously dark confections again. At my own leisure. Without any deadlines. And now, so can you!

from Chris Kelso

There are many imitations of horror—some are as subtle as a smudge of mustard on a Jackson Pollock painting, others tear through your entire system like a derailed coal cart—but no one permutation is more effective than the other.

Compiling *Terror Scribes* provided me with the unique opportunity to offer a home to some of the best horror exponents from around Europe and North America. Along with my mercurial editorial confederate, Adam Lowe, we were faced with the unenviable task of whittling submissions down to a select few, on the kind of tight deadline that Adam seems to relish but that anyone else thinks is lunacy.

I think the results have cumulated into a satisfying collection, furnished with nebulous, original tales guaranteed to set your teeth on edge and give you bouts of gooseflesh. From the home-grown talent of Sue Phillips to prolific US gore-hound Deb Hoag, from the satirists to the psychopaths to the traditionalists, everyone is well represented. We received some excellent stories from long-time Terror Scribes members, alongside some dazzling contributions from the newer members—and let's not forget our downright peculiar compatriots from across the pond, who were invited to bring just a little bit of bizarro anarchy to the order!

We are not oblivious to the fear *Terror Scribes* will evoke. Quite the contrary, we're advocates of it . . .

TABLE OF CONTENTS

WELCOME TO THE JUNGLE
by John Palisano

Michelle remembered the black business card and had a vision that it would be her way out of obscurity. "Always follow your gut," she said. She never got in trouble whenever she listened to her instincts.

She'd woken up after another anonymous day as an extra more tired than she'd felt in her entire life. Even her coffee didn't seem to do much to rouse her. She thought about calling Pam and telling her how it went. They'd both moved out to L.A. within weeks of getting out of Palmville, Texas High School. Pam settled in with a good casting company while Michelle beat the boards pursuing an acting career. She went on the occasional audition, but she never landed anything: another blonde in a sea of blondes. How would she ever stand out?

She grabbed the business card and looked it over. *Dusty Palace. Jungle Productions.* There was a snake-like drawing at the bottom. He'd introduced himself the night before at the Frolic Room, her favorite neighborhood bar. He'd directed two movies she'd actually heard of, *The Longfellow* and *Hounds Of Hell*. After he left, the bartender, Mike, told her he thought the guy was sleazy. *Aren't they all?* she thought. At least she could call him . . . find out what he was about. So what if it was straight to home video? So what if she had to be in a horror movie? She didn't mind. Whatever the project, at least she might be seen in something that had distribution. She certainly didn't want to pantomime to invisible dance music for fourteen hours a day for the rest of her life.

She looked him up on the net. Everything he said checked out—his company website, his IMDB credits. He was legitimate. "Wow," she said. "This could actually be something."

"So glad you called." Dusty talked warm and slow.

"I just wanted to find out a little bit more about the shoot next week. I mean, what's it pay? How long will you need me for? That sort of thing?" Michelle asked.

He laughed a little. "Now you sound like an actress."

"Well, I came here to act," she said. "Otherwise it's not really worth it to me to be here. I mean, I can make more at an office job back home in Texas, and work a lot less hours. It's not like I'll ever be seen doing extra work, anyway."

"I hear you," he said. "Well, look, I can't offer up too much more than two grand for the day without seeing how you act. I'm sure you'd be good enough for one of the girls in the dungeon scene, though."

"Okay. That sounds better."

"Are you good at being scared? Are you okay with nudity? Being topless? Can you scream?"

There it was. She heard Pam's voice in her head telling her not to call him. Fine. She'd test him. "I'm great at being scared. Honestly? The other stuff? Not really. I'm not sure I want to go there just yet."

"Fair enough," he said. "I've got other girls for that, but you did say that you're okay with being scared, maybe dying onscreen, maybe a love scene, right?"

"Sure! What's a little blood and screaming?" she asked.

"Right. Well, look, we're going to do that scene in two days. Here's the deal . . . "

"Are you nuts?" Pam asked. "You shouldn't be doing sleaze like that. Just stick with the extra work. It'll begin to pay off. Everyone in the industry has long hours. It's a given: The extras, the PAs, the entire crew. Heck, even those of us in the office, we all work long days. I even have to read scripts on the weekends a lot of the time."

"He's offering two grand for one day."

The line was silent.

"Really?"

"Yes."

"Get it up front."

"He's paying me as soon as I get there," Michelle said as she paced her studio. "That's rent and food for an entire month. And I don't have to wait three weeks for the check, either."

"Take it. Just be careful."

Sun Valley felt like an entirely different state. There were farms and horses. Houses spread out more. It reminded her of some of the border towns she'd grown up with in Texas, so she felt immediately at home. She thought, *this is going to be great. This was a good move.* Her little Toyota Yaris pulled onto the side of the road and she patted her GPS. *Best invention ever*, she thought.

The house was larger than she expected. She saw cars lined up and down the street. She wondered where the crew vans were parked? She hadn't seen any. Where was Craft Services? Were the actors being held inside? She saw none of it and just assumed they were in another location. *Ah, so this is what indie film is like*, she thought while she proceeded to the front door. *This feels really small.*

A handmade sign taped to the door read: WELCOME TO THE JUNGLE. The bottom had the same snake logo as Dusty's card. "Cute," Michelle said.

There was a lavender bush growing right next to the door and its smell mixed in with that of stables and horses. It reminded her so much of Texas that she shut her eyes for a moment and imagined she was home again, right on her Daddy's front porch.

The door knob rustled and she got her composure. Then she put on her bravest smile. Again, her stomach was in knots from the nerves. One day, she knew, it would all be familiar to her and she'd walk right into these situations as easy as iced tea.

Of course, it was Dusty who had opened the door. "Michelle!" he said. "My Michelle! Welcome to our little place in paradise city."

The cottage seemed perfectly interior designed with all sorts of traditional southwestern themes. The walls were painted sandy with Aztec blue accents. Every surface looked fussed over. There were people sitting on the couches. One was reading a script. The others joked and laughed.

"You have perfect timing. We need to get you changed and down to set."

"Down?"

"The basement."

"Oh, right. I just don't see where this place would have a basement."

13

"That's why we chose it. It's rare in L.A. to find a house with any kind of basement."

Michelle met Rebecca, the wardrobe person. She had Michelle keep her jeans, but changed into a white blouse. "The blood will show up better," she said. They both laughed.

"Speaking of that? Where's all the crew trucks and stuff?" Michelle asked.

"These low budgets . . . we have to carry everything in our trunks," Rebecca said. "Craft services is pizza. Dressing rooms are bathrooms. You get the idea. I'm doing lights, too, by the way."

"It's already a lot more fun than the other set I was on this week," Michelle said.

"Let's make it even better." Dusty reached into his pocket and gave her an envelope. She looked inside: Twenty hundred-dollar bills. It was impossible for her not to grin ear to ear.

The basement was hot and unfinished, so one could see the exposed rock walls. The floor wasn't much more than a layer of sandy dirt. There was a naked woman chained to the wall. She didn't look up or respond when Michelle and Dusty entered.

"What's the name of this movie?" Michelle asked. "I forgot to ask."

Dusty frowned. "*Appetite*," he said. "Some poor fellow, played by me by the way, has a monster chained up in his basement and he has to feed it live kill every few days to keep it happy, or else."

He gestured to a huge mound about as high as their shoulders on the far side of the basement. It looked like a giant red crab coiled in on itself. Each of its claws had a shiny dagger affixed.

"That's our special effect," Dusty said and laughed.

"It looks real." Michelle said, stuttering. In fact, it looked very real. There was something about it . . . a presence that touched her instinct. Something about it just wasn't right. She thought that maybe it was a giant puppet, but she couldn't see any wires coming out the back. Maybe there was a guy inside to puppeteer it.

Dusty waved a hand under his nose. "It stinks in here something fierce," he said. "We better hurry up and shoot this sucker."

Dusty picked up a handheld video camera off the washer and

dryer unit. "That's what we're shooting on?" Michelle asked. Rebecca the wardrobe girl, and grip, apparently, walked closer to the naked woman. There was another set of cuffs hanging near her.

"You can shoot Hi Def with this thing. It's better than what George Lucas used on *Star Wars*. If it's good enough for George, it's good enough for me."

Michelle was beginning to rethink having called him. Was she just in some terrible exploitation movie? Was this a mistake after all? Maybe she should have listened to Pam. Still, two thousand bucks to be scared of a giant crab monster is still two thousand bucks, she knew, and it'd get distribution.

"We just need you to put your hands up in these cuffs," Rebecca said. "Then we can shoot."

Michelle stepped over to the cuffs and turned backward. She raised her hands, smiled, and said. "These are, like, real chains?" She had a nervous pit in her belly, just like when she rode the rollercoaster at the theme parks growing up.

Rebecca cuffed her. "These are actually cheaper than the prop ones. Don't worry: They're perfectly safe."

Dusty opened his camera, turned it on and walked over to Michelle. "Okay, so here's the scene. She's going to get eaten, and all you have to do is scream and act terrified of big old Red over here."

"Okay!" Michelle said. "But once this is over I've got to see how that thing works." She nodded to the giant crab monster.

"Oh, you mean Red?" he asked, then nodded with a smile. "Sometimes a magician shouldn't reveal his secrets, right?"

"I guess," she said.

"I don't want your performance to suffer. I want this to be real."

"Action!" Dusty called.

Red unfolded slowly and gracefully. Michelle thought it looked like a one of those Transformers toys, or like a blooming onion, only more organic. Dusty held the camera rock solid. Red moved, creeping along the basement floor. It'd gotten almost an entire head taller since it unfolded. Four thin arms on each side closed in on the naked girl like two hands coming together.

"Farrah!" Dusty said. "Wake up! Look who's here to see you!

It's Red!"

The naked girl looked up from her daze and saw the monstrous thing in front of her. Then she thrashed in her restraints. "Let me go! Let me out of here! Come on! Please!"

Michelle did her best to keep her face looking as though she were terrified, even though she wasn't. She kept staring at the beast, studying it, recording it in her brain. The craftsmanship, she thought, was outstanding. Who'd need CG when they could make real objects look so life-like?

Farrah screamed. One of Red's hands slashed her across her belly with one of the knives. A curved slit opened and she bled profusely and quickly.

Michelle wondered how they were pulling off the effect. She thought that maybe Farrah had worn a false stomach pre-loaded with blood. Michelle thought they were quite clever. They could make it look like it was all one continuous take, and by using a handheld camera, they could tie into the whole reality TV phenomenon.

Red split in half horizontally. His eyes opened at the sides of his head: Even those seemed super realistic. It reminded Michelle of when she once swam with dolphins . . . she could see the intelligence in their eyes, just as she saw the intelligence in Red's. It was some magical trick.

Then Red opened his mouth, which seemed to take up the entire middle of his body. He had rows and rows of shining metal, shark-tooth-like teeth. Something else struck Michelle as funny: The smell. The air around them filled with the most rotten stench, like a hundred dead teeth, mixed with vinegar and spoiled meat. It came from Red.

She wracked her brain. Maybe they'd made him with animal parts to make him more realistic? No. She knew that wasn't it.

Red advanced toward Farrah and opened his mouth. The bottom jaw unhinged and fell to the floor. Knife-shaped teeth scraped along the dirt floor until they were just under her feet. She whimpered and screamed. "This can't be happening," she said. "No. Please. No."

In a blink, Red jerked forward and swallowed her entire bottom section. Some of the teeth gave her little slices.

Then Red clamped his mouth shut, like a giant shark. Farrah screamed and Michelle screamed, too. It was so real-looking!

16

Please let this be fake, she thought. *Please God let this not be happening.*

Something clicked in Michelle's head. She realized none of it was fake: Not a bit. Farrah's insides drooped from her top half. There was blood everywhere. Her head was slumped and she'd stopped moving. Her skin had gone ashen.

Red chewed on the bottom parts of Farrah. Michelle saw one foot and bit of leg before she turned away. She couldn't take any more. Tears streamed down her face and she shook uncontrollably.

Please let me live through this, she thought. *Please!*

She heard Red chewing for a few moments. *Pretend it's not real. Pretend it's just a big puppet. Don't worry about it. Act!* Then she sensed his warm breath on her. She wouldn't open her eyes . . . she refused to look . . . she refused to do anything other than what she had been hired to do, which was to act scared.

Act scared!

Then the beast's breath was away from her and she heard Dusty. "Here's where I need you most," he said. "Red here wants to copulate with you." He folded the LCD display of the camera down flush, turning it off.

"What? Someone's dead here!"

He smiled. "Is she really dead or is it just a special effect? I'm not telling."

Michelle was speechless. What was he telling her? Was Farrah truly dead? She looked over to the remaining half of the woman. It was too real . . . the smell of the blood was real . . . how could it not be real? She'd seen it in front of her own eyes.

Dusty said. "Come on. You'll be fine. You'll be famous for this. It'll be unforgettable."

Red made a grumpy noise and inched closer.

"Anyone who sees this movie will never be able to forget this scene with you and Red," he said. "What do you say?"

"I . . . don't . . . want to," she said. "I don't do nudity. Is she really dead?"

Dusty got up in her face. "Do you really want to find out if she's dead or not? Why don't you just do the scene, take your money, and go home? I thought you wanted to act! Do whatever you have to do to make this moment happen for me!"

Michelle felt her eyes well up. How could she have gotten

17

herself in such a position? Did Grace Kelly really need to get choked by a telephone cord in order to become famous. "It's not really going to . . . ?"

"We'll just make it look that way. Don't stress." Dusty's voice was very low. "You're just going to have to die in the end."

"Like Farrah?" Michelle felt sick. "I don't want to really die."

Dusty winked. "That's why they call it acting, you know?"

Michelle shut her eyes. *Can I trust him? That thing bit Farrah in half. Who says it won't do the same to me?* Michelle thought.

She said. "Just make it classy, okay?"

He laughed. "Not sure how much class is going to be involved with Red dry-humping you," Dusty said. "But I'll do my best." He unfolded the LCD on his camera and pressed a button. "Here we go. Ready?"

"Okay," she said.

Dusty moved closer toward Michelle. She could see that he had a much longer body than she'd originally seen. For some reason, Red reminded Michelle of a slinky as Red stretched out. He was some kind of horrific snake, she believed, like one of those fabled gigantic anacondas: Only Red was, well, red, and his head was closer to being nothing but mouth, teeth, and the six spindly red, dagger holding arms jutting from the rim of his mouth, three per side.

Dusty moved to her right side and got a different angle. She could almost see what he was shooting on the LCD. She looked at it from the corner of her eye: Michelle didn't want to ruin the shot by looking directly into the lens. The last thing she wanted to do was have to re-shoot the scene.

"Good," he said. "I'm going to be quiet now. I'll move around you two, but just be natural. Remember: pretend you're chained up in this crazy guy's basement and he's trying to feed his pet monster. If he doesn't feed the beast, it will eat him!"

Michelle said. "Okay."

"Okay . . . so . . . " Dusty said. "Action!"

Michelle felt Red's heaviness at her feet as it slowly crept upward. Red put his arms out. The daggers made a perfect halo shape around her face. Michelle instinctively made a whimpering sound. The daggers were so close, so sharp, and so very real. *Those are the same ones that I just watched cut Farrah. This thing could kill me in a blink.*

She shut her eyes for a moment again. Reaching down deep inside to the core of her training, she knew she had to use any acting tool available to her to make it through.

She searched her memories for something that really scared her. *You need to believe that this thing is fake. Then you need to be scared of something else . . . something from your past.*

What scared Michelle more than anything? A memory of a helicopter trip as a young girl flashed inside her mind. She'd been riding in the back with her father. They'd barely lifted off, and the pilot banked them to the right, when her door suddenly swung open. Her father grabbed her with both of his arms, holding her. She'd had on her seatbelt, so her father's reaction was more instinctual than lifesaving, she knew. Michelle, in that moment, looked down onto the river below them, across to the shore side landing area where they'd taken off. She was filled with dread that she was about to slip out and fall to her death. That was the feeling! She played over the helicopter moment in her head again. Her stomach tensed and she felt the exact same numbing fear.

Red slithered up and on top of her. She opened her eyes to find one of his looking right at her. He had to turn his head to his left a bit because his eyes were on the side of his head, like those of a fish. He blinked once.

She knew he was real!

No!

I'm going to fall out! Fall right down to the ground and that's the end of it! That's what I'm scared of happening! Nothing is worse . . . nothing is worse than that!

At her thighs she felt two nubs hardening. She looked down and saw a pair of thumb-shaped organs pushing into her. Thank God she had her clothes on.

It's all pretend. Nothing's real. Simulated.

"Okay, everyone hold on a sec," Dusty said. She looked up at him and saw Rebecca in the background quietly watching the scene. Her face was cold and expressionless.

Dusty went somewhere behind Red where Michelle couldn't see him. He returned a moment later with a plastic jug. "We'll need some blood for this one," he said.

He worked his way to her middle and poured it on her thighs, hips, and belly. It was warm. *That's human blood. From Farrah, or maybe someone else.* She tried to psych herself out of the thought. *No way. The blood's just been sitting in a hot basement for God knows how long. Maybe he just made it on the stove or something. Don't effects people make their own blood by cooking it with Karo syrup and red food coloring? It's cheaper than buying it from the supply shops, especially if you need a lot, right?*

Only problem was the blood smelled like blood, too.

Dusty said. "I'm ready," and grabbed the camera again. "Rolling."

Red's thumb-things massaged her thighs, searching for the place where they dipped downward between her legs. Michelle clamped her thighs together as hard as she could. No way was this thing going to get that close to her.

She sensed Dusty moving his camera down toward Red's thumb-things. Then he started panning the camera upward. She looked down so she wouldn't look directly in his lens again. She just let it happen without trying to force a scared face. Maybe if she kept it simple the scene would be scarier? Wasn't that what she was taught? Don't do anything. That was one of her acting teacher's voices in her head.

Then Dusty panned back down.

The blood had soaked right through her clothes and she felt numbness starting at her hips and going all the way down to her feet. It was what she'd imagined an epidural would be like.

She could still feel the thumb-things working faster and faster, but instead of hurting her, Red's weight was making her tingle. *Probably the blood rushing down from being hanged,* she thought. *There's really just a big special effects monster on top of me. That's all.*

Red moved faster. Dusty moved to the opposite side and panned up and down rapidly.

The thumb-things managed to spread her legs just a little, but not enough to get to any sensitive parts. It seemed to be working harder now that it'd gotten a small break. Michelle writhed on the chains. She wanted the scene over already!

Then the thumb-things managed to get between her legs deeper and Michelle screamed. "No!"

You're going to fall out of the helicopter. That's the only thing that's real. That's the only thing to be scared of. The rest of this is just

Hollywood.

The thumb-things moved quicker: It reminded her of when people would flutter their first and second fingers to simulate walking. It did not feel good at all, especially with the blood starting to dry and stick.

She looked down the length of Red's body and could see small ripples moving up and down his sections. As Red's skin moved, the circular bones stretched through. It was as though he were shivering.

Dusty kept shooting.

Then, as quickly as Red's assault started, it stopped. At least it looked that way for a brief moment. Red's face inched back away from hers. Dusty stepped back to get the whole scene.

Red opened his mouth and Michelle swore he was smiling. He moved his head from side to side, checking her out with one eye and then the other. Michelle wondered what Red was doing.

He slashed at her face with one of the daggers. She felt a hot pain flare across her right cheek, stretching from just under her eye to her chin.

She screamed, despite herself.

Red unleashed a rather giant tongue and rolled the tip. He used the tip to lick the slash he'd made top to bottom.

"No," Michelle said.

Red pulled his tongue back inside his head and shut his mouth.

Michelle looked down and could see she was still bleeding heavily. She felt as though she might pass out. *Is this what happened to Farrah right before he bit her in half? Am I about to die? How can I get out of here?*

Red backed away, slithering off her body. Michelle was relieved not to have his weight on her. She could see the nubs near his bottom, now flaccid and pale. She had an idea.

The nubs.

It had to be!

Even though she could barely feel her legs, she tried moving them. They wiggled. Her brain still worked!

Could she strike him?

No. He was too far away.

Dusty said. "All right. Take two!"

Two? Hadn't he gotten what he needed with one? She'd been cut, for real. How would that edit together? Well, she didn't think continuity would be high on Dusty's priority list in the end.

The nightmare started again, with Red bulking his way toward her.

As soon as his little nubs were close enough, Michelle kicked them.

Red raised in the air with all he had. He lifted up and his back touched the ceiling. It was his turn to scream! His voice was hoarse and deep, like a sick sea lion.

"Shit!" Dusty screamed.

Michelle looked down at his nubs. They were no longer pale, but red, and not from being turned on. Michelle kicked them again. The pitch of Red's scream rose. His eyes rolled back and he shoved his arms up toward the ceiling, where he stuck each dagger deep and into the woodwork.

He cried out again, his eyes locking with Michelle.

This is it, she thought. *He's going to kill me for that move.*

Red dropped back down, his arms whipping out from the ceiling. Chips of wood fell all over. He swung them around and violently punched them into a circle around Michelle. They were sharp enough to stick into the rock.

His mouth opened and she could see the little specks of blood in his drool. Had that been her blood?

Then Red tried to pull his daggers free. He couldn't. He pulled several times, but he was totally stuck.

"Cut!" Dusty said. He hurried up toward Red. "It's enough. Stop this!"

Red kept right on yanking with his arms.

Dusty said. "You're going to hurt yourself!" He looked around the basement. "We'll find a way to get you free."

Michelle felt something at her wrists. She jumped! It was only Rebecca with the key to unlock her. She was so busy staring straight ahead; she hadn't even noticed Rebecca rush up to her. In a moment, Michelle was free. Her legs were so numb and she felt incredibly wobbly without the chains to hold onto.

She ducked and bent, feeling some of the blood had dried to her clothes already. She noticed she was trembling. Her heart was beating fast and her eyes were watering. Overhead, she felt Red's violent jerking ever-so-close.

Standing up on her own, and still only a few feet from Red, Dusty jumped in front of her. "You can't leave! We're not done!"

"I'm done." Michelle pushed past him and made it nearly to the stairs. She hurried. In back of her, she heard Red struggling.

She heard Dusty. "We have to stop her! If she tells anyone . . . she's supposed to die in the end! You shouldn't have let her go!"

Someone grabbed at her shoulder. Michelle spun round and Rebecca cold cocked her. "We're not through! I need this movie for my IMDB credit!"

It barely registered. Maybe because of her adrenaline, or maybe because she'd grown numb, Michelle was able to shake Rebecca's punch right off. She returned the favor.

Rebecca went right down, holding her jaw, and cowered. "Screw your credits!"

Dusty was right behind her. "You!" he yelled.

"Me!"

Red broke free from the ceiling and dropped back to the floor with a hideous howl. His eyelids were slightly drooped. He turned to face Michelle.

She took the moment, with Dusty standing between them, and shoved him toward Red as hard as she could.

Dusty was surprised, said. "Hey!" and fell toward Red.

Then he stopped moving. It took a second for Michelle to realize Dusty's back had met a handful of Red's daggers.

Dusty looked up and choked up some blood. He reached his hand out. "Please," he said.

"No," she said back, and gave him another kick. The daggers went deeper. Michelle looked down and saw Dusty's feet hovering: his entire weight was carried by Red's daggers. Dusty's eyes shut and Michelle turned and ran toward the stairs.

She didn't look back. She heard slicing sounds. She heard moans. She heard Rebecca scream.

Michelle ran up the stairs.

The scene behind her got extremely quiet.

Don't look back.

She made it through the short foyer and right to the front door. She heard some kind of scraping behind her. She grabbed the front door handle and opened it. She hurried outside. Her car wasn't far.

Do I call the cops? Do I go to the Emergency Room? What?

Michelle made it to her car. Her keys were still in her front pocket, and although they were sticky, they worked. She patted her butt and felt the envelope with her cash still intact. *Thank God for small miracles.* As she climbed in, she heard a roar coming from the house.

From behind a curtained window, she saw Red. It'd made it up the stairs! It watched her with one of its eyes. Michelle wondered if Red had killed Dusty and Rebecca, and if they'd come after her. Would Red dare come outside and expose itself? She couldn't know, and wouldn't wait to find out. *Always follow your gut*, she thought. *Gut's telling me to get the hell out of here.*

She did see the sign on the door, the hand-printed one that Dusty had made that read: Welcome To The Jungle.

Michelle couldn't drive away fast enough.

Later, Michelle received a text message from Pam. "How'd the shoot go?"

She replied. "I'm retired."

John Palisano's *journey to horror fiction is a strange one. For a while he toured with with rock bands, while writing songs, poetry and fiction. His first fiction publication was at Emerson College, where a short film was produced from an early foray into scriptwriting. After college he moved to Los Angeles, where he took an internship with Ridley Scott. He learned much, and worked on many big budget films, as well as producing a couple of low-budget films himself. But he found the demands of filmmaking tiring and instead began writing fiction. He discovered that placing his stories with professional magazines was more difficult than financing films, but he continued to write anyway. Many years later, he now faces the impending release of his novel* Nerves *from Bad Moon Books, which is due out in the winter of 2012. In the meantime, he has lots of short stories appearing soon, and several movie projects, too.*

THE THIRD POSSIBILITY
by Sue Phillips

Diina leaned close to her husband who was still deep in slumber. She studied his face, unlined, untroubled despite all that had gone on, and said. "Let me go Freddy." There was no response. She had expected none.

Would she ever feel again? Her chest rose and fell and she knew she was breathing, but nothing touched a single nerve. Freddy murmured softly, words he would not remember when he woke. Holding one hand up she studied the ragged lines that crisscrossed its surface like a livid spider's web, seeming more substantial than the skin they covered. Would they ever heal? She rose from the bed ever conscious of the cord that bound her. It allowed her liberty within the house, but try as she might, she could not get outside. Many times she contemplated breaking it, but it was also her lifeline. Without it she could not survive.

She went into the bathroom, going through the motions of showering and dressing for the day, pulling on the same blue cotton long sleeved shirt and grey skirt she wore every single day. She brushed her hair and put it up the same way she always had, gazing in the mirror but not really seeing, and slipped on those same gleaming black leather shoes before going downstairs to the kitchen to wait for Freddy's alarm to wake him and bring him down for breakfast. Diina sighed, but with no feeling, there could be no satisfaction, no relief.

After an hour or so there was a small commotion upstairs. Freddy was stumbling out of bed and straight into the bathroom. She went back up and watched him shower and shave while the iron heated up. He was almost fanatical about his shirts and had never allowed her to involve herself in either washing or pressing them.

She said. "Why are you keeping me here?" but her words were lost in the hiss of the steaming iron. Her voice was faint nowadays. Before the accident, she had been able to belt out commands with the best of them. When she got the promotion she knew she had made it, but it came at a cost. For all the claims of equality, female warrant officers were rare and there was a point to prove. She had had to harden up a little and had lowered her voice tone to add authority. Whether it worked was debatable, but she had a mighty yell to back it up.

He slid the grey-blue tie under the crisp collar and tied the knot exactly according to regulations. If promotions were awarded on smartness, Freddy would be a group captain by now. The Royal Airforce (never RAF) was already her life when she and Freddy met five years before on a detachment to the Falklands, he too was a career serviceman and there was always an undercurrent of competition between them. She had moved up the ladder faster than him and she knew it rankled, but that was his problem to deal with and she had never concerned herself too much with his feelings on the matter. It wasn't as if they ever worked together and rank was irrelevant once the uniforms came off.

Detachments, usually abbreviated to dets, were a normal part of military life. They tried to volunteer for the same postings where possible, but it sometimes happened that while one was away the other was home. Diina often wondered whether he remained faithful during these times, many did not, but there was an unwritten rule: what happens on det stays on det—nobody asked and nobody told.

He was tying his shoelaces now, neat bows on gleaming black leather, breathing a little heavily with the effort of bending over. Freddy was only as fit as he had to be and his admin role did not require him to do much running around.

"Let me go Freddy." No response.

He ate breakfast with a paper napkin tucked into his neck to catch any spills.

"Can you even hear me?"

He washed up efficiently and fished keys from his pocket to unlock the door, glancing briefly at the photo on the fob, her face, suntanned and smiling, framed by the white pillow she was lying on. She had taken it herself in Afghanistan with her mobile phone shortly after she arrived and sent it to him, eager that he should not forget her while she was away. He had her listed in his contacts as Gina, a simple error, but he never bothered correcting the spelling. An emotion flashed across his face as it did whenever he looked at that picture. Anger, sorrow? She could never tell. Then out he went, locking up behind him leaving her inside, ignored, unreleased.

After Freddy left there was always a period of blankness. Try as she might, Diina could not maintain her presence quite so fully without him and so she drifted vaguely around the place, as securely held as if he had chained her to the wall. At last his shift was over and he returned to change before going out again. Diina continued to ask him to let her go and he continued to ignore her.

Once a fortnight he did a big grocery shop, but bought none of her favourite foods. She preferred coffee, he only bought tea. She enjoyed beef, he opted for chicken. It was as if he did it on purpose. The cupboards contained nothing that she would choose, unless it happened to be his own preference too.

"Why Freddy? Why can't I leave?" She said his name often these days, hoping it might help her gain his attention. "If it hadn't been for the crash I'd be long gone, you know that. I was on my way to Innsworth, you were staying here. It's not as if we didn't try to work it out, but you were always so jealous. As if that wasn't bad enough, you broke the cardinal rule Freddy. What happens on det stays on det, simple enough. How was I supposed to react? Three weeks after my promotion and you're home from Germany touting that bloody Kara around, not even trying to be discreet. It wasn't my fault you haven't made it past corporal, but you did everything you could to humiliate me until I had no choice. When the posting came up, I took my chance to leave you, start afresh.

Was it you who messed with the car? Details of the crash are hazy, but I'm sure I braked. Braked and nothing happened—that's not true, it did—something most definitely happened. They say your life flashes before you when you think you're about to die, but the only thing that flashed in front of my eyes was the bloody lorry as the car slid underneath it doing about eighty. I should have died then.

Comas are funny things you know, some say you can hear what's going on, others say you can't. Nobody mentioned the third possibility. I watched you, watched myself lying there. Saw the nurses come in and out, keeping me clean, changing all those drips, checking my wounds and wondering why they didn't seem to be healing. You knew why, didn't you? Every day, whenever you were alone with me I saw you pulling the edges of the cuts apart. I felt it Freddy, it bloody hurt, you smiled when I groaned, but there was

27

nothing I could do to stop you. Mind and body totally separate, but some things cut through the gap.

How did I never see that cruel streak in you before? Just took it as the everyday barracking that's so much a part of service life, but with you there was more to it. The jokes, the mickey taking, you weren't laughing at that, it was the pain you saw in the eyes of your targets. That's what did it for you. Everyone thinks you're the man now. Stood by your wife even though she was leaving you, even though she was disfigured by those terrible injuries, but you loved it. That photo album on the laptop, full of pictures of my wounds: what would your mates think if they found it? But you keep it secret, even I haven't managed to find out the password and I watch your every move."

Freddy was leaving the house again, now wearing jeans and a polo shirt. Through the window Diina saw him get into his new car—a replacement paid for with her insurance money. As he drove off, he seemed to drag the life from her, leaving her faint. Would he ever release her? What if something happened to him while he was out—a crash... she'd be stuck in this house. Alone.

A key sliding into the lock of the front door heralded the arrival of the agency nurses, a middle aged woman and a girl of around nineteen. Not quite alone then. They did not seem to know each other well, there was a distance between them and the conversation was light, avoiding personal subjects. Diina followed them as they climbed the stairs, the younger woman hanging back to keep pace with her colleague. She paused at the first door, her hand resting on the handle.

"Have you been here before Esme?"

The older woman shook her head. "No, but I've heard it's a bit . . . "

"Not just a bit. Look, we'll be in and out, just get her done and away. Don't look too hard, I've had people throw up just at the sight, and it's a right pain to clear up. Hold your breath, we do the necessaries and mark it down on the sheet."

Esme squared her shoulders and her mouth tightened. She caught her companion's eye. "Right, well, thanks for the warning Jen. I'm ready. Sooner we go in, the sooner we'll be out."

Jen pushed the door open and they whisked into the room. She picked up a pink folder from the bedside table and ticked half a dozen boxes on the top page, adding the date and glancing at Esme. "I always do the paperwork first, means I can get out quicker. Right, quick once over with the wash wipes and check her pulse, temperature and blood pressure, change the drips and make sure they're running properly."

Esme was staring at the occupant of the narrow hospital style bed and Diina had that strange jolt she always got when she looked at her physical body. Pitifully thin, face so badly crushed it bore no resemblance to the photo on Freddy's key fob, and almost every inch of skin etched in red lines, only breathing because it was connected to a ventilator. The cord was short now. It always maintained a straight line between body and spirit, slipping through solid objects as if they were mist.

"Oh the poor thing! But I thought you said she was in a coma?"

Diina could understand the woman's perplexity. Her body was writhing and twitching as if locked in some terrible dream. Should she slip inside and try to take advantage of the activity? She knew she was kidding herself. The movements were involuntary and, according to what she'd heard from others caring for her, not uncommon in such cases. What was left of her brain could not support conscious thought, only this continual movement. If she once slipped back inside, she could be stuck. Her prison would shrink from the house to a small, wrecked body. A living corpse.

"Makes you wonder why he didn't just leave her in the hospital," said Jen. "I mean, he doesn't exactly bother much with her. Look at those sheets—doubt if they've been changed this side of last month."

"Can't we do it for her? Seems criminal leaving her in that state."

"Yes if you want to lose your job for time wasting." As she spoke, Jen was taking Diina's body's temperature and blood pressure, marking the measurements down in the pink folder. "Best we can do is give her a wash and put her in a fresh nightie. That's all we're paid for and times running on. Let's get to it."

"But if she gets an infection, won't we get the blame? Wouldn't take a moment to change—maybe her husband doesn't know how to do it with her in the bed."

"Come on then, quick, but if anyone asks, you did it while

29

I was in the loo."

Seven minutes later Diina's living body was washed, changed and lying in fresh sheets with the drips and tubes that took everything needed into and out of her body replenished to prevent her from dying. To say they were keeping her alive was essentially an overstatement. Diina planted an out of body kiss on Esme's cheek as she bustled out of the room. Esme raised a hand thoughtfully towards her face, but then let it drop. She glanced back at the now closed door. "How are they going to manage it?"

"Manage what?" said Jen, already hurrying down the stairs.

"The birth. How does a woman in a coma give birth?"

"Oh for pity's sake Es, if you're going to be like this with every patient we visit today we'll still be at it at midnight! They'll probably do a caesarean. Now let's go. Only twenty minutes left for the next three and they're on the other side of town."

Diina went back into the room after they'd gone. Being alone with herself made her nervous in case her body should suddenly swallow her up and she'd be forever trapped. There was always the chance that consciousness would reunite the two entities separated by the accident, but she had heard doctors say that there was little chance of recovery, that she was brain dead and (privately) that if it weren't for her husband's insistence that they save the baby, they would have switched off the respirator and let her slip quietly away.

The swollen belly heaved as her unborn child moved in its tiny prison and Diina felt nothing. Any hopes she might have entertained that she could communicate with the soul inside faded weeks ago. There did not seem to be any connection and her spirit body had remained slim, not mimicking the pregnancy. She tried to imagine Freddy as a father. Would he be gentle, loving? He had fought hard to have her at home, but paid her scant regard, except when he chose to amuse himself. All the care she received was from the agency nurses. And there was his cruelty. Even now he worried at her injuries like a dog with a rag doll. What kind of a life would the child have with that for a father? But—when he'd had a drink he sometimes bent over her and rested his hand on her belly, feeling the baby's movements with that same strange look on his face he had when he looked at the key fob photograph.

When Freddy returned home a few hours later he was drunk: too drunk to drive, but he somehow managed to park the car and get himself to bed before falling into a heavy, snoring sleep. There was some small relief in that, he would not torment her tonight at least. Diina lay beside him, uncertain why she did this, but unable to prevent herself, having gone through the actions of undressing and washing first.

The long hours of night enfeebled her. "Let me go Freddy," she said over and over again. At one point his snoring stopped briefly and her voice seemed clearer than ever in its silence. He began to speak, slurring but distinct.

"What happens on det stays on det," he said. "but the evidence comes home."

"How? What evidence? That little tart? You didn't have to parade around with her like that. Why were you so cruel—still so cruel?"

"What happens on det—they took photos. Did you know they take photos, videos? Slip the phone under the covers. Share 'em round. Everybody gets a sneaky peek. That lovely smooth skin. Think I wouldn't recognise it because there were no marks, just smooth, perfect skin? Think I wouldn't know? Wouldn't be so keen now, would they. That smooth, perfect skin covered in scars, cuts. Sliced." Then he was snoring again.

"Freddy, you know I never joined in with that. I'm a lifer—was a lifer. You don't get yourself a reputation when you've got to dish out orders the next morning. No Freddy. I don't know whose pics you were looking at, but unless you took 'em, they're not of me.

Is that what turned you against me? Thinking I'd been up to that? You're such a fool sometimes Freddy. Such a total prat."

"Whose baby is it? Can't be mine can it?"

"Well who else's, you fool!"

"Bet it's got lovely smooth skin like its mother."

"Freddy you wouldn't. That's your child. It's done nothing. Promise me. Promise you won't hurt the baby." She put her hand on his arm to shake him, but she was just an insubstantial fetch and it passed straight through the flesh uselessly. He began snoring again and nothing she said or did rouse him until morning when the cycle of washing and dressing recommenced. He hadn't really heard her. She knew that. He was just talking in his sleep and she was filling in the gaps.

The body in the bed grew thinner, the belly more distended and, though it dragged, time was passing. Her health continued to be monitored by Jen and Esme. Occasionally the doctor called and checked her vital signs, which the machines kept annoyingly vigorous, despite the fact of her true state. He would listen to the baby's pulse and lay his hand on Diina's belly, feeling for movement. As soon as he was satisfied he would fill in those all important charts that nobody read, and leave her to her constant rhythmless dance.

When Diina had been pregnant for twenty-four weeks, Freddy went away on a six month detachment. Jen and Esme continued to call in once a day. The doctor had stepped up his visits to once a week and noted in the folder that her wounds were finally beginning to heal. In the middle of the third week, an hour or so after Jen and Esme had changed her sheets before dashing off to their other charges across town, the baby began kicking frantically and then seemed to settle down more still than it had been for a month. Her belly tightened briefly. There was no pain, just sensation. A few minutes later it happened again, and again a few minutes after that, transmitting a ripple of pain to Diina's fetch.

Diina watched in fascinated horror as the contractions continued to strengthen. It was too early. The baby could not possibly survive. In any case, how could it be born if she could not push? The contractions would pass. They had to. But they did not. Pain coursed through her ever more powerfully, contractions growing stronger until felt the agony that was causing her body to writhe more than ever. She moved closer to her body, wondering if she might be able to control things better from inside, but afraid of getting trapped, perhaps ceasing to exist altogether. At last, seeing no alternative she climbed onto the bed and rested on her own body, waiting to slip inside. Instead she found herself standing once more beside the bed. Her body had rejected her. She tried twice more, with similar results.

There was a sound. Tapping. No, dripping. Had her thrashing limbs knocked one of the tubes loose? She moved around the bed checking each in turn. All secure and functioning. The sound of dripping continued. A red stain was soaking through the top sheet, spreading across her groin. On one side, blood dripped steadily, rhythmically off the waterproof mattress onto the floor. The drips became a trickle and then a flow, creating a growing pool of bright red on the grimy carpet.

There was the gentlest of thuds under the covers and a faint flutter of movement. Desperate to see her child, Diina, the disembodied Diina, thrust her face through the sheet. Her little boy had somehow managed to get himself born and he was lying in a pool of her blood that covered most of his tiny body, looking about him with calm, dark blue eyes. The umbilical cord coiled around him and inside her. A moment later, a couple of contractions and the placenta was there, bigger than the child and no longer providing him with what he needed. He had to breathe on his own, but his lungs had not yet developed and there was no help. Only blood.

Instinctively, Diina reached in and lifted him clear of the scarlet pool, holding him close to her, hampered by a fine silver cord that stretched between him and an infant that struggled for breath beneath the sheet. As the battle was lost, so the cord thinned to nothing. Meanwhile, the flow of blood from Diina's body had slowed. Her complexion was grey and though the machinery kept her breathing, her own silver cord was also disappearing. She stood next to the body and that of her son, cradling that other body, the living spirit of her little boy. All the scars that had covered her had faded and her skin, in spirit at least, was perfectly smooth.

The infant gazed into her eyes and Diina felt a surge of love more powerful than anything she had experienced in life. "If we'd both lived," she said, still transfixed by those dark blue eyes. "I'd have named you Robert. How would you have liked that? For what it's worth, you are Robert to me."

How long she stood there cuddling him she did not know, but gradually she became aware that darkness was falling and that the bloodstains had dulled to brownish-red. A pale glow had begun to develop in the corner of the room closest to the door and as she watched it became more intense. The baby seemed to be straining towards it, though he made no attempt to wriggle from her arms. Diina had heard tales of the white light. Weren't ghosts encouraged to move towards it by people who wanted to be rid of them? And now she was seeing it for herself, but this light, it wasn't just white. There was something alluring about it, the brilliance reached out, filled her vision and yet it was what she glimpsed beyond it that she desired even more than that whiteness. What was it? The baby's spirit seemed to know, to be urging her on. Diina knew that if she

33

did, there could be no return. This was a one way door and so she had to be sure. But what was it? Beyond the light: what was it? She had to know and began moving a little closer. Not near enough for danger, but just enough to try and catch a glimpse. Closer still, she could almost work out what it was - her infant's soul safe in her arms, willing her forward.

All at once they were there, inside the light looking out. She could see it more clearly now, a sea of light atoms moving swiftly, faster than time itself - and such a colour. Palest blue mingled with lightest gold into a shade more beautiful than anything she had seen before. Above anything else she wanted to dive into that spinning, speeding blue-gold and as the urge took hold, so she joined with it, no longer Diina, all memories dropped away so that she was not even aware that her baby's soul had travelled into the melee with her.

Diina never saw Jen and Esme arrive to the shocking sight of her body and her dead baby lying in a drying pool of stale blood. Did not hear the scream of horror that escaped Esme's lips nor see Jen dial emergency services even though she knew there was little that could be done. She did not see Freddy return, summoned by the force's welfare service, to attend his wife and child's funeral nor see the look of thwarted frustration that quickly changed to grief when he thought someone might be watching. No she did not see any of that, nor grieve for her baby, for now they were both atoms of blue-gold light, moving faster than time and aware of nothing but the sheer joy of purest, untainted love.

Sue Phillips *is an award-winning writer. Black comedy and fantasy fiction rub along happily with books on healing and spirituality. Her more serious work has been seen in large circulation magazines such as* Prediction *and* It's Fate, *as well as in books from Capall Bann Publishing and Spiralthreads Books. Her articles and reviews have appeared in numerous magazines, including* Whispers of Wickedness, *where she ran Sue Phillips' Posh Parlour: a darkly dangerous place inspired by the work of Mr Sweeny Todd. Sadly the website closed in May 2009. The contents of the message board may resurface in some apocryphal tome in the not-so-distant future. In the meantime, it is possible to discover some of the secrets of Posh Parlour on Facebook (with, of course, the right map and the magic words). Her dark fantasy collection/novel,* The

Waldorf Street Paradox, *was published by Rainfall Books. It contains ten diverse stories that come together like a jigsaw between the prologue and epilogue to make a larger tale, subtly inspired by magic, the occult and a satirical sense of humour. Two of the stories, 'Images of Angels' and 'The Dark Mirror' have already won awards and Sue Phillips is the reigning International Supreme Terror Scribe.*

At the Water's Edge
by Sharon Kae Reamer
& Robert D. Rowntree

My wife's body felt lumpy against my right shoulder; pressure points struggling beneath her dead weight. *Fat bitch.* Firmer criticism of her eating habits may have helped, but the point was moot now.

Dropping her down onto the grassy bank, her body wheezed, expelling a last remnant breath. She'd liked it here between the sparse pine and the shore, something about the drowned buildings, the school's boiler chimney, the church spire and the old ruined house still visible above the waves. Romantic she'd called it.

Bloody gloomy; the low overcast made everything grey, and wet: a dampener for my Valium buzz.

Before Mary's accident—no that's not right, before I'd ended Mary's life, before I'd killed her; this place always gave me the shivers. The drowned villages and loss of history were oppressive and depressive in equal measure. Mary's enjoyment of the place bred resentment, a mounting pressure-cooker waiting for release. And oh it had come, erupting in glorious violence.

Had I really enjoyed it that much? The memory felt vague, distant.

That's not why I killed her, not her love of gloomy shit-holes. *At least . . .*

Retrieving the shovel I'd left earlier, I began to dig; Harry the grave-digger always said, a good seven by three, and six down, but the bitch didn't deserve that, no sir, no she'd get a shallow grave and no marker.

The sodden ground came away in big squelching slabs. Worms writhed. Drizzle fell.

Tie-dye blood seeped through the Laura Ashley sheets I'd wrapped her in—an improvement.

My shovel hit rock, and for a moment, with the metal ring of the spade fading I heard a young boy's giggle escape the nearby pines. Distracted, shovel in hand, I moved nearer the tree line. Nobody there, yet something played around the edges of my mind like an annoying fly. No matter; what's gone is gone and who gives a shit. Put the body in the hole and get out of here.

Stumbling back to the grave, guilt attacked. She'd needed to die, she really had. Snippets of conversation danced; *'You can't keep a secret like that. It's not right.'* Before my reply left my throat, she'd added *'I thought I knew you, loved you. But this, you're a monster . . . '* Yes, I'm pretty sure she'd needed to die.

Halting near the hole, fear stabbed and I dropped the shovel. I knew I'd put her body down, saw the depression where it had rested. Racing forward, I reached down and touched the compacted soiled, felt its wet granular texture. Shit, shit, bodies don't get up, don't vanish.

Sweat stuck my damp shirt to my back as damp air traced fingers across my cheek, and a child laughed.

Panicked, I hurled dirt into the hole and tramped it down. Coming rain would ease the boot prints.

Running back to the pickup I tossed the spade far out into the lake. The church spire jutted free of the water like an accusing giant's bony finger. I fumbled with my keys. *Not right, not right at all.*

Confusion dug holes in my mind. Rain splattered the windscreen, and as I reversed out of the parking space my gaze rested upon a faint smudge in the tree line. A small boy, grey as the day, pointed a scrawny arm out towards the lake.

What secret had she been talking about? Rain fell harder and the image was gone. What secrets?

The only thing I could think of, besides panic, was to start looking for Mary. The dead didn't just get up and walk away, did they? Straightening the pickup after a wet bend, I reached in the glove compartment and fished out *the* bottle; a few Valium couldn't hurt, not at the moment. After the panic eased and my heart stopped its drum solo, I tried to imagine which of my family or former neighbours might have interfered . . . scratch that. *All of them.* So, which one first?

The new-town sprung from the hollow promises of politicians gave a home to the few dozens of souls who had nowhere else to go. A faint haze of red-tinged smoke fought the early morning gloom. I parallel-parked in front of my father in-law's bungalow that, despite being less than a year old, managed to look run-down and seedy. The motor grumbled into silence. He'd have heard that if he was up. *Of course, he's up. He's always up.*

I gave the door a light rap. This was not a place I wanted to be. After waiting a respectable minute, I turned to go, relief making my shoulders slump. *Old bastard. He's haunting me, and he's not even dead yet.*

The door clicked open. "Jake?"

I turned back. "Morning, Connor."

"What are you doing up at this hour? Pulling an all-nighter again with that riffraff?"

The insult stung. "No, just looking at the old place again." A tremor shook my right hand.

"No sense pining after what's gone. Move on, like the rest of us. And Jake, you should take it easy with the pills." He nodded towards my hand. "With all the shit you took in the past, and now happy tabs; body and mind can't take it son."

"Sure." I turned to go. "Thanks for the words of wisdom."

"Tell Mary to come by this afternoon. Need her to clip my toenails again. Maybe I'll just call her myself."

"I'll tell her. No need to disturb her beauty sleep." I waved my good hand as I headed out to the truck again. Bastard. Always pointing out the obvious. At least it wasn't him. He couldn't have stolen her body himself . . . but he could have had help.

An odd thought struck me as I sat behind the wheel. *Had I killed Mary? Did Connor have a point?* Placing my still shaking hand on the wheel I gingerly eased the pick-up into first and drove off.

I sat for what seemed like a century in front of Gerald's place; a cosy cottage with a tidy postage stamp garden. What a knob. That Gerald had been Connor's first choice to marry his precious daughter Mary still rankled. Why shouldn't it? They'd been sweethearts way back when. Maybe she still kept it up even after we'd married. But I knew they hadn't. Gerald didn't have it in him, and I'd reminded him of that every chance I got. Never hurts to rub it in. Although maybe if he had, things might have gone differently . . .

As I got out of the car, something nagged, itched at the back of my neck. *Why had she called me a monster? It made no sense. I hadn't done anything to make her think that, had I?* Damned if I couldn't remember.

"Hey, Gerry." I knew he hated that, but didn't see any reason to stop calling him that now. Might look suspicious. Gerald didn't have to wipe the sleep from his eyes either. Early riser, he'd run the town's newspaper for well on twenty years. Knew everything. If it wasn't him, he might let something slip.

Gerald opened the door wider. I went in and leaned back against the countertop, crossing my arms.

"Coffee smells good."

"Help yourself," he said and took down two cups.

We stared at each other across the oval oak table that had been squished into the tiny kitchen-diner along with the other furniture he couldn't part with from his former two-story town home.

"How's Mary?"

"Could be better, but she doesn't complain. At least not much."

"You know, I've never wanted to interfere, but you should—"

"She's got everything she needs right now. That enough for you?"

I took a sip of coffee. It tasted off. Everything seemed off.

"Of course, Jake. She loves you. You love her. That's what counts, right?" He grimaced as he said it.

"She's thinking of traveling, give us some breathing room. This whole move hasn't been easy on her."

Gerald shifted in his chair. "Might not be a bad idea. You two were great back then, when you still had the band, with her at your side. She's still the same girl inside; even if she's gotten a little . . . want me to talk to her?"

I rose to go. "Nah. I'll tell her to drop you a postcard."

My home, my prefabricated dump looked much as it had before I'd left at five. A box, a nest of vile recrimination.

Before the mess, before Mary's inconvenient interference, I'd always felt a twinge of apprehension entering and now that feeling grew. Hadn't I only left the back porch light on earlier? Kitchen light blazed behind the roller blind; shadows moved within.

A grey fugue settled, clouding my mind in diesel-soaked cotton wool. It would only take a small spark to set it off. Just a tiny flash of anger.

Mary's greeting forced me to lean against the wall. "You could have at least let me know you were leaving early. I didn't know where you'd gone."

A small boy giggled.

No, I killed her. She's dead.

"What?" Her question punched reality in. "Cat got your tongue?" It was her favourite expression, one she used relentlessly to provoke me.

"Sorry love. It's a bit cold today and I didn't want to disturb you." What could I say. "Needed more Valium. Boot's all-night chemist, repeat prescription."

"You should make an honest effort to wean yourself off those. Being dependant is no good for anyone."

Did she really say that? Her? Images of her desperate neediness—hanging around the stage door, smiling from the stage wings—accompanied more pleasant memories. The parties, the hotel bedrooms, the soft brush of her skin, her lips—her lips—she'd done everything I'd wanted back then, and I didn't even need to ask. Memories long gone, drowned with the village and time. Fuck her. I'm not taking advice from a dead woman. But Mary lived and so I couldn't have—

"I told you, I—"

"Jake," sympathy softened her words. "you don't have to lie. It's okay to go back, to remember."

Remember . . .

Busking, a hat full of coppers. A small boy, five small boys, nine or ten at a guess. "Hey mister, you played in that band . . . yeah, what sort of music was that? Oh yeah, Rock-a-Billy bullshit." They laughed and giggled, waved their iPhones and downloads.

"There's room for all kinds of music." My voice sounded tense, angry.

"You fucking deadbeat," a nine year-old kid. "The Time Machine. What a shite name. Who'd you think you was, fucking time lords?" The other kids roared with composite derision. "My dad said you were rubbish then and that only twelve people turned up for your reunion gig." The talking boy dived in and snatched my hat. Coppers flew across the street.

"Hey. Give me that back."

I put my guitar down as the boys crowded, pushed and shoved, shoute. "Loser, loser." Round and round, pushing, picking, poking, closer and closer.

A simple reflex, a lashing out of pent up regret.

A boy went down, then another. Their taunts changed tone, became more aggressive. Nine and ten year-olds. "Fucking bastard. We'll stab you for that. Come when your back's turned and stick you like a pig." A kick came my way.

With the increasing violence, the street emptied. My truck parked a few feet away. I had size on my side and rage fuelled my actions.

Electric guitars can be lethal, both metaphorically and in reality.

But they weren't dead. Not that they didn't deserve it.

The school shut now due to the impending submersion would serve as a good place to lock the little bastards up. Just for a short while. The basement, a locker room, a boiler room, it didn't matter, just a lesson. Once fear cleared their evil little minds I'd release them . . .

Remembering? No. "Really, Mary. I just popped to the chemist. Take a look." He raised his shaking hand. "Needed some advice on this."

Mary looked and tutted, her eyes blazing. Recrimination lurked, barely congealed magma.

She slammed the passenger door as she slid heavily to the pavement. I gunned the motor. Mary whirled. "Where are you going?"

"Shopping. You gave me the list. Wouldn't want Connor to be deprived of anything."

"Aren't you coming in first?"

"And let Connor vent all of his frustration on me while you say nothing? Thanks. I had enough abuse this morning. I'll be back in a bit."

The Co-op was crowded with Mums shopping for dinner

and early shifters getting rid of a bit of their wages for a quick snack. Christ, even the supermarkets in Great Britain were imported. *Don't we do anything ourselves anymore? Yes, we drown people's existence.*

I shivered at the thought. Drowning. What would it be like? *A boy giggled, small bodies, floating, fighting for air, fighting to escape—*

"You're Jake, Mary's husband, right?"

The woman standing in front of me in the canned goods aisle looked familiar. She smiled at me and opened her mouth to speak. Was she one of Mary's friends? I tried to bluff my way past her. "I'm sorry, I don't . . . "

"Sally Robinson. My husband picketed with you in the weeks before . . . before the . . . " Her voice caught. She coughed and put a hand to her cheek. Her eyes blazed for an instant in pain and, I thought, anger. "I've been meaning to ask you something. Mary mentioned that you'd seen David that day."

"David?"

"My son, he's been missing since a couple of days before the town went under. She said you saw him and some other boys in the town. You might be the last person to have seen him."

I pushed my arm in front of her and grabbed a half a dozen cans of baked beans, the cheapest ones. Connor hated the cheap ones. "Mary said that? I don't know what she could have been thinking, Mrs Robinson."

Suddenly apologetic, she backed away.

Shopping for my eternally ungrateful father-in-law never sat easy with me. But his lists of fabricated errands or forgotten shopping served well as opportunities to get-a-way. This time it hadn't worked out well. But I wasn't ready to go back just yet. Mary's betrayal sat like a stone in my throat. There was someone I wanted to see.

Outside of Trev's tower-block I felt my drug saturation level must have dropped. As I approached the sewage-strewn entrance to the dingy flats the forlorn weight of the chore bit deeply. *You can't go back, nobody ever can.* My life now revolved around a grey fudge of doubt and shit—a boy giggled.

A couple of kids, grey and grimy, their faces smudged and blurry, slung bits of trash at each other—or at me. I ignored it. *They're not there.* Edgy from my exchange with Mrs Robinson, my knock on the door might have been a little heavy. No one answered.

42

I banged my fist again. "You in there, Trev? It's me, Jake."

A crash followed by the bolt sliding back. Two bleary eyes framed by wisps of stringy hair that didn't begin to cover his bald pate peered out at me. "Jake? What the fuck?" He swung the door open and shuffled back into the dark living room. I picked my way past empty pizza cartons and empty beer cans to the threadbare couch shoved against the wall. His collapse on one end was clearly a signal to welcome me into his home. I joined him by hugging the other end of the couch.

"You got anything to drink?" He peered at my empty hands as if I had flounced centuries of social tradition with insult. He stank. From what, I didn't really want to know.

"Trev. Hey. What the hell happened to you? Last time I saw you, you were waiting tables at that bistro."

He cackled and wiped his nose with the back of his hand. "Need a diving bell to do that now, eh mate?"

He pushed himself slowly to his feet and swished his arms through the debris on the floor until he found a half-full can of beer. He held it out to me, but I shook my head.

"What's with you? Married that posh cow, didn't you? Things work out?"

He eyed me greedily.

I refrained from shaking my head. *What was I thinking? Why in hell did I come here.* "Things? What kind of things?"

"You still gigging, man?"

I expelled a coarse laugh. "Right. Every night. Same as you."

He laughed and took a swig, made a face. "Where'd it all go wrong, mate? We had everything. Blondes with tits this big, freaking audience what loved us, money to burn. What happened?"

My hand began to shake again. I pushed my answer inward. *He's worse off than me. No sense shoving him further down.* I took a couple of tablets from my pocket, swallowed them fast.

"Saw that," Trev looked to my pocket. "spare a couple?"

"No. Medication mate."

"Fuck that. You've been splashing cash with those kids down at Barker's Corner."

Those kids . . . those other kids . . . *whatever happened to them.* I shoved ten quid at Trev. "The world forgot us, mate. That's what

43

happened. The Time Machine. We were, and then we weren't, just like our name. Just like our town. Maybe there's us, somewhere in the future, playing just like we used to."

He stuffed the money in his shirt. "Yeah, that's it all right. Catapulted into the fucking future. Why can't things ever go backwards?"

Why can't things ever go backwards? I reflected on the truth of Trev's words as I let the engine idle outside of my father-in-law's, knowing how much that would aggravate both Mary and her father. She slammed the front door in the same manner she had slammed the pickup door earlier. Screamed at me to get the shopping in and simpered while I unpacked in silence.

Mary continued to simper in the gloom on the way home, but as soon as we got into the kitchen, I saw the magma had boiled to the surface in Mary's eyes. *Once you would have welcomed that, mate.* I reached into the fridge for a beer. Mary grimaced and poured herself a glass of gin, small dainty one. There'd be many of those before the night was out.

Backwards. Let's do the Timewarp again—

"This just can't go on any longer," she said, pouring herself another. "Where were you?"

I shrugged. Took a long swallow. "Checked in on Trev. Hadn't seen him around lately."

"Lately? Try ten years."

"So? You're upset because I wanted to see how he's doing? Not like we don't have other things to pick on each other about."

"No, and that's not what I meant." Her head jerked back with the second sip. "Aren't you ever going to face up to it?"

I felt my hand jerking like a foreign object attached to my arm, the beer sloshed. My hand resided there at the end, as if it didn't need to do anything I told it to. "Face up to what? Look, I tried everything to prevent them from submerging the town. Gave up giving music lessons. It wasn't me who sold out, though. Enough people made money out of drowning the town. Like your old friend, Gerry. He did all right, didn't he?"

"Oh, god." She screamed and her hands flew towards the ceiling. Reminded me of a movie I'd seen once about an evangelical

44

preacher, and the ones saved because of him. *You can't save her. You can't save them either.*

No. My arm jerked, beer shot onto the cream carpet: Who buys a cream carpet? *Boys giggled.*

Mary turned and slammed her gin down on the draining-board. "It's always paranoia with you. Always other people. I've tried to talk to you about this, god knows, and all anybody ever tries to do is make the best of things, for themselves, and surprisingly for those around them."

"Your father never liked me. If he could have substituted Gerald for me—"

"Look at you. It's not about Dad or Gerald. It's about what you did, what you became." She moved to embrace me. "I do love you Jake. But this has got to stop. Now. It's for the best."

Backing away, I felt relieved when a knock came at the door. Mary appeared to relax, almost as if she'd expected the visitor.

"Put your beer away and I'll see who's at the door."

As Mary plodded down the hall, I wondered where the woman I'd married had gone to. The over-caring do-gooder at the front door didn't resemble her at all.

The beer bottle crashed into the bin as the front door opened. I stared out into the back garden and in the reflected kitchen a boy pointed at me. No. I, I—

"Jake this is Sally Robinson. She lived in the old town just like us."

Politely, I nodded to her. "Hello, nice to see you again," I said while quickly glancing about the Shaker cupboards and built-in appliances. Nothing out of order. No giggling children.

Mary sat her visitor at the table and moved to a chair nearby. "Sally's the head of a local support group that help people traumatised by the flooding. She's here to talk or listen. What do you say?"

Silence pushed into the room, crushed any doubt in my mind that things were about to change for the better. "Look, Sally is it? My wife is under the illusion that I need some kind of help and that the root cause of my issues lies with the flooding. And I can understand that. I'm on Valium and the GP's can't put a finger on it, so it's only natural to try and figure things out. Two and two and so on. I think you've had a wasted journey. I'm just feeling my age and having a bit of mid-life crisis on the side, call it aging rocker syndrome."

The women shifted in her seat. "Okay, that's a start. Some of my group were reluctant to believe their symptoms—inadequacy and feelings of guilt—" Anger burned her cheeks, two dots of bright red. "were linked to the flooding, but talking helped them realise how much they'd been affected."

Was she fucking kidding. "Okay, fine. Let's do it."

Sitting hard, my chair screeched across the floor.

Mary appeared pleased; perhaps this tête-à-tête represented her master stroke in my 'rehabilitation'. Sally said. "Can I relay my experience?"

"Sure, why not."

Tipping back, I fetched another beer form the fridge. Holding it out I asked. "Want one?"

She shook her head. "Perhaps tea, coffee?"

Mary rose to see to it.

"The flooding created a major upheaval in my life Jake and to this day I'm not over it. David was only ten. He'd gone out early on the Sunday before the flooding. Met his friends. Scooters, skateboards, you know how they are, kids, race around town, promise to be home." My beer tasted sour. "We waited up, phoned the police, waited and hoped. On the day of the flood, they dragged me from my home screaming."

Mary, you fucking bitch. I spared her a single glance. The magma had lessened, cooled. But I didn't understand what had replaced it. Triumph?

I stood. "Mrs Robinson please leave." *Basement, in the fucking basement. I only meant to . . .* A boy giggled.

"Jake?" Mary loomed.

"Now, Mrs Robinson." I moved around the table, lifted her by the arm and dragged her to the front door.

"What? Jake no, please, I can leave on my own." She shrugged herself free, turned to Mary. "I can't help you. I think it's time we turned this over to the police." She stiffened as she opened the door. "You should have come to me earlier."

For quite a while I stared at the slammed front door. Much like a door I'd forgotten, locked and secure. Small frightened voices tapping away on the other side. Forgotten.

"I thought it would help. Thought talking about what you two had in common might help you."

You can't trust anyone in Mary's little clique; not Gerald, not Connor and most of all not Mary. Had she fuckin' told her? A crack frayed at the edge of my mind, a widening sliver of pent up rage set free. "You bitch, you knew all along: 'this is Sally, she's had a similar experience'," my whiney imitation of her voice pathetic yet empowering.

Mary backed away. "I don't understand, what?"

"The boys, the missing boys. It's always about those fucking annoying little boys." My arm shook; a spasm ran up to my shoulder. "Snarling and snapping, and stealing with their scooters and skateboards and their, oh-so-funny jibes about music." Her eyes sparkled in the hall light.

She knew. Of course she knew. I had told her once. But she'd been all loving and understanding, all hugs and tears. That was then.

I knew. I'd done it. Not directly. But in effect. It had all happened so fast at the end. Last minute rallies around the clock, sitting in rows handcuffed to each other. They cut us loose, dragged us away. All I had to do was tell them about the school. Wouldn't have been any worse than what actually happened. *They deserved to die, just like Mary.* Anger and desperation. Had they made me forget? Or had I wanted to forget? Just one problem less to deal with. Now I had another problem. But it was a thick rope with only one knot in it. Knots could be untied. She was standing in front of me.

"Leave me the fuck alone for once, will you?" I marched into the tiny conservatory, grabbed the guitar I had leant up against the wall, plugged it in, turned up the dial. No need to make it sound pretty. Not now.

When I had calmed enough to sit back and take my fingers from the strings—it never shook while playing, odd that—I heard the sound of breaking bottles. My last six pack. I didn't have any money to buy more. I'd given my last ten quid to Trev. I got up, jerking the plug from the socket.

Her mascara ran, making her eyes look like dark holes with the fires of hate burning inside. How easily things changed, something once so good now bad, any chance gone now, like the town, *the boys.*

"What do you want from me?" I asked. "I can't change it now."

"You can't keep a secret like that. It's not right." I opened my mouth, but she pointed at me, just like the grey child in the window. "I thought I knew you, loved you. But this, you're a monster."

"And me? You and Connor killed me long ago. You're just as guilty as I am."

She lashed out with the beer bottle, a jagged edge. She went straight for my neck. My hand stopped shaking, tightened around the neck of the guitar.

Strings vibrated as the guitar swung through a vicious arc. Mary's stabbed glass bottle nicked the side of my neck as I dodged right. The strings held perfect pitch, a killing note. She had to die, be taught a lesson just like those kids. A small boy appeared, grey words from a grey mouth. *"Kill the Rock-a-Billy bastard, kill him Missus."*

The guitar crashed into the linoleum floor, Mary somehow moving her bulk out of its path. She smashed into the work surface, spun around brandishing a carving knife. *"When your back's turned we'll stick you like a pig."* The grey voice now held venom tinged with the urge for revenge. Maybe they'd have it now.

Mary advanced, eyes dark with blood-thirsty intent. She lunged, I jumped back. Her foot slipped, spilt beer maybe, and she fell headlong towards me, the calving knife waving in the air. I rammed the neck of the guitar forwards, forcing the headstock and tuning pegs deep into her mouth and throat. The guitar sung a gurgled note and the fire in her eyes grew. She pushed forward, slashing wildly, kept coming, step by step, her head slipping down the blood soaked neck, inch by squelching inch.

"Die you bitch, die."

Slumping to the floor, I wedged the guitar body in the angle between the cupboard and the linoleum. She took a long time to die, her hot blood dripping on me, her eyes fading cinders.

The grey boy appeared disappointed.

I wouldn't have thought a body held so much blood, the kitchen sloshed in the stuff; but the fucking guitar was still intact. I grabbed the bottle of pills and washed them all down with a straight shot of gin. Followed by another. Mary wouldn't be needing it now.

The room went out of focus, the tape was winding . . .

My wife's body felt lumpy against my right shoulder; pressure points struggling beneath her dead weight. *Fat bitch.* Firmer criticism of her eating habits may have helped, but the point was moot now.

Dropping her down onto the grassy bank, her body wheezed expelling a last remnant breath.

She'd liked it here between the sparse pine and the shore, something about the drowned buildings, the school's boiler chimney, the church spire and the old ruined house still visible above the waves. Romantic she'd called it.

Bloody gloomy; the low overcast made everything grey, and wet: a dampener for my Valium buzz.

A grey boy pointed from the pine trees lining the horizon.

*As a teen, **Sharon Kae Reamer** developed a deep love for speculative fiction including science fiction, horror, and fantasy of all sorts, and somewhere along the way acquired a close affinity to magical realism. Her written short fiction spans the entire speculative gamut. She has just completed the fourth novel of the Schattenreich fantasy series that includes* Primary Fault, Shaky Ground, Double-Couple, *and* Shadow Zone. *Her newest novel,* Gravity's Gift, *a tale of deep space with a touch of romance, is in revision.*

Robert D. Rowntree *began writing in 1997 after attending a writing class run by Derek M Fox. His first story was accepted by* Strix *magazine and then several more magazines took stories in quick succession:* Terror Tales, Dead Things *and* Sci Fright *to name a few. He continued writing and had further acceptances in* Unhinged *and* Hadrosaur Tales, *and sold a micro story for anthology in the States. Along with Lisa Negus, he penned a play which narrowly missed short-listing for the East Midlands Playwriting Competition 2001. It was well received and Robert and Lisa have had discussions at The Leicester Haymarket with a view to expanding the play for a future reading. He now has a regular writing slot with* Ideomancer, *interviewing other writers. Currently he's working on a novel,* Destructive Tendencies; *a film treatment; and several shorter pieces. He likes spicy food and has been known to enjoy a good night out. He lives with his wife Dawn and his two sons, Ethan and Aidan.*

ANGEL TRACKS
by Richard Farren Barber

The fat man stepped off the kerb belly first. If I hadn't killed him I suppose he'd still be standing there, dead eyes staring into the distance.

The impact threw the man's body up onto the bonnet of my car and rolled him across the windscreen. For a moment my vision filled with his faded red T-Shirt pressed up against the glass and then the screen shattered into a thousand fragments. I stood on the brakes and as the car stopped the fat man rolled off. As he fell to the ground I heard his head crack against the kerb.

It doesn't matter how many times you've hit someone, you still can't fully prepare yourself for the shock—the heavy thud that rattles through the body of the car. You feel it in your stomach first; like someone punching you hard in the guts; and then it rises up your throat to the back of your mouth.

The road was empty. I walked around to the front of the car. He didn't look too bad; lying in a small bundle at the side of the road. There was a pool of blood blossoming at the back of his head, crimson against the grey pavement. Like a halo. I crouched down beside him.

"Don't worry, it won't be long now," I tried to reassure him.

He opened his mouth to say something but all that came out was a wheezing breath.

"Don't try to talk," I told him. I watched the life slip from his eyes. His body hitched with the effort of one last, tremendous breath and once that had finished rattling through his body I knew he was gone.

I waited for the Angels to come.

When the call came I was out in the inspection pit, checking the joint on the downpipe of a Mondeo. The radio was blaring out Michael Jackson and my nose was filled with the familiar stink of oil and scorched air. The phone had been ringing for a minute before

Tim hurried into the office to pick it up. Now he stood at the door, calling over to me.

"James, you need to get this."

I looked over at him and I knew. Just by looking at him I knew. Maybe not everything but it was like someone had whispered into my ear: it's Sheila. Sheila and James Jnr, and I scrabbled out of the pit and ran across the garage floor.

The phone was lying dead on its side on top of the chaos of the office desk. I stared at it for a moment, as if I could see something seeping out of the earpiece, something slick and putrid. I didn't want to pick it up. I was disgusted with the idea of picking it up and yet I watched my fingers wrap around the receiver and I heard myself saying calmly. "It's James here."

"Mr Green?" She had a soft voice.

My throat closed up. When I spoke I didn't recognise my own voice. "Yes?"

"I'm calling from the General Hospital. I'm very sorry to tell you that your wife has been involved in an automobile accident. Both your wife and your son were brought to the General. Their injuries were too great and although the medical staff tried everything they could to save them. I'm sorry to tell you they died."

I stared out of the window. I could vaguely hear the official but kind voice of the woman. Her voice was distant and unimportant. Tim was standing outside the door of the office.

"They're gone," I said. Tim started to cry, I'd always known he'd had a crush on Sheila.

Gone. I kept repeating to myself over the days and weeks— as if I had to remind myself—the explanation when I woke up in an empty bed each morning and came down to an empty house. Gone. More than once I started off towards James Jnr's nursery only to remember en-route that I didn't need to collect him, that he was never going to need picking up from there again. Gone.

And eventually, weeks after that phone-call, I did what I suppose I knew all along I was going to do: I drove out to the crossroads where Sheila had been trying to make a right turn. Where the Artic had simply ploughed through her tiny Fiesta and crushed the life out of it. I stood on the side of the road, buffeted by the side swipe of the wind from passing traffic.

I crossed the road and I was almost to the white line when

I realised I hadn't even bothered checking it was clear. A car crested the hill, racing towards me. It slowed almost to a crawl and I saw the driver's angry face peering out the window, her mouth working soundlessly. "do you want to get yourself killed? What sort of an idiot are you?" I stared through her with dead eyes.

On one of the trees there was a scar weathered to yellow where Sheila's car had stripped bark from the trunk. Right here was where Sheila was sitting and over here . . . I moved just a few steps to my right . . . this was where James Jnr had been prised out of the vehicle. Small cubes glittered in the grass like false diamonds. Somehow coming here made the whole thing real in a way that nothing else had; not the empty house, not visiting the morgue, not James Jnr's shoebox coffin. I stood at the side of the road and I cried and cried and cried until I thought surely I had no water left inside my body.

I don't know how long I stayed there. Winter was folding over into spring and the sky darkened gradually. The cars flashing past had their lights on—low beams at first but as the sunlight leeched from the sky they came over the brow of the hill with their halogens glaring, pinning me back against the darkness.

That was when I saw them: A line of footprints leading away from the crash site. Two sizes—Sheila and James Jnr size. At first I didn't believe it, thought my mind was making it up to give me some comfort. You had to really look for them, but once I saw them it was almost impossible to ignore them, or to think of them as anything except what they were: Angel tracks. This is where they had died. This was where their souls had left their bodies.

I'd never been a religious man: births, marriages and deaths were the only times I'd stuck my neck through the door of a church, but as soon as I saw those silver footprints leading away from the crash site I believed. No, I didn't believe, I *knew*.

I tried to follow the footprints but as soon as I left the road it was too dark to see them. I came back the next night with a torch but that only took me a little further—through the first line of trees and over a fence into the wood before I lost them. On subsequent nights I sometimes got a little further. There was a comfort there— knowing something of Sheila and James Jnr had walked away from the crumpled wreck of her Fiesta, even if they were no longer here with me.

I came back every night, trying to follow wherever the footsteps would lead. Night after night, the trail fading over time, until the night came when I could no longer find any trace of Sheila and James Jnr.

And that might have been the end of it—leaving me to try and find some meaning in my life. Except that I was called out to the M1. Pete was off in Malaga for his annual week's debauchery and Tim was laid up at home with Swine Flu so when the call came in it was me, me or me. I knew they'd been protecting me—nothing said but since Sheila's death it had always been Tim or Pete's turn to go out and haul in the wrecks, but I couldn't hide from it forever so I got the flatbed out and chugged down to Junction 23.

One of the traffic cops filled in the details: some old codger driving down from Inverness had fallen asleep at the wheel. I waited in the van whilst they cut the guy free. They transferred him into an ambulance and it rolled away: no sirens.

As I walked over to the wreck I saw them—you couldn't miss them—amongst the shattered glass and debris on the carriageway; silver footprints leading across the hard shoulder.

I looked back at the cop. He knew. They all did. They stared up at me but then they looked away, one after another returning their attention to the crumpled mess on the carriageway.

The glow of the footprints was already beginning to fade. I stopped, crouched down beside one and reached out. The print crumbled beneath my fingertips and I felt a terrible guilt at destroying something important. Silver rendered to grey ash and blew away in the breeze.

I walked up to the policeman, holding out my ash covered fingertips. "What is it?"

He didn't even look, he stretched out his foot, dragged his toe over the tracks until they were gone. "We've got to get the road opened," he told me.

The fat man lay huddled in the gutter.

This time.

I knelt down beside him. "This was what you wanted," I told him. I'd seen it in his eyes—in that fraction of a second as I'd come over the hill and he'd chosen to walk out in front of me. And never mind the slight swerve of my car that had taken him into my path. I recognised that look, I'd seen it on the features of the others—and once you saw it you could never mistake it for anything else.

I stood up and looked around. Nothing. No silver footsteps leading his soul away.

"Come on," I shouted at him, if I was less in control of myself I might have lost my temper. If I was someone else I might have screamed and kicked at his limp, useless body.

"This time," I said to myself.

Every second I waited by the side of the road was a gamble. Soon someone was going to come over the hill.

"I promise—just this once." And I knew they must have already heard this from me so many times before. "I just need to see it again."

It couldn't just be... It couldn't just be that one time on the M1—because if that was the case then what did that say about Sheila and James Jnr?

It couldn't be that I imagined *that*?

Off in the distance I hear sirens—probably nothing to do with me but I don't want to take the chance. One last circle of the dead man and then I hurry back to my car and drive away. Another failure.

Just drive and drive and drive. It starts to rain and water smears the windscreen—everything out there is blurred and unreal and nothing matters except moving forwards.

Rain-tired taillights glow red from the cars up ahead. I can't tell you where I am—I stopped paying attention to the journey months ago and now there's only the motion and the sound of the engine and the water under the wheels and the steady swish-swish-swish of the wipers pulling me forwards.

I don't even think about it, not really, because if I think about it I might change my mind. Instead I push down on the pedal and the needle on the Speedo judders past 70, through 80 to 90 and with just the slightest pull on the wheel I drift off the carriageway and I hit the motorway bridge at nearly 100 mph.

Richard Farren Barber was born in Nottingham in 1970. He has had short stories published (or due for publication) in All Hallows, Blood Oranges, Derby Scribes Anthology, Derby Telegraph, Gentle Reader, Murky Depths, Midnight Echo, Morpheus Tales, Scribble, Shriek Freak Quarterly, The House of Horror, This is Derbyshire, *and* Time in a Bottle, *and broadcast on BBC Radio Derby.*

Richard was sponsored by Writing East Midlands to undertake a mentoring scheme where he was supported in the development of his novel Bloodie Bones. *The Literary Consultancy are currently submitting it to agents on his behalf.*

His website can be found at richardfarrenbarber.co.uk

51 WEEKS
by Rachel Kendall

We are members of something unique; a small collective, a thumb-sucking comfort. We are emotional refugees who fled the sanctimonious core of society, who seek to reconcile with the truest, most unconventional order.

We met on the internet, conferred electronically, planned telephonically and then gravitated to this one place, Pescara, Italy. A warehouse, hot with a vaguely meaty odour, plastic shards hanging like stalactites from a high ceiling.

The devil wears a sandy coloured suit. His flesh is tanned. The shades worn indoors and the sculpted beard betray his cool and his wealth. But there will be wealthier, more powerful demons above him. He is Tuvia. Tuvia is our guide.

There are twenty seven of us here. Some are people I have met before, some are new members. Some wear the expression of accismus, others' eyes dart nervously. We are teachers, officials, artists, and nurses, in blue and white collars. We are unemployed, unemployable, homeless, 'cured', bullies, bullied, pugilists and pacifists. And we have one thing in common—a need for satiety. Some of us have points on our license, criminal records for indecency, drug habits. Others own firearms, fucked up lungs, multiple piercings. And for us, nothing is ever enough.

Pescara is picture-perfect, a postcard paradise. Clear warm water, a blazing white sun, sandy beaches, coloured houses trailing flowers.

But we're all blinkered. We see only what we choose. Or, at least, only that which we're allowed to see. We sleep during the day and come nightfall we prepare to be shown our unHoly Grail.

I've been a member for four years. Once a year we all meet. It is our holiday and our reunion. For the other 51 weeks of the year we carry on as normal. We wait for the pubs to open so we can have that first drink of the day. We masturbate at the sight of lovers groping in the backs of cars. We steal the neighbour's kids' pet rabbit and saw off its ears before placing it carefully back in its hutch. We shoplift. We write letters to the editor. We have affairs and blackmail magistrates and lie on our tax returns.

What we want can be seen on a hundred different sites on the internet. But what we need is the chance to get involved. We want to submerge ourselves in the action, not sit alone in a room, staring at the monitor. Here is a group of like-mindeds to share the pleasure with. People we might meet in the flesh and start an actual friendship with. We help each other out, make suggestions, offer services, lend money, supply drugs. Hits and misses. I helped out a woman who went by the name of Rose (a woman by any other name . . .). She wanted to live out her rape fantasy. She lived a few hundred miles from me and I offered my services. We made plans. As she walked jauntily through the park near her four-bed, two-car home, I jumped her. I ripped and kicked and tore my way between her legs. Fucked her, pissed on her bloody face, kicked her a couple more times in the ribs and fled. It didn't fulfil any of my desires. I hoped it filled hers. I never heard from her again.

My first 'outing' with the group was in my home town of London. Tuvia led what was then only five members into the warm basement of an empty house with boarded-up windows and a pervasive smell of piss. Graffiti covered the walls inside and the toilet was clogged with shit. The squatters had to be forcibly removed before the body could be brought in. He'd been shot in the face; unidentified and possibly homeless, he'd been in the wrong place at the wrong time. Two of his fingers had been partially eaten away, by a stray dog, or maybe rats. His body had been cleaned up but his face was a mess. We were here to watch him decay. The heaters were there to speed up the process. The longer we were out here, the more money we had to part with.

So, we came and went as we liked for hours, days, weeks. One man vomited the first time he saw the body and didn't return. None of us spoke. We took our chairs or leant against the wall and performed our vigil around the corpse. We were not there to touch. We were eyes only. Eyes that widened further with every movement of flesh, every fluid and gassy ejection from every aperture. Our fingers merely held handkerchiefs over noses. Sometimes we went outside to breathe in the carbon monoxide from the day's mass of traffic. Going back inside was made harder by the fresh onslaught of decay. I found it easier to stay where I was. People brought me coffee and sandwiches, which I barely touched. I didn't want to miss a second of the show.

When Tuvia asked, I told. When he asked each of us in person and in private what effects the sight of the corpse had had on us, I told him none. I was disappointed, I said. I wanted more. It was all too passive, sitting and watching as nature did what nature does. It might make some people sick to the stomach, it might revolt others with its obvious mortality show, the reminder that this is how we will all end up. But what was it, really? It was nothing. It was a cycle. It was not enough.

I think Tuvia took note of my grumblings as the following year we ended up in Madrid at two in the morning, sitting behind glass on a second storey, watching a dog fight. Pit bulls. At least in part, these dogs had been bred to be fighting machines. Starved, beaten, kicked, they had been revved up like bulls before a fight. They ran at each other like they had been shot out of a cannon. I was impressed at first. The way their muscles rippled. The way their short legs pounded the floor. The way they tore at each other, ripping off a nose in one bite, taking out an eye, sinking teeth deep into the other's shoulder, through muscle, ripping off flesh till the bone was visible. Exhausted, they continued dripping blood, legs buckling, the chant of the men around them urging them on until one just gave up and the other tore its corpse to pieces.

"Why were we behind glass?" I demanded to know the next day.

I'd found the missing piece. Sitting on the edge of my chair, face inches from the clear obstacle, I'd been denied a right to be part of the action. I wanted to be down there where it happened. I wanted to be jostled by the crowd, smell the sweat of the men, be deafened by their shouts, wave money about, hiss and spit and clap the winner on the back.

"Too dangerous," was his answer. "These are very violent men. They know each other well. They've been face to face with each other for years. They don't take kindly to strangers. They're not here to put on a show for tourists."

"So give me something I can be part of," I spat at him. "It's what I pay you for. Give me something real, something I can touch and smell and feel."

The next outing was for me alone.

He took what I had said to heart and a few days later a black car pulled up outside my hotel room. I was alone at the time, drinking bourbon, lying on the bed staring at the stains on the ceiling. I wasn't prepared for three men to come knocking at my door, with guns and rope and heavily disguised voices.

When I woke I was back on my bed. Tuvia was sitting beside me. He cocked a brow when he saw me, shone a light into each of my eyes in turn. Perhaps for show, perhaps he was actually concerned. He nodded, satisfied.

"How do you feel?"

There was a question I couldn't answer in a flash. I felt . . . hungover. My head cracked and splintered, my eyes felt like they might roll out of their sockets. It was as though all the fluid in my body had been drained out. I was a pit of sand, and it felt like someone had been digging away inside me. Gradually I became aware of a pain in my genitals. What started off as a low throb and hum worked its way up to an acid burn as my foreskin began to peel off, followed by layer and layer of skin until I expected to find a bloody red stump in place of my cock. When Tuvia saw my pain he lifted the bed sheet (and here I discovered I was naked) revealing two metal spikes going in one side of my penis and out the other.

"Do you remember anything?"

I shook my head, closed my eyes, the pain almost visible to me. "Get them out," I said.

"Of course. But first, watch."

He pointed a remote control at the TV at the end of the bed and I watched myself in grainy black and white. The whole thing had been filmed, from my kidnap, to the S&M club, to the loss of my body in a mass of flesh, to the woman (man?) towering over me, my body on a rack, my penis limp, and the insertion of the spikes into my flesh. My face did not even register pain. Had they filled me so full of drugs I was completely numb? Blood, thick and black on film, covered my legs. They left me there, carried on cavorting around me. The screen faded to black.

The offending articles were removed from my cock and though it hurt to piss for a few weeks and sex was completely out of the question, there was no lasting damage. These people were not amateurs. Still, in the end, I had to ask Tuvia what was the point?

"You didn't like it?"

"There were many things I didn't like about it. I wanted action and you offered me a passive role again. Not only that but I was drugged beyond awareness. I felt nothing. I saw nothing. I asked you for something, Tuvia. Give me something."

And now, a year later, in a warehouse in Pescara, we wait for the devil to speak.

What he offers for our amusement has me turning on my heel and heading for the door.

"Mike," he shouts after me. "I need to talk to you after the meet."

I nod and head outside, lean against the wall to smoke a cigarette.

Watching people fight to the death. Men, high on angel dust and god knows what else, ripping at each other like animals. I've seen it all before. Here he is, suggesting a spectator sport yet again. Crude, yes. Dangerous and vile, of course. But passive all the same. After watching the dogs, I'd wanted to be a part of the crowd. But now I knew it still wouldn't be enough.

"I want to fight," I say when he comes out of the warehouse. "I want to get my hands dirty this time."

He shakes his head.

"I will not have your death on my hands. Nor any death from this collective. You know that. If you want to commit suicide, you do it on your own."

I shake my head in return. "I can win."

"No, you can't."

And then he takes my hand. "Come," he says. "I promise you will not be disappointed."

When I was a kid, a boy of twelve or thirteen, me and Gareth used to watch Mrs P undress at night. Peeping through the corner of the window where the net didn't quite meet the edge of the frame, we'd take it in turns to watch the luminous flesh slowly appear as clothes were shed. She always slept naked and always went to bed at least an hour before her husband. We'd get a full view of her bush, that beautiful mound of thick black hair, her wide hips and thighs. I would watch the way Gareth's mouth tightened when he was aroused, and his neck would get blotchy. Later we would shoplift from Smiths and play chicken with the cars on the main road. Always looking to get our kicks. He was killed in a simple automobile accident. A drunk driver rammed into the back of his parents' car, killing him and his dad outright. After that I started to steal into people's houses at night and take any crap I could carry in two hands. But without my look-out, my ally, I was no good and landed myself in jail more than once. Sitting alone in the cell I would think of Gareth. How he had been cheated in death. It had crept up on him and then taken him in one ear-splitting moment, by a drunken man, a regular, normal human being, soused, not even in control. A totally passive death.

The men have weapons. I thought they would be fighting bare-fisted but no, they both have metal scaffolding poles to fight with. They charge each other, weapons held high. One knock to the skull would be enough, but we want the fight to last awhile. So they aim low, shattering kneecaps, breaking ribs. There is quite a crowd here, and we are in amongst them this time, close enough to be hit by an occasional splatter of blood. We shout and jeer, clap and yell 'hit him hit him hit him'. The smaller man bites off a large piece of his tongue as metal crashes into the side of his head. He spits it out and grabs the other man in a half-nelson. They hold back a little more than the dogs, though they growl and wheeze and bark at each other. One is on his knees, vomiting, and the other takes the opportunity to kick him in the ribs. They don't hate each other. They probably don't even know why they're doing this. The survival instinct is as strong in these men as in any other animal. That is all. Kill or be killed. I can feel the pulse of the crowd. I have a semi-erection. Not far from where I stand, a man is masturbating furiously, eyes locked on the fight. We want a victory. For many of the people here, it's simply a business transaction: winner takes all. For the rest of us, we don't care who takes the crown. All we want is to witness a triumph.

It ends with a crescendo. Back from the brink, the smaller of the two men wins the war with an attack of blows to the head. The tall man is left with no face, his head mashed to a bloody pulp, his body black and blue. After much waving of money and pats on the back, the crowd begin to disperse, some happy with their winnings while others, dejected, return to the fringe they came from. Some stragglers wait behind. I wait for Tuvia, who is talking to a big man wearing tattoos and a holster. When they walk over to me I unfold my arms and stare hard into the man's steel-grey eyes. With a nod from Tuvia, he hands me the gun. I am blank-faced and blood-smeared. But he has seen something in me.

"Kill him," Tuvia says, pointing to the winner of the fight who sits on the floor sucking on the bloody end of dog-eared cigarette.

"But he won the fight."

"The rules of the game Mike. The winner must die as well as the loser."

"But—"

"No, Mike. If you can't do it, it's fine."

The tattooed man is getting impatient. I look down at the target. He is watching me, my face. Does he look smug, or is it my imagination? Does he *want* me to kill him? Is he daring me? I point the gun at his head and pull the trigger.

"So," says Tuvia as we walk away from the murder scene. "Did you feel something then?"

"No," I say. "I didn't feel a thing."

Rachel Kendall can't keep secrets. She is editor of Sein und Werden and ISMs Press. Her debut collection, The Bride Stripped Bare, *was released to critical acclaim in 2009. Her work also appears in* Cabala *(edited by Adam Lowe) and* Women Writing the Weird *(edited by Deb Hoag).*

ADRIFT WITH SPACE BADGERS
by Jeff Burk

The men, drunk on boredom, blood lust, and bathtub wine, cheered on the two combatants in the center of the ship's hangar.

Most planet-dwellers have heard of space badgers, but have never seen one in real life. They're nasty little buggers. They have claws, sharp teeth and are completely fearless. They look very much like Earth's honey-badger, but wear tanks of air on their backs. A hose connects each tank to a clear, glass, fish-bowl helmet covering the badger's head. These pieces look like equipment, but they are actually part of the space badger's body. The species evolved these appendages to survive in both the vacuum of space and in pressurized environments. Darwin never saw these little bitches coming.

Whereas sailors have to deal with rats stowing aboard ships—spacemen have to deal with space badgers. The feisty little creatures build nests inside of machinery and fuck up the workings of all sorts of internal systems if they're not immediately dealt with. Nothing is more annoying than to suddenly lose main power for a day or two and be stuck dead in space just because you've got a family of space badgers getting all cozy in the reactors.

Therefore, most people who work in space have no patience or sympathy for the little fuckers. It's considered standard practice to kill all space badgers on sight. Or if you don't kill them right away, you catch them and keep them for space badger fights.

Like the one the maintenance crew was watching.

They gathered around a barrel full of water, placing bets on which of the two space badgers trapped inside it would survive.

While space badgers can survive and navigate fairly well in vacuums, they really hate water. They can barely swim and their air pack only lasts for a short period of time before they need to refill it in an oxygen rich atmosphere.

There was no way either badger could escape the barrel. A small platform, big enough for just one space badger body, was the only safe haven above waterline. That's what they were fighting for.

The two thrashed about in the water; claws slashing and splashing, glass helmets clinking off each other and the platform. As one badger climbed, the other jumped on top of him, pushing him down under the water.

Each badger had a stripe painted down its back—one was red, the other blue. Red Stripe perched himself firmly atop the platform. Blue Stripe desperately clawed at him from below.

"Gentlemen, we may have ourselves a winner soon," yelled Lieutenant Hanson over the cheering men.

Blue kept trying to climb up to safety but Red swatted him with his strong paws and sent Blue tumbling back into the water. Stunned and tired, he struggled to move. Red's little chest heaved and sighed as he tried to catch his breath.

Blue made one final mad dash at Red, but Red easily caught Blue's helmet between his claws. Blue attempted to thrash free but Red held on tight and smashed Blue's helmet against the platform.

Clink, clink, clink, and then—*CRACK!*

Shards of glass plopped into the water as Blue's helmet shattered. The space badger fell limp. His head began to expand like a balloon until it almost completely filled what was left of the helmet.

POP!

The space badger's head exploded, spraying some of the men standing close by with blood, bone, and brains. They roared even louder.

"Red is the winner, settle up!" yelled Hanson over the cacophony.

Commander Gaines handed two hundred credits over to Hanson.

"Not your lucky day, eh, Commander?" Hanson said, grinning while taking the money.

"I'm lucky when it counts, Lieutenant."

Ensign Walker went to the barrel with a hammer in his hand. The winning space badger was soaking wet and shivering. Its eyes darted around at the crew, pleading, searching in vain for some method of escape. It saw Walker looking at it and swiped its claws along the side of the platform while hissing as loud as it could.

Walker smirked. He raised the hammer above his head and smashed it down on the space badger's helmet. The glass shattered almost completely away—all that remained was a jagged ring of shards around its neck. Its head expanded, and then—*POP*—it exploded.

The normal reward for the winning badger.

"Alright ladies, play time's over," yelled Gaines above the excitement.

The men quieted down and snapped to attention.

"Clean this shit up and get back to work," he continued. "We have a ship to keep working. I'll be on the bridge if anyone needs me."

Gaines grabbed a nearby toolkit and headed to the turbolift. Before reaching the door, he turned back to his men.

"And someone find out where those fucking space badgers are comin' from. Find them and burn them alive."

The U.S.S. Davis was a Super Freighter, capable of transporting several million tons of cargo across more than twice the distance of a standard freighter ship. Commander Gaines had been the chief engineer of the ship for more than two decades. His job was to oversee the ten person engineering department and keep the ship moving, the air flowing, and the gravity going. On most missions, the worst he had to deal with were a few blown out connectors and some loose wires.

The doors to the turbolift opened and Gaines stepped onto the bridge. It wasn't much of a bridge—nothing like the ambassador and war ships had—just a few tech stations that monitored the status of the ship, and a view screen that took up the entire front wall. Right now, it displayed only empty space and pinpoint stars.

Four officers monitored the display screens and Captain Ingles stared at the view screen. Bored.

Gaines went over to the navigation station. Lately it had been acting up a bit and was calculating their arrival at Depot Station 23 above two hours later than what other calculations were determining. That's not off by much, especially not for the three month mission they were on (transporting 350 million barrels of quadrotriticale). But you really don't want the navigation system acting up at all. The last thing they needed was to get lost, with the nearest starship over fifty systems away.

Gaines knelt down and popped off the circuit panel. He

looked over the mess of wires and bolts but nothing was obviously damaged. That meant he was going to have to check each circuit manually until he found the problem.

Shit. This is going to take hours.

"Captain, a large object has been detected three hundred meters off our starboard bow. About two hundred meters across, four hundred long."

"That's almost as big as us," said the Captain. "How'd it get that close without our sensors picking it up? View screen, now."

A gigantic creature filled the view screen. It looked like a blue whale—the kind of animal one would normally see swimming peacefully on Earth. But this beast had three rows of teeth in its gaping maw. Its body glowed a strange and unnatural neon blue. The monster flapped its four pairs of flippers slowly in space and turned to face the ship.

Gaines had heard of these creatures but he never thought he'd actually see one—a Behemoth.

A spaceman's nightmare, the Behemoth was the most feared creature in space. Nobody really knows how many ships have been lost to Behemoth attacks over the years. The space whales have some way of evading ships' sensors. Only two ships have been known to escape a direct Behemoth attack.

The monster darted forward with astonishing speed straight for the freighter ship.

"Evasiv—" began the Captain, but was cut off as the ship shook violently. The men on the bridge went tumbling. One of the officers flew head first into the computer screens. His head whipped back and twisted around—snapping his neck. The corpse fell to the floor.

The main lights went out and the emergency lights turned on, bathing everything in a red glow.

Then the female robotic voice of the ship's warning system began. *"Warning. Warning. Extreme structural damage sustained. Engine core overload imminent. Crew is advised to evacuate. Crew is advised to evacuate."* The message repeated itself.

Gaines looked around the bridge and locked eyes with the Captain. There was a large cut across his forehead, spilling blood down his face. The ship shook again as the Behemoth continued its attack.

"You heard the lady," said the Captain, smiling. "Time to—"

His windpipe was crushed before he could finish. The paneling above him gave way and several tons of metal, wire and other duct work fell on top of him. Instantly mashing him to a gooey pulp.

Gaines bent down and picked up his toolbox. He wasn't sure why—he just operated on autopilot. He hopped into the turbolift and punched the button for the flight deck. Repeating the steps he had memorized in emergency drills.

When he reached the deck, he had to crawl under metal beams and through loose wires to get into the corridor. He singed his hair on a small fire burning in a fallen air duct. When reached the evacuation area, the escape pod doors all glowed green, indicating that the pods were present and ready to launch. Either Gaines was the first one to get there, or no one else was going to make it off the ship.

He ran straight for the nearest green oval-shaped door and was ten feet away when his feet caught on something and he fell flat on his face. He looked back and saw Lt. Hanson. The officer was trapped beneath a heavy sheet of metal. It covered most of his body, which was why Gaines hadn't seen him lying there. Hanson gripped a hold of Gaines' feet.

"—Warning. Warning. Extreme structural damage sustained—"

The computer continued its alert.

Gaines tried to shake his feet free, but the injured man held tight.

"Let go," yelled Gaines as he kicked.

"Help . . . " Hanson whispered.

There was no time. Gaines swung the toolkit into Hanson's head. There was a loud *crack* and the man moaned. Gaines sat up and brought the metal box down again and again and again. Hanson's body began to convulse and Gaines hit harder and faster. Each blow emitted a wet slushy plop, but still the grip on his feet did not weaken.

"—Crew is advised to evacuate. Crew is advised to evacuate—"

He stopped hitting when there was almost no more head left to smash. Gaines reached down and pried the dead man's hands from his feet. Finger by finger.

Gaines stumbled to a standing position, toolkit still in hand, and the ship lurched to one side tossing him into the wall, right next to the pod.

"*Warrrrrrrrrnnnnnnnnn sssssssssd—*"

The warning system shut off and the red emergency lights went out. The only source of illumination was the green glow of the escape pod doors. Gaines hit the button on the door and it rose up smoothly. He threw himself in and the door slid shut.

The computer system inside the pod whirled to life.

"*Ignition in 3, 2, ...* "

The pod jerked as it separated from the U.S.S. Davis. Gaines looked out a porthole and saw the Behemoth biting huge chunks out of the freighter. There was almost nothing left of it—nothing worth salvaging anyway.

A blinding flash of white light exploded from the center of the wreckage. Gaines backed away from the porthole rubbing his eyes. They burned. And all he could see were throbbing white clouds.

The pod pitched suddenly. First down and then up, hard. Gaines' feet left the floor and he was hurled through the air. His head hit something and his body crumpled down.

He tried to stand but he could not get his limbs to work. His vision obscured by white blurs, then grey, then black.

Gaines sat up rubbing the back of his head. His hand brushed a hard bump the size of a walnut and sharp pain shot through his head. He winced and brought his hand where he could see it. Blood. Cradling his head in both hands, he inspected the wound with his fingertips. He gently poked. It felt like an ice pick to the brain every time his fingers made contact but he was relieved to find nothing serious.

He stood up, and while his legs felt wobbly, he didn't appear to be injured in any other way.

He went back to the porthole and looked out. The U.S.S. Davis was gone. Millions of tiny hunks of mangled metal floated aimlessly in space. The engine must have gone nuclear.

There was no sign of the Behemoth.

The interior of the escape pod was about twelve feet wide by twenty feet long with an eight foot clearance. It was one long room with a cockpit with a hyper-strong glass shield surrounding it. The walls were storage cabinets and computer banks; all colored the same shade of metallic gold as the floor and ceiling. The porthole in the docking door was the only other view outside.

Gaines went to the cockpit and sat down. A quick glance at the control panel showed all the pod's systems at normal operational levels. The blast from the ship didn't seem to have damaged the escape pod. Thank God.

He did a scan of the surrounding space for life signs or emergency signals from other escape pods. It took the computer under a minute to complete its operation. Nothing. It appeared that Gaines was the only one who made it off the ship.

He plotted a course for the nearest starbase. It would be a long trip—about two weeks stuck in that tin can. But the pod was stocked with food and water. He would be fine. He finished entering the coordinates and hit ENGAGE.

Nothing happened. ENGINE FAILURE flashed in bright red letters across the screen.

"Shit," he muttered. Maybe the blast *did* damage his pod.

According to protocol, his next course of action was to send out a distress call. He recorded a brief message giving his name, title, ship of service, location and request for immediate assistance. When he finished he pushed SEND.

MESSAGE FAILURE.

"Shit!"

He sat back from the panel. He couldn't move the ship and he couldn't call for help. He spun around in the chair to look over the escape pod and see if he could think of anything else to do.

His eyes immediately latched onto the toolkit that was lying on its side in the far corner. He could fix the pod. It might take a while but he knew he could do it.

If he worked quickly, he figured he might still have enough supplies to get him to the starbase, even with the extra time spent fixing the ship. The standard escape pod was stocked with thirty days, worth of food and water along with a variety of medical supplies.

Medical supplies . . .

Gaines remembered the lump on the back of his head. He touched it. It still hurt just as bad but the bleeding stopped and the swelling was going down. He should wash it off.

He opened the first cabinet. It was empty. There were a few brown crumbs and an empty energy bar wrapper but nothing else. He went to the next cabinet and opened it—it too was empty. And so were the next two cabinets.

"What the fuck . . . " said Gaines, as he looked from empty cabinet to empty cabinet. Every escape pod was inspected before leaving dock to make sure they were properly outfitted. There's no way this should be possible. Yet here he was.

He had no choice but to get to work on fixing the pod.

He grabbed the toolkit and took out his screwdriver. The access panel to the main circuitry was located in the center of the floor. It was purposefully easy to access just for situations like this. Gaines unscrewed the four bolts that held it in place and hoisted up the heavy metal panel.

At first, he couldn't make sense of what he saw. Where there should have been a mess of wire and motherboards, there was a solid, heaving mass of brown fur. Suddenly a dozen little heads in glass helmets popped up.

Space badgers.

They hissed at Gaines.

He calmly placed the metal panel back in place and screwed the four bolts back in place. He could hear the space badgers on the other side, scratching with their heavy, sharp claws.

He went back to the cockpit and did a scan of his pod for life-signs. A minute went by and then a second minute. After three full minutes had passed and the computer hadn't finished conducting its scan, he began to get worried.

Please don't fail on me too.

After five minutes there was a loud *beep* and the screen read SCAN ERROR—TOO MANY READINGS IN TOO CLOSE PROXIMITY—CANNOT ACQUIRE FIXED SCAN.

Holy fuck, they were nesting in here, Gaines thought.

Scratch, scratch, scratch, scratch.

The noise came from all around him. Gaines heard the space badgers scratch beneath the floor, in the ceiling, and from inside all the walls. When he opened the panel, it must have riled them up.

Gaines sat still, looking around the small cabin that suddenly seemed much smaller, listening to the animals move about. It sounded like there were hundreds of them.

Well, I guess I know what's messing with the pod.

It took him a full hour to thoroughly search the entire pod but he safely, and sadly, confirmed that there was no food or water anywhere on the ship. The space badgers must have ate and drank it all. There were also no medical supplies, tools, or weapons. In fact, there was nothing that wasn't bolted down. Even the emergency space suit was missing. The space badgers had cleaned the pod of everything. Why they did that, Gaines had no clue.

He sat back in his chair and his eyes quickly began to feel very heavy. All the stress and physical exertion were taking their toll on him.

He must have fallen asleep but he snapped awake to the sound of claws scurrying on metal. He looked across the pod and saw four space badgers digging through his toolbox. On the wall next to them, one of the metal panels had been bent forward providing a two foot hole in the wall. Through that, Gaines could see nothing but fur as dozens of space badgers moved within the walls of his pod.

"Hey," he shouted while standing up.

The four space badgers whipped their heads up and turned to face Gaines. Each held a different tool in their claws and they were as still as statues. Suddenly, three of them made a dash for the hole in the wall. The fourth dropped the tool it was holding, grabbed the handle of the toolkit, and ran—trying to take all the tools with it.

Gaines chased after them. By the time he reached the other side of the pod, three of the space badgers had already escaped with their prizes. The fourth was trying to pull the toolkit through the hole but it was too bulky to fit.

Gaines grabbed the kit and pulled back but the space badger would not let go. He accidently hit the latch and the kit spilled open, dumping tools on the floor. Other space badgers darted out of the hole and snatched up the instruments from the floor.

"No no no no." Gaines said. Acting out of reflex, he let go of the kit and tried to scoop up the tools from the floor. Each time he tried to grab one, a space badger claw would shoot out, scratch him, and steal the tool. In moments, the space badgers pulled all the tools through the hole and even the kit itself.

Gaines kicked the bent out metal panel. "Fuck! Fuck! Fuck!" he yelled with each kick as he bent it back into place.

When he'd closed it enough to keep out the space badgers, Gaines slumped to the floor and looked at his hands. They felt like they were on fire. Each one, covered with dozens of bleeding scratches. In some spots, the cuts were so deep that the blood flowed down his fingertips and dripped onto the golden metal floor.

He looked around and saw that the space badgers had missed one tool—the screwdriver. Gaines darted across the floor on his hands and knees and greedily scooped up the tool.

Those Goddamn pests got my food, my water, my medicine, and now my tools. All I got is this fucking screwdriver.

He sat on the floor looking at his one tool. If he was going to get this ship moving again, he needed to figure out how to get all the space badgers out of its interior.

He sat for a full half-hour thinking over the situation, when finally an idea came to him. An absolutely insane idea. But if it worked, he could escape. If it failed, at least he'd be dead sooner that starving or dying of thirst.

He went to work right away. First he addressed the panel the space badgers had bent out. He unscrewed four bolts and it fell to the floor with a *Clang!* Confused space badgers blinked at the bright light from the cabin and half-heartedly hissed at him.

Gaines ran to another wall and unscrewed the first panel he came to. Once it was removed, more confused space badgers spilled out. He unscrewed another panel and another.

Once he removed all six interior wall panels he went to the panel on the floor—the same one where he first discovered the space badger infestation. Now the other badgers had adjusted to the light and were angry at being disturbed. They jumped at his legs and scratched while he unscrewed the final bolts, frantically trying to finish his work.

Finally the last bolt was out. He pulled on the panel and tossed it aside. The interior of the cabin filled with space badgers. They poured out of the openings in the walls and floor.

Gaines kicked the animals aside and made his way across the room to the cockpit. He sat himself down in the chair and strapped all three seat belts—two across his chest and one across his lap.

He pushed buttons on the control panel while space badgers

scratched his legs, tearing open dozens of wounds, and began to climb his command chair.

The screen read OPEN DOCKING DOORS? EMERGENCY OPPERATING OVERRIDE YES/NO.

Gaines took a deep breath and pressed YES.

The docking door began to open. Then all air was violently sucked out of the escape pod. The force spun Gaines' chair around and scores of space badgers flew out the door.

The animals poured from all of the open panels. They just kept coming and coming. Gaines felt his lungs threatening to burst and his eyes felt like they wanted to leap from their sockets.

Finally, the atmosphere seemed empty of space badgers—except for one that had its claws dug into Gaines' calf muscle. The pull of the vacuum wrenched the wounds wider, and the animal still hung on. Gaines kicked at the beast with his other leg. He didn't know how much longer he could hold on. His lungs were screaming but if he tried to take a breath it was all over for him.

Just when Gaines thought he could take no more, the space badger lost its grip and went spiraling through the pod and out the door. Gaines' hands thrashed atop the control panel and hit the button reading CLOSE.

The docking doors lowered shut and immediately, the life support system adjusted the atmosphere to normal. Gaines gasped for breath.

He hit buttons on the control panel starting a full system scan. In moments the screen read SYSTEM SCAN COMPLETE: ALL SYSTEMS NORMAL.

Gaines almost started crying.

It worked. I have control of the ship again.

He replotted the course to the closest starbase. Sure it would take him two weeks, and he didn't know what he was going to do about food, water, or all the open wounds on his body—but at least he was moving.

He paused and looked out the glass screen. All around the ship hundreds of space badgers floated in space. They thrashed about and tried to space-swim their way back to the escape pod or to other hunks of floating debris. It would still be another half an hour before their air ran out and they choked to death. Gaines wished he could stay to watch that.

The stars directly in front of his escape pod suddenly looked very weird. It was like they were shimmering and shaking in place. The area turned a familiar neon blue as a huge mass revealed itself in front of the small ship.

The Behemoth was back. It must have had some kind of camouflage system that enabled it to blend into its space background. Gaines finally solved the mystery of how Behemoths can so easily sneak up on ships.

Not that it mattered.

The monster was attracted to all the space badgers floating around. They had nowhere to escape—and neither did Gaines.

He furiously attempted to finish punching in the coordinates but he was too late. The Behemoth's jaws snapped shut around the escape pod and the hundreds of space badgers.

Jeff Burk is the cult favorite author of Shatnerquake, Super Giant Monster Time, *and* Cripple Wolf. *He is also the Editor-in-Chief for* The Magazine of Bizarro Fiction *and the Head Editor of Eraserhead Press' horror imprint, Deadite Press. His influences include: sleep deprivation, comic books, drugs, magick, and kittens.*

You can stalk him online at jeffburk.wordpress.com and facebook. com/literarystrange.

SLEEP DEEPLY
by Mark West

Tom Davis noticed that his throat felt dry at the exact moment the car alarm went off, shattering the stillness of the night with its piercing scream. He tried hard not to hear it, tried to block it out but couldn't.

"Bugger," he said and sat up. He pressed his earplugs in deeper but the sound wouldn't go away and the more he thought about trying not to hear it, the more it penetrated and rattled around his brain.

He flicked his blindfold up and looked at the clock, the digital numbers swimming a little whilst his eyes focussed. It was 3:47, he'd been in bed since 11:25 and he was desperate to go to sleep. Not that being desperate would help. Tom had suffered from insomnia since he was fifteen and he cursed his affliction

He flopped back onto the bed and coughed. Should he go and get a glass of water or not? His breath hitched in his throat so he swallowed a couple of times and decided to stay where he was.

From outside, he heard a front door slam and then a rapid series of beeps that stopped at the same time as the alarm.

"Thanks a lot, mate," said Tom as he smoothed the duvet against his chest and tried to clear his mind. He wished Amy was lying next to him, she would have helped him through the night.

They'd met, three years ago, at the Wildebeeste Club in Chaton. He was more tired than normal, tripped and bumped into her. Apologising, they'd both noticed a spark and talked through the night and started to see one another.

He explained about his affliction and she was intrigued, having never had a sleepless night in her life. She helped him with his rituals—the ear plugs, the blindfold to block out the light, the silence he needed to try and sleep and the patience for when he invariably couldn't. However great their love was though—and he believed she truly did love him, as much as he loved her—some things cannot survive the strain of one partner being awake a good day or more a week longer than the other.

She left him in the March and it cut him to the quick. His insomnia got worse and, desperate for a cure, he re-read the same books he'd read in his teens. Pills were prescribed by a doctor who'd tried too many things on Tom already and he invested in a state of the art blindfold and ear-plug system that seemed to have been designed by the military it was so comprehensive.

Nothing had worked. It was now early October and the nights had drawn in so much that it was perpetual darkness to Tom. His job didn't inspire him like it once had and he pined for Amy. It seemed like he had nothing left, except for this bloody gift that he'd now had for thirteen years. Unlucky thirteen, someone had once said to him when he was in a betting shop. He didn't put much store in superstition—when you spend most of your life awake, magic and miracles soon explain themselves—but how everything was coming together this year could make him change his mind.

He looked back at the clock and saw that it was now 4:02. He groaned and pulled his blindfold back down. He had a meeting in five hours and twenty eight minutes when he would try and sell some bods from Unilever on the idea of having a pig advertise their new washing powder. He had to sleep, he had to win this account— everything had to work for him for a change rather than try and hobble him, every step of the way.

The worst thing he found about his insomnia was how loud his body was—the blood in his ears, the clicking in his jaw, the sound of his breathing and the pulse in his wrists. Everything was as it was during the day obviously, but at night, with silence around him, it became a cacophony of noise, a concert in the Royal Albert Hall with the Tom Davis Body Orchestra, conducted by No-Sleep-Brain. That was bloody annoying because it didn't matter what you did, that orchestra started at one o'clock in the morning and they kept going, no fag breaks, no tea breaks, no nothing for hours. Night after night, hour after hour, minute after bloody minute.

He felt short of breath, coughed and breathed in deeply.

Why couldn't it stop, why couldn't it all stop? He wanted Amy back but knew it was a lost cause and the anticipation of the boredom of thinking the same thing over and over—all night—was starting to drive him insane.

He felt short of breath again and breathed in.

Baboom Baboom, went the blood in his ears.

Flick swish, went his eyes.

Tick dribble, went his mouth.

He listened for his breath, waited for it to make its appearance, like the first violin.

It wasn't there. He felt short of breath again.

BREATHE.

He inhaled. He listened for the pulse in his wrist and felt it, like a bass echo—bu-bu, bu-bu.

He couldn't breathe.

BREATHE.

He inhaled but felt full, as though he was trying to eat something and his mouth was still full from the previous bite.

Exhale! Exhale!

Breath whooshed out of him like a punctured balloon.

What was going on? What was happening to him, why wasn't he breathing?

Inhale. Exhale.

His could still hear his pulse, the clicking in his mouth, the soft shuffle of his tongue along his palate but there was no breath. Cold fear roughly caressed his heart and he inhaled so deeply that spots danced before his eyes. He swiped them away with a leaden hand, exhaled and inhaled again quickly so that not a moment was lost. He sat up in bed, panicked, in an attempt to keep his airways straight, all the while keeping his breathing going—inhale, exhale, inhale, exhale. He pulled off his blindfold. What was happening?

He stood up, the simple act requiring more exertion than he realised. Inhale—quick, quick—exhale. Keep it going.

Taking deep breaths and very quick exhales he worked his way to the bathroom, pulling the light switch and temporarily blinding himself. He thought about how painful the light was on his eyes and then felt tightness in his lungs.

Inhale. Exhale.

He opened his eyes slowly and walked to the sink, looking at himself in the mirror. His hair looked like Elvis' on a bad day, which was normal. He eyes were slightly bloodshot and that too was normal. He felt another tightness in his chest.

Inhale. Exhale.

"Jesus, what's going on?" He ran a hand over his face and through his hair. He tried to think about anything unusual that might have happened that day and then felt giddy, his vision filling up with white spots. Looking in the mirror, he saw the faraway look in his eyes.

Inhale. Exhale. What was happening? Inhale. Exhale.

He looked into his own red-rimmed eyes and something in his tired, frantic mind clicked into place. Although it didn't make sense it seemed like his lungs weren't on automatic anymore, they were running on manual, for some reason. He wasn't aware that that could happen and the fact that he would go down in medical history as the man who had to think about breathing didn't cheer him up at all.

White dots all around.

Shit. Inhale. Exhale.

No, that was just ridiculous. How could someone simply stop being able to breathe?

Hang on, if you stopped breathing.... He pressed a hand against his chest and was comforted by the steady beat of his heart. He wasn't dead then, which was a relief.

Inhale. Exhale.

Breathing had become his life's soundtrack over the years, accompanying his night sweats and strains to get to sleep. Amy had once confided in him that she sometimes worried that she'd stop breathing, that she wouldn't be able to draw enough breath and that she would have to concentrate on breathing for the rest of her life. The fears, she'd said, sounding embarrassed, usually only lasted for a few minutes until she forgot about the process and let her body get on with it again. He'd laughed, telling her it was silly, that your body didn't just stop breathing. At that time, he'd spent twelve years of nights listening to his breath, hearing it whistle out of his nose, sing out from between his lips, pump into his lungs, keep everything going. He knew it didn't just stop.

Inhale. Exhale.

He rinsed his face and breathed deeply, the exertion crippling his lungs. He dried his face slowly and carefully and walked back to his bed, taking four or five revitalising breaks on the way.

He laid down, the clock reading 4:14. He didn't care any more because caring meant thinking and thinking seemed, for some reason, to mean not breathing. All this could be a dream but he didn't want to test it out.

Inhale. Exhale.

He was terrified. What was he going to do—he couldn't think about breathing all the time. Or could he? If he didn't think about breathing, he didn't breathe—it seemed as simple as that.

Inhale. Exhale.

Okay, that seemed to work okay, you just add the inhale and exhale on the end of your thoughts.

'Yeah,' he thought, 'and look like a complete idiot.'

But then it occurred to him that being in marketing, if he said inhale and exhale at the end of each sentence, people would think he was creative and eccentric. He'd never lose an account and progress further up the ladder than he'd ever thought possible and, who knew, he could even end up a partner.

Inhale. Exhale.

This could be used to his advantage, this could really start to make things happen for him.

He yawned. Sleep was coming, thank God. It had been a long time coming tonight and, what with the presentation tomorrow, he needed some sleep, any sleep, if only an hour at the very least. He could then awake refreshed, win the contract and suddenly be on the fast track to promotion that had been promised him eight years ago.

"This is it," he said, to prove the point.

Inhale. Exhale.

He felt sleep start to come, welcoming it with the delight that only a true insomniac can. He listened for the blood in his ears, the clicks in his mouth, his breathing...

Inhale. Jesus, that was close. Exhale. Inhale. Exhale.

Horrible realisation crossed his addled mind—he needed to think about breathing to keep breathing. When was the only time he wasn't aware of thinking? What was the one thing he welcomed more than anything?

Inhale. Exhale.

He began to cry, his breath catching in his throat, his tears running down his cheeks.

Inhale.

"You bastard," he yelled, to whatever it was that had given him the gift of insomnia and now laid this dirty trick at his feet.

Exhale. Inhale. Exhale.

His sobs caused havoc with his inhaling and exhaling so he tried to calm down and slowly his breathing got back to normal. He pulled his blindfold down and stared into the perfect darkness.

Inhale. Exhale. He put the words to a rhythm. Inhale, huh huh, exhale, huh huh. It worked for quite a while.

Then, at 4:57 am, Tom Davis, still humming something under his breath, fell asleep.

It was almost four days before Tom Davis was found. Amy Worth, worried because she hadn't been able to raise him on the telephone, used her key to get into his flat. She found him in his bed, blue lipped and pallid, a beatific expression on his face.

Mark West is a member of the British Fantasy Society and a proud Terror Scribe of long-standing. Rainfall Books published his collection, Strange Tales *in 2003 and his short novel* Conjure *in 2009, whilst his novel,* In the Rain With the Dead, *was published by Pendragon Press in 2005. His novelette* The Mill *appeared in the BFS-shortlisted anthology* We Fade to Grey *and has since been published as an ebook by Greyhart Press. He can be contacted through his website at* markwest. org.uk. *This story was originally published in* Enigmatic Tales *in March 2000.*

SCARRED
by Deb Hoag

I

Jauncey Hunter had his first fracture when he was four months old. When he was two, the old man ground a cigarette out on his arm.

People say that Child Protective Services are too quick to rush in. That they see an innocent bruise and concoct a whole imaginary history of abuse and neglect.

Not in Jauncey Hunter's case. The welfare agency never came for him. His horror went on and on, in the dreary cabin that stank of fried onions and his old man's boozy shit. Nobody rushed in to rescue him. The neighbors surely heard his thin high screams of pain, the old man's curses and laughter.

But no one ever came to rescue *him*.

Because everyone was scared of the old man. They sat behind closed doors and thought, "as long as it's not me."

Teachers looked silently at his battered face and took his toneless excuses and did nothing, remembering the last time they had seen the old man rolling through the school, glowering and threatening, a rageful flush burning in his face. And they looked away, not wanting any of those bruises for themselves, not wanting the old man targeting them for reprisal, revenge.

Jauncey's old man snapped two of his fingers - one as an experiment, to see how hard it would be to do, the next because he liked the sound of the little bastard's screams so much.

Police took a measured look at what they saw on the boy and thought about that psycho in Belleville who had barricaded himself in his house, kid and wife hostage, and ended up killing two officers before he shot his family and himself. And in a measured way, they decided that the risk outweighed the benefit.

The old man burned the word. "fuck me" across Jauncey's

back with cigarettes. Just for fun, he burned an arrow pointing down over the boy's softly fuzzed butt cheeks, pointing at his ass. Then he followed his own advice and sodomized his son. Not for the first time.

The local social workers looked at a bulletin board where a tattered newspaper clipping detailed the serial rapes and beating of a dozen CPS workers by a man who felt Child Protective Services had wronged him. They remembered the rivulets of sweat that ran from the old man's forehead and armpits, the huge rotten bulk of him, the indecent hot eyes, the meaty cruel hands, and decided to wait until more evidence came to light.

As a graduation present from junior high, Jauncey received a concussion, a broken tibia, and the first blast from the old man's new Taser. And the second, the third, the fourth . . . after that, Jauncey lost count.

After all, the boy went to school, right? And he backed up his old man's stories one hundred and one percent. Surely, if something was going on, the boy would say something, wouldn't he? How old was he now—fourteen, fifteen? Old enough to speak up for himself, if something was going on, God damn it.

And then, Jauncey received a present that really mattered.

It came in the form of a closed head injury, when the old man tripped him and he fell against a hard pine stump, knocking himself senseless.

The present was: *Freedom.*

That night, Jauncey went to sleep with swelling and pressure concentrated around the sensitive frontal lobe of his brain. The area of the brain responsible for certain higher functions, among them empathy, conscience, a sense of right and wrong. Even the ability to love.

Some researchers have a more Darwinian take on what is contained in that section of the brain. "The herd instinct" is something they toss out. That desire to comply, to devote oneself to the good of the group, to obey rules and laws whether one believes in them or not.

It's also the area which generates the feeling of fear, of

reasonable restraint, of dread and regret and reverence.

The swelling increased, pushing the frontal lobe against Jauncey's skull. Delicate cells were crushed, nerves that raced signals from one section of the brain to another destroyed forever.

The brain may heal, but it does not regenerate. What is destroyed stays destroyed, whether it's the ability to warm and open in the face of love or the ability to say to the self. "no, I won't. That wouldn't be right".

All those things were cut off from Jauncey's experience like a lump of butter cut off the stick.

He was sixteen now, a big boy, taking after the old man. He was smart, smart as a whip, although he rarely saw the opportunity to put that intellect to good use.

Today was going to be that day.

He lay in bed for a few minutes, savoring the sensations that were flooding him. Or, he mused, the absence of them. He had no idea why everything had changed from one day to the next, only that it *had*. It was like he had been listening to really, really loud music for a long time—wasn't there a story about that somewhere? About a society where smart people had to wear headphones that deluged them with senseless noise all the time to make them dumber, where ballerinas had to drag along heavy weights when they danced, good looking people had to wear ugly masks, some shit like that? Whatever it was, whatever had changed, the fear was gone. The headphones were off. The dread, the horror of waking up to another day on a stained mattress in a filthy cabin, wanting to die, afraid the old man would follow him even in death if he tried to escape that way—it was all gone. Except that now, for some strange reason, he no longer wanted to die. No, not at all.

The solution to all his troubles, the answer to all the bruises, breaks, fractures, sprains, cuts and burns was suddenly, glaringly, obvious.

He would kill the son of a bitch.

Really, really slow. The idea made him smile. Pack 16 years worth of torture and abuse into a few weeks. A little creativity and he was sure he could pull it off. Who would come to the old man's rescue? Nobody. He'd cut out the bastard's tongue right off the bat and take his time for the rest.

First, he had to get the old man in a manageable state. Not too hard, when he put his mind to it. He slipped out and down the rutted dirt road to the McNally's house, quietly twisted open the unlocked back door—*careful,, careful!*--and padded down the short hall to the liquor cabinet. He laughed pulling the nearly full fifth of Jack off the shelf, hearing McNally and his wife nattering in the living room.

His heart beat a little faster thinking they might hear him and come to see what that noise was, but he realized it was excitement, not fear. A rush, wasn't that what people called it? He'd lived in bowel churning fear for so long he'd never experienced anticipation before, but he decided he liked it.

He wished they *would* hear him, so he could swing the liquor bottle and bash in their fat, stupid, fearful faces, their avoidant eyes, their guilty half smiles of acknowledgment whenever they passed him by in the street.

Sure, that smile seemed to say, *we know. We all know. It's our little secret now, isn't it? But we're afraid of him, too. Better one small, defenseless boy to bear the brunt than our well-off, well-fed, well-tanned fat-ass selves, isn't that right, boy? You don't really mind, do you? Those screams are an exaggeration, aren't they? Surely, you don't hurt that bad. If you did, someone else would know, would do something, wouldn't they?*

But they didn't stop their yackety-yack-yack-yacking for long enough to hear a bowling ball hit a china cabinet, as far as he could tell. So he pulled out his dick in the kitchen and pissed all over their pressed wood kitchen table and the stupid-ass penguin salt and pepper shakers that lived there.

Then, feeling immensely satisfied, Jauncey zipped up his pants and swung out the door, leaving it swinging gently in the early morning breeze.

Before he presented his gift to the old man, Jauncey did a quick search of the old shed out back, the old shed that smelled like grease and gasoline, the shed that was bigger than his bedroom and

84

the witness to many of his beatings. There was a tree handy to the shed, where any number of dispirited hunting dogs had been tied. Sometimes Jauncey had been tied there, too, to make it easier for the old man to hit him when he was getting tired, when his arm was getting tired …

Amused by the memory now, Jauncey searched the shelves, looking for an old paper packet of pain pills that the vet had given them for some long ago dog that had tangled with a bear when the old man was out hunting. Whistling, Jauncey smashed the pills with a hammer, and then dropped them into the whiskey bottle.

Hiding a chuckle with a cough, Jauncey bent his body back into the familiar subservient posture and walked back in the door of the trailer. "Hey, pop? I found a bottle of whiskey out by the truck. You must have set it down when you were coming in last night, and forgot to pick it back up."

Hair of the dog is a damn good thing when you're nearly 300 pounds of greasy, hungover rat guts. The old man had swallowed half of it before it even occurred to him to look that particular gift horse in the mouth. And by then, it was *way* too late.

The thing was, Jauncey discovered, it was also *quite* a bit of fun.

II

Keenan Bowers was a product of too much methamphetamine and a temporary shortage of rubbers at the local drugstore. His mother had abandoned him in the backseat of an unlocked SUV that still had that yummy new car smell, and while the people to whom the SUV belonged had no interest in keeping the squalling infant for a second longer than necessary, they had taken the time to turn him over to the proper authorities.

He had screamed and shaken and cried through the weeks following his birth, a shriveled little thing that looked more like a tiny wretched mummy than the plump, smiling babies that the baby food commercials invariably showed. Nobody was exactly what effect the drugs had had on his brain, what circuits that should trip hadn't and what circuits hadn't tripped that should have. He was odd, and oddly fragile in some ways, something the foster care system had little patience for. So he was pushed and placed and pulled and replaced until he could no longer remember how many families he had stayed with, how many times he had gotten the back of someone's hand, how many times something he loved had been stolen, forgotten, discarded or broken.

Keenan didn't like cats. They creeped him out, the way they stared, the way they wouldn't come when you called them, like they knew something nasty about you that they'd blurt out when you least wanted them too. And even when you got them in your lap, when you petted them nicely, and told them what good, good kitties they were, they'd still flex those needle sharp claws and leave you with your blood leaking out little bloody holes they made in your leg without even caring.

No, Keenan didn't like cats. Not at all.

Dogs, though, were a different story. Dogs were friendly. They wagged their tails, they pushed their noses under your hand—nudge, nudge—practically begging you to pet them. They'd chase a ball if a guy felt like throwing one. And if you told a dog your secrets, you could bet he'd never, ever tell.

Keenan liked dogs quite a bit. Whenever he got put in a home had a dog, he always figured it was a good sign. After all, if folks liked dogs, they probably wouldn't mind a boy too much, would they?

At age twelve, he was still scrawny, with flapping hands and eyes too large for his thin face. He hated school, where he got made fun of a lot for his hand-me-down clothes, for his gullibility, his daydreaming. He had poor impulse control, which got him into plenty of trouble in his short life. Mostly of th. "sit down, Keenan! Shut up, Keenan! How could you *do* that, Keenan?" variety.

He didn't know, either, honestly. It baffled him as much as it baffled his legion of teachers and foster parents.

So when Keenan saw the big, sandy-haired man in the park, throwing a ball for his clumsy, flop-eared beagle puppy, it never even

86

occurred to Keenan to be cautious; to keep walking. Stranger danger and all that stuff they taught him in school? In one ear and out the other, as the saying goes. His glowing eyes glued to the dog, Stranger danger was about as far away from his thoughts as the drought in Africa.

"Hey, mister! Can I throw the ball for your dog for a while?"

And Jauncey Hunter turned slowly, surveying Keenan like he had to give the matter careful consideration. Keenan waited in an agony of anticipation for Jauncey's decision.

Finally Jauncey smiled, shaking his shaggy hair out of dishwater gray eyes as he did it. "Sure. My arm's getting kind of tired anyway. But Buddy here is getting pretty close to his dinner time. If you want to come back to my house with me and help me feed him, then you can have a good, long game of catch with him afterward. How does that sound?"

And as simple as that, Keenan hopped into Jauncey's completely forgettable, comfortably middle-aged van, and disappeared from Perkosee Park.

III

When Keenan came to, he was lying on a narrow bed in a small, rough-timbered shed. There was an ache in his head and a disgusting taste in his mouth. He blinked, and then hauled himself laboriously up into a sitting position. He was hampered in this by the thick leather cuff that anchored him to the metal bed frame.

He could see the puppy, now moving restlessly in a small wire cage on a high wooden table. It looked like a workbench, bare of tools. There was a vise bolted to the far end of the table, and shelves above it where a bunch of junky looking stuff was stored. The man from the park was doing something with the cage, fiddling with the door. When Keenan sat up, he turned and smiled.

"Hey, mister," said Keenan. He tried to match the smile, but a wave of nausea gripped his stomach like a fist.

Keeping himself from puking took all of Keenan's concentration for a minute, but when his stomach settled, he tugged experimentally at the cuff. "What's going on?"

The big man pushed himself away from the workbench and his smile widened. "We're going to play a game. You like games?"

"Sure. What are we going to play?"

The man opened the cage door and took the puppy out. The puppy wagged his tail and licked the man's hand. Quick as a snake, the man's fingers shot out and grabbed the puppy's tongue.

At first, Keenan thought it was a joke, the man holding the little pink tongue, the puppy's rump up in the air as he tried to pull away from the man's grasp. But when the puppy started whining, Keenan shifted uneasily. "Hey, mister. I think you're hurting him. Maybe you should let him go."

The man just grinned and held on. The puppy's whining turned to that high, screeing sound that's halfway between a moan and a cry, rising as the pain got worse. The man picked the puppy up and dangled him, as the puppy shrieked and its oversized paws clawing desperately at nothing.

Keenan leaped to his feet, heart pumping furiously. The cuff kept him from standing straight, but he reached out and grabbed at the man's free arm, trying to get his attention. "Mister, put him down! Please put him down! You're hurting him! Stop it!"

The man gave the boy a sly look, and bounced the helpless dog in the air once, twice. Then he slowly lowered the puppy back to the table, shoving him back into the cage. The little dog cringed into the corner, still screaming, as the man shoved the door shut and clicked the lock.

"You didn't like that game? I've got another one. Let's see what you think of this."

IV

Jauncey leveraged himself up from the bed, away from the boy who had been nearly crushed beneath him. The boy's body was covered with clammy sweat, his skin pale from shock. He had stopped screaming long ago, needing every bit of energy he had just to keep breathing.

After much experimenting, Jauncey found that, like his old man, he preferred the young to the old, boys to girls. Although, Jauncey conceded to himself with a smirk, he was much more *diversified* than his old man, who had only one victim as far as Jauncey knew. Jauncey was working on two dozen, and baker's dozens at that.

In his considered opinion, children made much better victims. Kids were so much more hopeful, in every way. Hopeful that they could convince him to stop, hopeful that someone would rescue them, hopeful almost right to the very end that heaven, at least, would reach out to them and end their pain. Most adults had no such illusions; they weren't nearly so much fun.

Girls weren't nearly as much fun as boys. He'd finally decided that girls, somehow, already knew on some fundamental level that they were going to get it. Boys were so much more shocked by the whole thing. For girls, it was just a matter of who and when. Some rich shit-for-brains hubby after they graduated from high school and were married nice and proper in a church somewhere, or some asshole john in a stinking hotel room, that big prick was inescapable in the end. The thought made him smile. A joke! He'd made a joke. He thought about sharing it with the shivering boy on the bed, then decided to go grab a beer instead.

As he walked around the bed, he trailed his fingers against the wires of the puppy's cage. The little dog cried and tried to back into the corner.

Looked like the dog might turn out to be smarter than the kid. At least for the first round.

V

In the days that followed, the man always followed the same pattern. He would enter the little room, filling it to bursting just by stepping through the door, and start with the dog. When the boy could no longer bear the puppy's screams of pain, when a protest forced from him by his conscience, regardless of his intentions, the man would smile and turn to him.

Then the pain would start. And go on, and on, and on, until his mind short-circuited and went away. Most often, the man would stop then, uninterested in proceeding if Keenan was not an active participant in the pain.

After the man tired of whatever he was inflicting and left, Keenan would pull together the shattered pieces of who he used to be and wait for the next onslaught. He dreamed of rescue, plotted his escapes, which were many and brilliant and always entirely in his mind.

Sometimes, Keenan would stretch out on the bed full length, his body straining away from the leather cuff, and reach out with his feet to to the tall table. If the man didn't jostle the cage too much when he took the puppy out and put him back in, Keenan could reach the cage with his foot. Sometimes, he could feel the little dog's soft fur, the shivering that matched his own. Shivering that didn't come from cold, but from whatever terrors had been inflicted on them that day.

Keenan would whisper to Buddy when gaps in the plank walls told him it was dark out. Secrets always seemed safer in the dark. He would talk about foster homes he had lived in, friends he had made, things he would eat when he got away from the man.

"Ho Hos, Buddy," he whispered. His voice was hoarse. The man had done things to him that day that had made him beg for mercy. The things had gone on for a long time. So had Keenan's screams. "You break 'em open and lick all the cream off, then eat the frosting, then throw away the rest. You're going to like 'em so much! I'll use 'em to teach you to do tricks, Buddy. And I'll never, ever hit you if you don't get them right. No matter how much you screw up. I'll never, ever hit you . . . " Hot tears slid down and hit the thin wool blanket.

Keenan had started to think he would never, ever get away from the man. Neither would Buddy. He couldn't see the little dog so good anymore, because of something that the man had done to Keenan's left eye. But he didn't think Buddy was feeling so hot. The puppy didn't cry out so much anymore, no matter what the man did to him. Keenan thought maybe Buddy was starting to give up hope.

Keenan wasn't feeling so hopeful himself.

Slowly, fighting a thousand aches, he inched down the bed as far as the cuff would let him. The skin under the cuff was rubbed raw and bleeding from futile attempts to get away from the man's tortures. He stretched out a battered leg, forcing it high enough to reach the table, inching along in search of the dog's cage. Unexpectedly, his foot found the cage a good two inches closer than it usually was.

The puppy edged closer inside the cage, pressing his body against the wires, so that boy and dog could touch.

A daring thought shot through Keenan's brain, and he reached with his toes, curling them around the vertical wires and pulling the cage, and the little dog, toward himself.

As if the puppy understood what Keenan was doing, it made soft fearful noises, the kind a small child might make, caught in by a night terror. There was no way this would end well. The man would come back, catch them, and the punishment would be terrible.

"Shh, shh, Buddy, don't make any racket," said Keenan, and continued pulling the cage toward him with his toes, but he could feel the entire cage shaking with the dog's fear. "He's gonna get us anyway, Buddy. We might as well be together when he does."

He eased the cage closer.

Closer.

It balanced precariously on the edge of the table.

Keenan gave it a last, gentle tug, and the cage fell.

He thought he'd be able to catch it, but his aching muscles were slow and the cage crashed to the floor.

The dog gave out a little shriek.

"I'm sorry, Buddy," said Keenan, swinging his body around on the bed so he could reach the door of the cage with his hands.

Keenen pulled out the long nail that served as a linchpin on the door and eased the little dog out. He cradled the puppy gently,

91

burying his face in fur that had gone patchy and dull. One of the dog's paws was horribly maimed. It had been crushed in a vise. His ears were ripped and torn. His left eye was gone, burned with a cigar. Ichor crusted around the oozing socket.

The dog moaned and squirmed closer, licking Keenan's arm.

For a minute, the briefest sliver of time, they were simply a boy and his dog.

The door crashed open and the man burst in.

"What the fuck was that noise?" he screamed.

The man stepped inside, crowding out air and light with menace.

His eyes swept the bed, the boy and the dog curled together. "Well, isn't this a nice moment," he sneered.

The boy shifted, shoved the dog under the bed, out of the man's easy reach.

Keenan half knelt, half stood on the bed, looking at the man with steady eyes.

"I guess we're both about used up," he said. "Why don't you just finish this now?"

"You think you're ready to die, you little fuck? You have a lot of pain to go yet before I'm gonna let you go. A lot of pain. I'm gonna cut that fucking dog open and pull out his guts. Real slow, just like I did to my old man. And when the dog dies, I'm gonna cut off your dick and your balls, and I'm gonna make you fucking swallow them before I kill you, you fucking bastard."

The man grabbed Keenan by the throat with one big hand and lifted him off the thin mattress.

He held the boy up in the air, face inches away, and bared his teeth as Keenan choked and gasped for air.

The puppy darted out from under the bed and sank his teeth into the man's calf.

The man gave out a strangled scream.

As hard as he could, Keenan slammed the nail from Buddy's cage door into the man's greasy ear.

The man screamed again, this time a high, thin scream. He reached up with a hand suddenly gone vague and useless, as if he were going to pull the pin out, but seemed unable to grasp it.

He dropped Keenan back on the bed. The boy stared up as the man started to topple, not sure which way to roll to keep the man from falling on him.

The man took a step back, then fell to the floor. His eyes were wide and unfocused.

His body twitched.

Keenan had lived for a while in a foster home with a kid that had seizures, and he knew what they looked like. He thought maybe the man was having a seizure because of the nail, buried several inches deep in his brain.

The little dog growled loudly.

A thick line of drool flowed sluggishly from the man's mouth to the floor.

A stink filled the room. The man had pissed himself.

Keenan and the little dog watched as the man shuddered and flopped on the floor.

After several minutes, the man stopped moving, except for a ragged panting breath that came and went.

Keenan looked at the little dog. "He's got a knife on his belt, Buddy. I could cut my way out of this cuff. Think it's safe to try and get it?"

The little dog looked from the boy to the man and growled again, as if to say. "I got your back, Keenan. Go ahead."

Slowly, Keenan reached out and grabbed the sheath of the knife.

The man moaned. Small bubbles formed in the spittle on his lips. His eyes were fixed on a spot on the wall.

Keenan tugged the blade free, slowly, slowly.

After a full minute, when the man showed no reaction at all, Keenan began to saw frantically at the cuff on his wrist.

The little dog sat at his feet as he cut, cut, cut. The leather, stained with Keenan's blood and sweat, separated reluctantly.

Finally, the cuff fell away. Keenan stood and took wobbly steps away from the bed that had been his whole world for eight weeks. He looked down at the man on the floor, and felt the heft of the bitter sharp blade in his hand. He could almost feel the knife slipping through the man's pasty flesh to the organs below, tasting blood, tasting heart blood, slitting the throat and watching blood fountain up until the man was dead—as dead as he had promised to make Keenan and the little dog.

It wasn't in him. Keenan opened the door and whistled softly for the little dog. He threw the knife in a scrubby bush and began to hobble slowly toward freedom.

VI

It took nearly an hour of labored walking to reach a main road. Keenan had followed the drive that led away from the man's disreputable cabin, and found a rutted dirt road. The light of the moon was thin, but it looked to Keenan like more tracks ran in and out along the left hand side of the road than the right, so that's the way he headed. Buddy followed, limping on three paws.

After the first mile, Buddy just laid down and quit, and Keenan ended up carrying him, teeth gritted against the effort. "Neither of us have had much of anything to eat," he explained to Buddy. "You know what I'm gonna eat once we get back to people?" Obligingly, Buddy licked his hand, as if encouraging him to go on. The boy looked down and smiled before he continued. "Ice cream. About a gallon. Cookie dough. Or maybe chocolate mint chip. What do you think?"

The little dog sighed and snuggled in, closing his good eye. Keenan, his bare feet raw, staggered on through the cold night air.

The road seemed to go on and on forever, but just at the point that Keenan might have given up, curled up on the ground somewhere and floated away, the slight breeze carried a noise to him. The sound of a motor of some kind--a car? No, a truck. A big one. Diesel. Then a car. He walked faster now, and realized he was close to some kind of major road, because he could hear one vehicle after another zooming past.

With a last burst of his failing energy, Keenan made it to the

94

top of a small embankment and crested it to see a paved road.

He half fell, half raced down the gentle slope. He held the puppy with one hand and thrust the other out in the air. "Stop! We need help!" he said, stepping out into the road in front of an oncoming car.

As the driver slammed on the brakes and swerved to avoid him, Keenan collapsed on the road.

The car screeched to a stop, straddling both lanes. Other cars coming up behind him had no choice but to stop, too.

The driver got out and ran to Keenan were he lay on the pavement.

The boy was starved, bones protruding sharply from skin that was bruised, cut or bloody over his entire body. He wore a pair of filthy cotton underpants and nothing else. One eye was swollen shut, and a finger on his left hand was gone, a small oozing stump in its place.

There was the sound of car doors slamming, as people got out to see what was going on. They approached Keenan cautiously. He looked more like a small, demented skeleton than a boy.

"I didn't hit him," said the man Keenan had stepped in front of. "I swear. He must have passed out or something. He just collapsed on the pavement right in front of my car."

"I called 9-1-1," another man said. "They'll have an ambulance there in a few minutes. Anybody got a blanket to put over him till they get here?"

Keenan's lids fluttered. His good eye opened and he fixed it on the man who had just spoken. "I'm alright, mister, but I think my dog is awfully thirsty. Could you find him a drink of water, do you think?"

A teenage girl crouched down to inspect them both. She looked doubtfully from Buddy to Keenan. "Kid, your dog is in pretty bad shape. I'm not sure--"

Somebody said something sharply, and she stopped talking, stood up, took a step back.

A woman came forward with a water bottle and poured some into a paper cup, offering it to the dog. Buddy lifted his head to lap it up weakly then sank back into the safety of Keenan's arms.

In the distance, Keenan could hear sirens. He frowned and lifted his head to look at the small crowd gathered around him. "There's a really bad man back there. There's a road right behind that little hill. Follow it back to a trailer a couple of miles back. He's in the shed behind the house."

And with that, the little dog still clutched tightly to his chest, Keenan fell back into unconsciousness.

As he was loaded into the ambulance, he roused briefly as the EMTs debated what to do with the dog.

"He's not going to make it," said one. "I can run him to the shelter after we drop the kid off. Jesus, it's going to take a frickin' miracle for the kid to make it."

Keenan opened his good eye and looked at the man who had spoken. "He saved me," Keenan said earnestly. "He needs help. We'll help him, right? I can't get better if he can't."

"Well," said another voice, after a moment's silence. "I guess that's that. Dog goes to the hospital too."

"Docs are going to love that."

"Fuck 'em. You heard the kid. Package deal."

On the stretcher, Keenan smiled.

VII

When the police made it to Jauncey's house, he was still alive, still sucking in those faint, rattling breaths and bubbling spit at the corners of his mouth. But he was completely unresponsive to the crowd of lawmen and EMTs that surrounded him, loaded him onto a stretcher, took him to the hospital. He died two days later, without ever regaining consciousness.

Investigation turned up twenty-six bodies on Jauncey's property. The older ones varied in age, in size, even in sex, but the last thirteen or so were much like Keenan, young boys, on the cusp of puberty, defenseless against the outpouring of sadistic rage that seemed woven into the very fibers of Jauncey's being. Each one had been buried with a puppy.

There had been no one to mourn them, or even miss them, when they had entered his orbit. No one but Keenan. When he finally turned eighteen, was out on his own, he had found out everything he could about each and every boy. When he could, he got pictures of them, old school pictures, file pictures from social services, and put them up on the narrow halls of his home. When he was alone there, except for Buddy, he talked to them as if they were old friends.

VIII

A thin, pale man in his early thirties sat on the park bench, clad in a black suit and spotless white shirt. He wore dark sunglasses in heavy frames. He was a study in black and white, except for the sunny white-gold spill of hair that flowed down to his collar and across his forehead.

A puppy played in front of him, a stick in its mouth, staggering here and there as the weight of the stick overbalanced it first this way, then that.

A small girl was working her way with deliberate nonchalance toward man and puppy.

The man studied her intently from behind the dark glasses. Long, thin fingers stilled and came to rest on the back of an decrepit-looking dog at his side on the bench. The dog had only one eye; its left leg was missing as well. Its fur was traced with scars and bald patches that had never grown back.

The little girl drew closer, looking from the puppy to the man.

"Mister, is that your puppy? What's his name?"

The man pulled his glasses down, so that he could get a better look at the girl who stood in front of him, twisting shyly.

Keenan looked her over carefully. Like Buddy, he only had one working eye, but unlike the dog, he'd been given extensive plastic surgery and an excellent glass eye, and now you would have to look very, very closely to see the thin star-burst line of scars that led away from that meticulously reconstructed socket.. "That's Rosebud," he said, finally. "It's a *she*."

"Carli, what the hell are you doing? Get the fuck away from that guy. What did I tell you about talking to people you don't know?"

Buddy growled softly, low in his throat.

A fat man approached, a faint aura of sweat and semen seeming to announce his arrival. As he approached, the little girl's face closed up. She shot Keenan a desperate look. "My name's not really Carli," she whispered urgently, then fell silent. She turned her eyes to her feet and couldn't seem to bring them back up.

Keenan stood and gave the fat man the same careful study he had afforded the girl.

The man grabbed the girl by the shoulder and brushed past Keenan with hard, hot eyes. Buddy's growl got louder. Even the puppy was still, watching Keenan and the fat man with interest.

As he passed, Keen reached out to touch the man's arm. It was a light touch, almost casual, but the fat man spun around and raised a hand, as if he would smash Keenan without even thinking about it.

Once, maybe. Never again.

Keenan grabbed the fat man's raised hand and effortlessly stepped out of the way, turning so that the fat man ended up with his arm pinned behind his back. Keenan reached up with his other arm and wrapped it around the man's neck. He put his lips close to the man's ear and said pleasantly. "Bill Withers, you are under arrest for multiple counts of kidnap, sexual assault of a child, and murder." The fat man started to splutter and tug at Keenan's arm, and Keenan turned him so he could see half a dozen other men in SWAT gear approaching, faces grim and fierce.

Over the fat man's shoulder, Keenan smiled down at the little girl. "Hi, Cindy Perkins, age five. I know some people who are going to be really glad to see you. How would you like to go home?"

Deb Hoag has been writing professionally for going on 20 years, starting at a weekly alternative newspaper in Detroit, Michigan, The Metro Times. *Her work there included answering phones, editing, writing a column and organizing such events as the Detroit Music Awards and the newspaper's yearly photography contest and Best Of issues. In the early '90s, Deb went back to school and was awarded a PhD in clinical psychology at the University of Detroit-Mercy. Since embarking on her new career, Deb's worked on the White Mountain Apache Indian Reservation in a variety of mental health positions, and is currently the in-patient therapist at the psychiatric hospital in Show Low, Arizona. Her novels* Crashin' the Real *and* Queer and Loathing on the Yellow-Brick Road *have both been published by Dog Horn Publishing, where she also edits the* Women Writing the Weird *series.*

HAIRY PALMS
by A.J. Kirby

When he was a boy, Remus Coley's ma warned him so many times about what would happen to him if he continued to beat the meat so frequently that even now, as he finished off, he didn't feel any pleasure or relief. He snapped his hands out of the marigolds and his cock out of its own glove and then guiltily started checking his palms for hair. He lifted one hand then the other in front of his face, wondering how they looked both slapped-ass, new-born fresh but also calloused and work-worn. Of course, there was no sign of any hair.

'Get a grip Remus,' he muttered to himself, closing-up his favourite magazine *Hairy Harems*. His drained cock lay slug-like across his thigh, mocking him, reminding him of the utter pointlessness of his actions. Grim-faced he wiped himself down, zipped-up, and reached over to the mini-fridge for a beer.

He took a satisfying swig from the can and creased his foamy lip into a sneer. He was too old to still believe in old wives' tales. Too old to hear that old crone's voice every time he even reached for the zipper. Nevertheless, the fact remained: he only masturbated at the shack in the Paulson Woods. Could never do it at home even though it was a couple of years since she'd passed. Hence every Friday since he'd been able to drive, he'd run on out to the truck as soon as the five o' clock bell rang, leaving the factory, the house, and back when she was alive, the old crone behind him.

When he was at the shack, he could live the high-life just as his daddy had done before him. Indeed, there still remained a portrait of Remus' daddy on one of the least decrepit walls of the shack. It showed him grimacing over a huge caught carp he was clutching in a meaty fist. It showed him as Remus remembered him: a shaggy-haired, whiskery kind of fellow who was not overly impressed with his lot in life; a man who liked to talk with his fists and ask questions later; a cruel, vindictive little man who'd made family life almost impossible. After he'd died, at least according to Remus's old ma, daddy had become a bona fide saint as well as the ultimate judge. That most of the magazines in the shack were just about the only thing daddy had ever passed on to his son was beside the point. That daddy clearly used the shack for *exactly* the same purpose as his son was one of life's great *unmentionables,* even now.

Remus drained his beer, tossed the can on the floor—no need for pleasantries here—and immediately reached for another one. Already, he was starting to feel a little drunk; that old temper of his was about to get a work-out, he could sense it.

'Goddamn hairy palms,' he laughed.

But as his laugh echoed back to him off the bare walls, it didn't sound nearly as confident as he meant it to be. He was uneasy. And it wasn't just that whenever he thought about his parents, he felt a real sense of guilt. No, it was something else. Something new. It was those rumours he'd heard about the animal loose in the woods. Those rumours, which chimed jarringly off-key, reminded him of something he didn't ever want to think about . . .

Taylor Gray looked like the great movie director he'd been pretending to be for most of his life. He had the big shaggy beard, the unkempt hair and the rapidly expanding paunch that suggested he spent most of his time sitting on his ass in a darkened room. The way his sausage-fingers shook as he held the rented camera was the only thing which called this image into question.

'One more time, Slim,' he barked. 'From the top.'

Slim Drake sighed. 'Don't you think you'd be better at playing the wolf? You already got the hair for it.'

Taylor ignored him; wondered if Kubrick or Jackson ever had such trouble with their leads. Doubted it. But then, their casting couch hadn't been out back of Romi's Bar. They hadn't had to make their own props either, nor had they had to rent their goddamn cameras.

Think of the money, he told himself. *Think of the career I'll have after this film is shown.*

He fingered the record button, but then had another thought.

'This time try to make the wolf's movements more realistic. We can't have our lycanthrope saying "shit!" every time he stubs his toes . . . '

Slim laughed like a drip-tray.

'That wasn't supposed to be funny,' warned Taylor. He'd have to start rationing the whisky now. They weren't here for a good time, they were here to try and fake a film which would set them (*him*) up for life.

'You seriously think anyone will believe us?' asked Slim.

'It's amazing what folk *will* believe,' said Taylor. 'Especially if they see it on television. Now: all-fours please . . . Lights, camera, action!'

There really was no need to call for lights. There was nobody *on* the lights. It was just him and Slim Drake. Him and Slim and the hundreds of extras; the tightly packed trees. Slim hunkered down onto his paws, shook his wet flanks then started pacing round in circles like a caged animal. That was good; Slim was starting to *get* the movements now, becoming less self-conscious. The shots of whisky from the hip-flask had helped, of course, but there was also something about the woods themselves which seemed to be affecting his lead's performance. The trees seemed to be closing in around them, the air thickening with the stink of decay. It had made the both of them a little *Blair Witch* crazy.

Taylor spied him through the viewfinder, blurred the image a little, upping the authenticity ante much as it pained the director in him. Now the image wasn't a hundred percent. Slim's wolf seemed far more lupine, far more real. The costume wasn't great, but in the half-light of dusk in the Paulson Woods, the mange looked good, Taylor had to admit it. All the hard work of stitching together the skins of the road-killed foxes and dogs, all of the night-shifts he'd put in actually collecting the things in the first place, had proved worthwhile. Not that he'd have ever got into the skins himself, of course. The shop-bought fake blood which he'd liberally applied around the wolf's chops looked good too. And then there was the natural, kinda hunched way Slim held himself. Slim, he knew, had injured himself in a drink-driving accident, way back in the mists of time. He had an air of desperation about him, just as a wolf which had been forced to live off the scraps of the land would have looked. Everything was coming together now. Soon he'd have his fake masterpiece. Soon he could start negotiating with the TV studios.

Slim Drake sniffed around the trunk of a tree and then gave off this guttural growl. He turned to face the camera, all hollow yellow eyes, all bestial depravity, all Friday Fright Night. He was really getting into it now, like the woods had brought out the primitive in him. When he snarled, a shiver rattled up and down the director's spine. 'That's good,' he whispered. 'Scary. Keep doing that!'

Slim didn't miss a beat despite a compliment which was so rare it might as well have been *bloody*. He slunk into a darker place, where the trees were thicker, where the stink of decay grew even stronger. Taylor followed with the camera, picking his way carefully through prickly branches, cursing as he went. The wolf was starting to move too quickly now, like he was in single-minded pursuit of something. Soon he'd lose him and all of this great footage.

'Slow down,' he panted. 'You're going too far!'

The woods were almost impenetrable now, pressing in all about him. Roots reached up and tried to make a grab for his scurrying feet, thorns clawed at his face. And the mist was setting-in now too; icy tendrils crept up from the ground itself.

'Stop!' he called. 'Cut!'

Ahead, Slim was almost out of sight, eating up the ground with his lurching stride. He didn't stop. Taylor pushed himself over fallen trees, through a small stream, under overhanging creepers, his heart jack-hammering away in his chest, the acrid taste of the whisky on his tongue. But it was no good. He could no longer pick out his lead. In fact, he could barely pick out anything. Suddenly, the mist was heavy around him like a blanket.

Christ! he thought. *What if I can't find my way back?*

The scream cut through the atmosphere like a foghorn. So ear-piercingly loud it could have stripped bark from the trees. So chilling it could have frozen blood. Taylor stumbled, felt the ground rushing up at him, reached out with a hand to stop himself and realised too late he'd landed with his full weight on the camera.

There goes my two-hundred dollar deposit right there, he thought. *What the hell was Drake playing at screaming like that?*

He staggered to his feet, brushed himself down, assessed the damage. The camera was ruined, wouldn't even turn on. But that was the least of his worries. The mist was all around him now like snow. He couldn't see more than a couple of feet ahead of him. And now he'd fallen, he couldn't even remember which direction he'd been walking in.

'Slim?' he called, trying hard to keep a note of fear from entering his voice.

There was no answer. He forced himself to start walking. Slim couldn't have gone far. Most likely, he'd just stumbled in the mist. Most likely he was just holed-up somewhere, waiting for it to clear.

Taylor didn't want to think about the other possibility. But he couldn't help but recall the whisky-soaked closing-time conversation which had started him on this trail. The rumours of a big stray dog, 'like the hound of the Baskervilles', which haunted the woods. The tales of what this big dog had done to the farm animals, to the deer. Of course, in the fug of Romi's Bar, Taylor hadn't believed a word of it. It had been all he could do not to laugh in the bumpkin farmer's face. But now he was out here, and now he'd heard Slim's scream, everything seemed plausible.

What if this wolf is out there in the trees stalking me? he thought. *What if it's just waiting for me to have another stumble and then it'll be on me: biting, tearing, clawing?*

For a terrible moment, his legs started to give way. He was going to curl up into a ball and play dead, just like he used to as a child when those bullies used to beat on him in the yard at school. For a terrible moment, Taylor was about to give up. But then, the businessman in him started to speak-up: *Okay, say this thing is real. Say there really is some werewolf in the woods. And say I somehow manage to get the camera working again . . . Cher-ching!*

Almost immediately, it was as though his lifted spirits acted to lift the mist. As he blinked into the evening light, he realised he had somehow managed to stumble into a clearing. Here, the woodland was not as tightly-packed but still the trees surrounded him, encircled him, watched him like sentries. Directly in front of him was a big old elm; it had shed its leaves, which drifted into browny-yellow piles, big as burial mounds. Flanking the elm was a haphazard collection of skeletal beech trees, almost choked by the dense green bushes which seemed to have leaped up everywhere. Mushrooms, large as skulls, grafted themselves onto everything. The stench was terrible, like death.

Think of the money, he told himself, and started to walk on. There was a narrow path, at first glance almost completely buried by leaf mulch, which led out of the clearing an up a steady slope. At the top of the slope, he thought he could pick out what appeared to be a small shack. He made for it, still nursing his broken camera, hoping to coax it back into life. Now he had a purpose, he barely gave Slim a second thought. Slim Drake had survived a car wreck *ferchristsakes*; should've seen the state of the car they cut him out of.

The shack was really not much more than a wooden lean-to. Probably it had been used by hunters once upon a time, but now it looked abandoned. Nature was reclaiming it; weeds choked the doorway, a tree appeared to be growing out of the smashed window, the front steps appeared almost overwhelmed by leaves. Only, the closer Taylor got, the more he began to think it wasn't rotten leaves at all but something else. Something mangy; something hairy . . . The stink was starting to get worse too. Smelled like the abattoir up at Netherbridge.

By the time Taylor was close enough to see what was really on the steps, his nose had already given him ample warning. By the time he got close enough to see how Slim's throat had been ripped out, he'd already thrown-up twice. And by the time, he'd steeled himself to roll the body of the poor old drunk over and look into his terrified face, Taylor was already crying. Whatever had attacked Slim Drake had clawed off all of his fake whiskers, his fake hair and his fake snout.

Taylor sniffed, spat away some leftover bile and then crouched over his camera. If he could just get a shot of Slim's face so mangled, everybody would have to believe him. If he could just get the camera working for two minutes . . . one minute . . . then the footage would be priceless.

The first growl echoed back off the empty shell of the shack, through the clearing, up the path and mainlined straight into Taylor's heart. He fell forward, onto the already cold body of his lead actor. He curled himself into a foetal comma and tried for all he was worth to stop shivering and crying. The second growl sounded, if anything, even closer. Even angrier. The wannabe film-director in him longed to open up his eyes, to at least look upon the beast before it did to him what it had done to Slim. The child in him wanted the ground to suck him up, make him invisible. The child in him was also, no doubt, responsible for him pissing himself, just as he had in the yard all those years ago.

Then Taylor felt the beast's hot breath on the back of his neck, carrying with it the overwhelming smell of death. He felt the beast's bloodied whiskers pricking into him. He heard a third growl: strangely monstrous and soothing at the same time. Somehow, he understood it was a growl from the beast's lupine belly—a ravenous, cavernous *hungry* growl. The growl told him it would all be over soon.

But the beast wouldn't put him out of his misery yet. It continued to sniff at him for some time, as though confused by the vinegary aroma of urine Taylor was giving off.

'Just let me die,' he sobbed.

He was shaking so much now the broken pieces of the camera started to rattle in his hands. Shaking so much the beast placed a heavy paw on his shoulders as though to stop him. Taylor felt the claws ripping through his check-shirt and into his flesh. But what was even more terrifying was the startling warmth of the padded parts of the beast's paw. How he could feel its racing heartbeat through it. How that heartbeat felt at once human and at once something so *out there* it could scarcely be believed. Still, Taylor couldn't stop himself from shaking.

106

The beast, it seemed, was confused by the rattling sounds. It lowered its head and started to nuzzle the camera, dripping blood, gore and death upon Taylor's hand. Then it started to wrap its huge jaws around the camera, ready to swallow it, Taylor's hand still strapped in and all. And as it bit down, miraculously, the camera started to make a whirring sound. Miraculously, it started to creep back into life. Startled, the wolf began to back away a little.

And now the wannabe director in Taylor just *had* to look; had to check whether the camera was pointing in the right direction. Had to check whether the little red light was on again and whether he was now in a position to record the last moments of his life. He opened his eyes; they were narrow-slits at first but gradually wide saucers once he took in the scene.

First, the camera was working again. Indisputably working. Its little red light danced jerkily from side to side, in time with his rhythmic shaking. Second, the beast. The beast was far larger than Taylor could have possibly imagined. Rearing up on its back legs as it now was, it must have been eight-feet tall. Eight-feet tall and comprised almost entirely of burgeoning muscle, bear-trap jaws and fierce, poisonous yellow eyes. Yellow eyes which were full of a wild kind of intelligence. Yellow eyes which immediately locked-on Taylor's and told the story of exactly what would happen next.

Taylor held up the camera in a bloodied hand and watched as the beast lowered itself onto its haunches and readied itself to pounce. Like a domestic dog, its rump twitched back and forth, generating the required energy for the leap. Unlike any domestic dog Taylor had ever encountered, it seemed to laugh just before it did so. And the laugh sounded so bitter, it could only have come from the human side of the creature.

When it came down to it, it was *Taylor* who howled like a wolf. Howled and screeched and pleaded until the beast ripped out his throat and the only noise left available to him was the weird kinda clicking noise which half of his tongue made as it slapped against his teeth and his non-existent lips. His tongue kept flapping, like a great red surrender flag, right until the end, when the beast started feasting on his heart from a newly-opened cavity in his chest.

Remus woke up feeling guilty as sin; like he'd been caught right in the act of doing something terrible by ma. But for the life of him, he couldn't remember what he'd done. Must've got stuck into a few too many of those beers, he reckoned. Must have started on daddy's old magazines again.

Straight away, like a nervous tic, his eyes darted down to his hands, checking for hairs on the palms. And for a moment, through his blurred early-morning eyes, he really thought ma's old tale was true. For, at first glance, his hands were thick with a rusty-brown substance. He screwed up his eyes, shook his head clear of the beer-cobwebs, and then took a second look. The brown substance was still there, but immediately he knew it was not hair. No: it was something else entirely, and Remus thought he knew what it was.

Foreman Tipper at the factory once got one of his paws caught in one of the machines. Before anyone could get in there and push the emergency stop, it had chewed off three of his fingers. When they pulled him out, his hand was ejaculating blood all over the place; it was a goddamn fountain. Anyways, Boss-man Reed wanted to keep the injury in-house—the factory couldn't afford any more health and safety disasters—and so they'd kept him up in the smoking room, shaking and whimpering away until the bleeding stopped. When he came down to see Boss-man Reed again (and be granted full foreman's pay for the rest of his life), he was pale as fish-flesh and his ruined south paw was coppery-brown with dried blood.

Coppery-brown.

Remus took a frantic inventory of his body-parts, secretly praying he hadn't done anything stupid. (Once he'd nearly followed through on a guilt-mad desire to make a John Wayne Bobbitt out of himself.) But everything appeared to be in full working order.

So if it isn't my blood, it must be someone else's, he thought, feeling a surge of almost sexual excitement. He pulled himself out of bed and lurched across the dilapidated floor of the gingerbread shack, kicking half-empty beer cans out of the way as he went. By the shack's drunk-looking door he found the first of the magazines, his favourite: *Hairy Harems.* Only, it was now so badly ripped it looked

108

as though it had been passed through a paper-shredder. And it was so covered in blood it looked as though it was being viewed through only the red side of a pair of old-style 3D glasses. Scattered over the lip of the doorway were more magazines, fluttering in the breeze: *Unshaven Havens, The Overgrown Lady Garden,* and *Au Naturel.*

'Shit,' breathed Remus, bending down to pick them up and feeling an ache in his legs. As he did so, he clipped the door and it swung open with a creak, letting in cold reality.

Outside was a scene so shocking it took his breath away. It was as though the whole forest floor had been daubed in red paint. And there were *things* hanging from every branch of every tree. Horrible, snaking *red* things, like guts. Remus screwed up his eyes, sure that when he reopened them, he'd see something different; that it had only been a trick of the fierce early-morning light.

It wasn't. If anything, the scene was even worse upon second viewing. Now his bloodshot eyes started to make sense of the confusion. It wasn't simply a mass of blood and guts and hair and filth, like something accidentally run over by a combine harvester. No, it was more like a scene of sacrifice. Like the clearing was a space for bloody, ritual killing.

He picked out what looked very much like a face; ripped from the mouth right down to the throat, but a face nonetheless. It was kinda grafted onto the trunk of a tree. He picked out what looked like an immensely hairy leg hanging from the roof of the shack. He picked out what was definitely a human hand in amongst all the mangy fur and tatty hair gathered right at the centre of the clearing.

And then Remus felt his insides leaping out of him as though they were on their own suicide mission. His heart threatened to hammer its way right out of his chest. His bowels groaned in warning. He dropped onto his haunches and tried to take deep breaths, but new worries assaulted him almost immediately. What if one of the farmers happened past the shack and saw the bodies on his steps? What if a policeman chanced his way out here?

Quickly, he dived back into the shack, and reached under the mouldy-looking bed for a spade. He'd bury the bodies; that's what

109

he'd do. Before any interfering busybodies visited. Before any blame could be apportioned to him.

He stepped past the bodies, not even looking down at them, and made for the edge of the clearing, where the leaves had drifted deeper, where it would be easier to hide something like a body. And at some instinctive level, like he was remembering a dream, Remus felt as though he'd performed such a task before. He felt as though he'd done such a thing so many times he could get by on auto-pilot. But what kind of a person becomes adept at burying bodies?

Remus dared not think about such a sticky question. Instead, he allowed his spade to break ground and started to dig. Surprisingly, he found the digging easier than he'd expected. Like he'd suddenly grown stronger than he'd ever given himself credit for. He *ploughed* into the dirt and leaves with an intensity which bordered on the maniacal, barely even pausing to wipe the sweat off his brow.

Only when a good, grave-sized hole loomed in front of him did he even take a moment to look back at the shack to check whether any small animals were interfering with the bodies. And only then did he see something glinting back at him from right next to the human hand he'd seen.

'What the fox hat?' he asked himself in a voice which sounded almost exactly like his daddy's. Although he did hear *some* voices quite a lot of the time, Remus couldn't remember hearing that particular voice in a long time. But he didn't have time to start wondering about the whys and the wherefores. Not when the glinting thing had caught his eye so.

He approached the bodies gingerly and pulled up his shirt so it covered his nose, before reaching down for whatever it was had caught his attention. And when his fingers touched upon the video camera, at first he couldn't work out just what it was he was touching. But he pulled it up nonetheless, and with it came the half-eaten hand of Taylor Gray.

Remus tried to shake the strap loose of the hand, which only made the scene more terrifying as the hand responded almost as though it were waving to him. In his desperation, he kicked out at the dead hand and finally its rigor mortis grip was broken.

110

With trembling fingers, he lifted the camera up to his face and clicked on the 'play' button, *knowing* the camera wouldn't work, *knowing* nothing would have been recorded. So he was startled when a crackly image started to emerge on the small viewfinder screen. A crackly image which appeared to be of these very woods; it had the same russet-brown leaves, the same dense foliage.

Almost immediately, the camera found its subject; it started to focus on a large dog, or a wolf. And then Remus started to laugh. Because it was definitely a man dressed up as a wolf, and a drunken man at that. Hell, the wolf kept stubbing its damn toes and cussing all the time.

Remus watched some more and laughed less. The man in the wolf suit's acting skills appeared to be improving the longer the film went on. After a while, when the camera followed the wolf into deeper woodland, Remus thought it hardly looked like a man in a suit at all. It looked real.

Abruptly, the film stopped and then jerked back into life again, showing a different scene. This scene looked remarkably like the clearing he was standing in right now, only it was filmed from a funny angle, as though the cameraman was lying down. *These modern film-makers,* thought Remus; *too clever for their own good.* He was almost going to stop watching when he caught sight of the wolf again, and this time he was even more impressed. Whoever had done the special effects for this low-budget flick deserved a goddamn Oscar. For this wolfman looked *stacked* in the kind of way that only a real honest-to-goodness animal which hunts and *feeds* can be. It looked as though it was bursting with power and with rage.

Remus watched with terrified eyes as the wolf destroyed the cameraman in so comprehensive a manner as to leave no doubt as to whether it was a man in a suit. And then he watched in awe as it sunk low in the middle of the clearing and howled at the waning moon. He could have sworn werewolves, lycanthropes, whatever you wanted to call them, only came out when there was a full moon, but then he realised that being pedantic about such things was patently ridiculous. This was no fairy-tale. This was real; the video proved it.

And then came the real shocker. As Remus Coley watched,

the film showed the wolf kinda bucking and bending into its own body. Clicking and crashing and transforming itself into something else, into the man that he saw in the mirror every day he dared look. And when he saw that, he almost dropped the camera.

As if on auto-pilot again, he staggered back into the shack and flopped down into his mouldy old chair by the beer fridge. Absently, he picked up his marigolds and the last condom, wondering what to do. The plastic felt nasty against his fingers. Nasty and forbidding. He flung them away into a far corner of the room and then, without allowing himself to think, he unzipped his fly with confident hands.

Suddenly, he was feeling more turned-on than he ever had in his miserable little life. His cock sprung obediently to attention and he dropped his trousers. And remarkably, he heard his daddy's voice once again. *That's why they call it the blood lust, son,* it said. And Remus smiled and started to stroke. He continued to stroke even when the soft hair started to poke its way through the calloused skin on his palms. He continued to stroke even when it didn't feel like his hand any more but rather like the paw of *something else*. For the first time in his life, Remus Coley really felt alive. The picture of his daddy seemed to smile down upon him from the wall, at last happy his son had discovered the real family jewels.

When he finished up, Remus didn't feel the least bit guilty. Instead he was hungry. Hungrier than he'd been in a long while. As he thought about what he fancied eating, he let loose a howl of victory.

A.J. Kirby is the award-winning author of three novels and over forty short stories. He is a sports writer for the Professional Footballer's Association and a reviewer for both The New York Journal of Books *and* The Short Review. *He was runner-up in the Dog Horn Prize for Literature (Fiction) 2010 and winner of* The Big Issue in the North's *Genre Fiction Award 2011, in Association with* Polluto *magazine. His work appears in* Cabala (2011) *and* Bite Me, Robot Boy (2012), *both published by Dog Horn Publishing.*

GALLERY GREEN
by Jan Edwards

The Gallery had grabbed the usual bouquet of design awards and sufficient brickbats to start a reasonable sized wall. Karrin though it was 'pretty bloody amazing'. From the pavement, staring up that blue-black facade, she was certain that, love or hate it, no one standing in its shadow could avoid feeling some kind of awe. That overwhelming sense of mortality, normally reserved for cathedrals and palaces, inspired by a column of steel and apparently seamless glass rising six stories above the street. This was the brand new, and highly controversial, Tate Modern, Bristol, and she knew the world would beat at its doors whatever words passed on either side of that debate.

Above the entrance a rank of feather flags snapped and flapped the exhibition's multi-hued logo to the wind in a brashly sophisticated welcome. Beneath them a chattering crowd of lesser beings were segregated from the Celebs by ubiquitous metal barriers. Less-privileged photographers lacking press passes snapped and whirred their glass eyes as she passed. Spectators, there to gawk at the glitteratti in their black-tie designer-splendour, eyed her suspiciously. The more knowing Arties, who were camped out for the following day's public opening, dismissed her as a nothing, a nobody.

She still felt uncomfortable being here. This rarefied end of the Art-world always unsettled her. She felt vaguely fraudulent. Yes she had a couple of minor local exhibitions to her name, but hardly Turner Prize. Cameras clicked and flashed, and she could almost hear a few hundred pairs of eyes slashing at her back with two questions. Who is she? And why does she get in so easy? Knowing her invitation was the real deal did not stop her feeling that way; and the security guys, handing back her invitation with such scepticism, backed that up. She had that certain feeling they waved her through only because the Holographic-Ticket could not lie.

Walking into the building clutching her holographed invitation was such a buzz, and she smiled. Russ had always referred to these events and the people in them as the Art-ificials. 'It's not

113

the real world,' he had said so very often. 'It's not art. It's money. It's a sell out. It's a bloody con.' *But that was B.B.,* she thought. *Before Becki.* Now it was all changed, and even he, the great artiste, had plunged both feet into the murky waters of commerciality.

She was so late, so *very* late, and Becki would be furious. *Best opening in years and she'll say I've blown it,* she thought. Her own tiny gallery had been quiet all day, until a couple of browsers sauntered in right before closing. 'Just looking,' they'd said. It had got *so* late she had almost decided not to bother. Once she passed through the Tate's main foyer into the Grand Hall, however, she knew that staying away would have been her biggest mistake. This was everything the promos had promised and more. Muted lighting reflected off the pale marble floor and walls. Pale metal stanchions supporting the six floors, and, ultimately, the infamous cone shaped glass roof that gave the project the subtitle 'Cornetto Tower'.

The ground floor was one vast atrium with glistening spiral of stairs running up to the top floor. From there the glass ceiling cone poked upward into the night, and from that darkened structure shards of pure colour were apparently hurtling toward her in jagged swathes. She knew this piece—knew the artist, in fact. Russ Willis was an arsehole. A total git of epic degrees. Yet he had conceived such as this. She stared at the installation, feeling her pride and loss in familiar stabbing twists of the gut. 'Destruction of the Rainbow' was an old friend. She had seen its tiny prototype, and helped in the cutting of its glass sections. It was the *only* thing she had ever seen him working on. His obsession and his reason. Yet still she was unprepared for the real beast. It was breathtaking. The shattered spectrum, carefully edged in finely hammered silver, held in a timeless free-fall, as each piece lazily twirled on gleaming steel chains. Swaying in the updraft, despite their weight, they nudged at each other, whispering and tittering amongst themselves at each new visitor who dared to stare. It diffused the wall lights into a mosaic of shifting patterns on the pale floor. She had stepped into the maelstrom, unwary and unprepared, and she paused, vaguely disconcerted that the floor itself seemed insubstantial, like the rippling surface of a clouded lake.

Her dress of white silk and silver trim was caught in the same dance, as tiny mirrored decals on wrap and dress sparked flashes of colour like tiny lights, so that she felt like some very small, and very pale, Christmas tree caught in a psychedelic vortex. It made her vaguely nauseous.

A movement lower in the spiral caught her attention, a glass lift gliding toward the top level, mirrored by its twin descending on the far side, synchronised like pendulum weights, marking the hours, the minutes, the moments.

She tracked its path avidly, glad for any distraction against the rainbow's glamour. From its destination on the top floor came faint chinking from glasses of a very different kind, along with soft twin hums of music and voices. Unmistakable sounds of 'launch party' seeped from what the programme had condescendingly informed her were the 'Discourse Arena' on the sixth floor.

Karrin crossed the few last metres, stepped into the waiting lift car, and came out at eye level with the shattered Rainbow. She made a deliberate effort not to see it, but to look through it to the other side—all anticipation of the art and the artists she could rub shoulders with. He would not get in her way tonight, not even by proxy.

She searched the crowd for Becki, Chief Curator and her oldest friend. There had been a time, of late, when they had not been friends. There had been a time, not very long ago, when they had been close to killing each other. Over a man, of course. When best-girl-friends stopped talking it's always over a man. But best-girl-friends are friends forever, and once that fanny-rat had cleared the scene they were back to guzzling wine, and giggling, and comparing tales of his chipolata-prick, and his terminal-halitosis.

Karrin glanced at the Rainbow and sighed. She should be over it all by now. Art was art, to be appreciated whoever gave it life. What else was there? 'Forget him. Bastard little toad,' she muttered.

Becki was waving to her, and had left a bevy of art's finest maestros and divas and ingénues to join her at the glass and steel balustrade. She slid her arm beneath Karrin's to link them together as they stared for a moment at the Rainbow.

'Is he here,' Karrin whispered, finally.

Becki laughed quietly. 'Are you really asking me that?'

'I guess not. He's got star billing.'

'Karrin—understand. The Rainbow was already commissioned. And even if it wasn't—it is special. Enjoy it for what it is. As Art. Then move on. But enough of him. What kept you? I was beginning to think you'd bailed. Cold feet again?'

115

Moving away from the barrier, with arms if not mind still linked with her mentor, Karrin forced herself into calm. Becki often avoided answering merely by ignoring the question, an arrogance that she, Karrin, had to ignore in turn. 'I know Becki. I was so held up in the shop, a couple of time wasters who would not take the hint.'

'Should have shut up shop early. God, Karrin. This is a chance for you to get out of that bloody back alley of yours and make your name.'

'Can't just close. You should know that. And not so much of the back alley,' She grinned and hugged Becki's arm. 'I'm making a nice profit this quarter, thanks to the last two artists you sent me. Best shows I've had. Thanks. I really will owe you.'

'Course you will.' Becki grinned tugged her toward the throng, her arm still looped with Karrin's in a gesture of sisterhood for all to see. 'You do know I'll collect. No matter. You're here now. Come and meet Benny. He's setting up a new exhibition that I think you two could really connect. I'll set you going then it's down to you. Circulate darling. Get your face under the right noses.'

Not advice Karrin could afford to ignore. She circulated herself to standstill and then drifted to the bar for a fresh glass to ease the next round, hugging her Blackberry to her breast like a baby. More names and contacts had gone in it tonight than she'd collected in years of slogging round the circuit on her own. Becki had really come up with the goods. *She is so going to own me.* Awash with so many names and faces, and so much red wine, she was more than happy to park herself in a quite corner whilst her friend did her 'thing' with the departing guests.

She took a fresh glass and wandered off to view one of the halls that she had not had time for yet. The party had circulated in sections covering the big Names and of course the Installations that the press always loved so much. She wanted to see the Outsider Gallery. *Its one bit I have an 'outside' chance of ever being exhibited in. And I need to walk off this damn wine. I need a clear head. If I get half the things I've been promised tonight? I'll be in there damn soon,* she told herself.

She glanced at her watch. Almost one a.m. Surely Becki and her staff had kicked out the last few by now?

The two women had arranged a late supper. *But at this rate*

116

it could turn out to be an early breakfast. She sipped the last of her wine and pulled a face, realising she had been clutching the glass by the bowl and turned it from room temperature to blood heat. It hit her stomach, acid and unrelenting, to join the rest of the evening's quota.

Not good on an empty gut. She rubbed at her forehead and tried to focus on her surroundings. She had come full circle back to the top floor now and stepped out of the lift as she had at the start of the evening.

The rainbow shards claimed her attention yet again, glittering now with eerie intensity under dimming lights. Somewhere she could hear Becki's strident tones wafting up from the atrium floor. Looking over the balcony Karrin glimpsed the last few guests being ushered toward the exit.

With their going a quiet settled and only the rainbow was left whispering in soft tinks and chinks as thick chunks of coloured glass collided in slow motion. The sound was mesmerising, doubly so in her wine induced haze, and she watched the sheets of silicate swaying for some moments without any real thoughts running through her mind. Swallowing the last of the wine in her glass regained her attention. She grimaced and ran her tongue around her front teeth to push off the gritty wine lees that lingered there. *Becki needs to speak with her caterers,* she thought. *The wine waiters are crap.*

Across the space, through the glass forest, a movement caught her attention. The lift had opened and someone stepped out. 'Becki?' she called. 'Can we eat now?'

The half obscured outline paused—looked at her—turned away. She recognised it—him. 'Russell-fucking-Willis. What the hell is he doing here now?'

Rhetorical question, she thought. *Of course he's bloody here. He's one of Becki's star turns.* She stared at him through the evidence of his stardom, which twisted and turned between them. He was staring straight back at her his familiar face framed momentarily in a wafting section of green, pitted, glass. It distorted his features, throwing his image back at her as a rippling gargoyle. She shuddered, gripping the rail in front of her; fighting off the panic that numbed her legs and fingers and face.

Six floors below Becki was crossing the floor, her heels clipping on marble sharp and clear, pausing directly under her now, on the edges of vision waiting for the upward car. Across the void the far lift was preparing for descent.

'Russ? What are you doing here? Hey!' She ran around the gallery barrier, and called out to him again. 'Russ?'

She could see him, smiling at her. Waiting. Watching. A few paces more and she would reach him. She stopped some three metres short. 'Have you been here all evening?' she said. 'I didn't see you . . .'

'I've been here all night, Kara mia, and I've seen you.'

'Oh.' She was thankful at being too shocked to blush. The idea of him watching her was creepy, which helped her raise some rapid defences. Before today she had always relapsed into the gauche student in his presence, eager for her Master's approval. But after a year of bitterness and a lot of very expensive therapy--He was just a really creepy guy. She was an artist. She ran a successful business. She was her own person now. 'Really?' she said. 'You surprise me, though I wasn't really looking.' That tautness around his lips was heartening. *A hit.* She thought. *Go on you slimy bastard. Say something else. I'm ready.* 'Glad you made it,' she added. 'Glad you've arrived in fact. Nice to know someone else from our class actually has a living the way they intended. From their art.'

'Oh, I'm here,' he said. 'Always will be.' He nodded at the Rainbow. 'Immortality. It's what we're all after. Right?'

'Depends on how you go about it, ... So, you and Becki— she says you're not together now.'

'No need.' He nodded again at his glass memorial.

Glancing at the shards Karrin had to smile. All that angst and jealousy, wondering what Becki had that she didn't. And really? she thought. It's nothing. He's a user. A lying, cheating snivel-nosed loser. 'So, good for you,' she said aloud. 'What next? More rainbows?'

'No. Once the statement is made—once it's out there— anything else can only be a reflection.' He grasped the balustrade and looked down. 'I have one final statement though. And I wanted you to be the messenger.' He took a last look at her, and waving his fingers at her in mocking farewell, swung up onto a seat running along the side and stepped out into the air.

Watching him fall wasn't like slow motion. Not as such. But she would play those few seconds on constant repeat, so that it did get to feel that way.

His hair lifted, his shoulders hunched in that odd way that they always did when he walked. One leg, then the other, arms bent and out, almost as if he were steadying himself for his descent. Almost as if he intended to catch the updraft and fly up and out of the atrium and became a part of his precious rainbow.

What he did was plummet. She turned away, stomach boiling and imagined falling with him. She did not see, but she heard him hit the ground, and his body made a curiously musical, bell-like sound. Loud, deafening, and then the black cloud came down in a high-pitched hum, as though she was enveloped in an impenetrable, cloying, swarm of insects that wrapped around her head, as dense as velvet and cold as glass. She knew there were other sounds, voices, some close and some away off down that long black tunnel. Karrin hung in stasis, vivid glimpses of colour whisking past her in blurred gyrations. In her memory the Rainbow was forming, bursting, and reforming, over and over in kaleidoscopic tumult.

Then Becki was beside her trying to pull her hands together, and shouting at her to;

'Stop screaming and listen'.

'I have to get down there. He needs help,' Karrin leaned back, struggling weakly at the hands clasping around her own.

'I imagine he's beyond help,' said Becki. 'Wait with me, Karrin. Security has everything under control. The Police will want to speak with you I think.'

'Police? He needs ambulances, paramedics.'

'The Police will be here for you, not him.'

'What?'

'I saw, Karrin. I saw what happened.'

'But . . . '

'I saw what you did. I never imagined you would react that way.'

She seemed sincere. To all intents and purposes Becki was the concerned friend calming and reassuring. On the surface she was all that Karrin could want under duress, yet she had the feeling—'Saw?' she whispered.

'You were arguing, Becki said. 'Don't you remember? And then you tried to lift him up, he fell . . . '

'No. No, that wasn't the way. He climbed up.'

'I saw, Karrin.'

119

It was not true. Karrin knew it. Becki had not seen her do anything, she couldn't have seen it. She couldn't have. 'I need to see,' she moaned, and ran to the stairs. Becki did not attempt to stop her.

At ground level she stopped to look at the remnants. Crimson smears ran through the gyrating swirls, marking the place where Russ had fallen. In the centre of the smears lay a cream coloured blanket; rumpled and blood soaked.

Karrin stepped forward. People were talking to her. She ignored them. They were distant, far and far away, and without words. She did not understand or need to listen to them. They were nothing. Droning insects returned to keep the people away. High and insistent, breaking through to the centre of her skull and messing with her senses.

A few steps closer, and she could see smears of blood all around her. Spatters had streaked the closer stanchions and gouts of scarlet gloop were pooled nearest to the blanket in thick, viscous lumps—looking more like jammy rice than blood spill. She swallowed hard and forced her bile back down her throat. Yet she could not help herself from staring.

Someone was next to her, holding her arm. Becki.

'Where has he gone?' Karrin turned dull eyes toward her oldest friend. 'Where . . . '

'Probably the ambulance guys already scraped him up,' Becki replied. 'The little cockroach was still breathing when I got to him. He wasn't for long. He's dead, Karrin.'

'Poor Russ. I never thought he'd . . . '

'I saw, Karrin. I read all those emails you sent him so I know you wanted him dead. No one will blame you. I can't blame you. Me least of all.'

'No. He jumped.'

'Karrin. I saw,' Becki replied. 'I saw what you did.'

'So the Police are here? It's not fair Becki. I never did it. Believe me. I never killed him. You have to know that. Please Becki. Help me. Please.'

Becki glanced around her. 'Let's get you somewhere safe, shall we? Then we can think.'

The familiar face before her was wavering, the voice distant, and through it there was something Karrin felt she should be doing, had to be doing. Something she should be saying—to someone—about something. 'Me?' she mumbled. 'What happened?'

'I saw,' Becki said. 'But they don't have to know, do they?'

Nothing works like bad publicity to make yourself a name in art. From here in her own rooms she could earn a mint. Not that she would ever get to spend that much of it. There was little to spend it on in a private and very *secure* nursing home. She could paint all she wanted, and sell almost everything, and no one ever knew what she did—what Becki said she did.

She has to be right, Karrin thought. *If I could remember, then it would all be good. Maybe I could get out of here? If I could ever see what went before that bloody blanket. If I painted as Camera obscura, seeing what went before.*

Her subject matter seldom changed. Rainbows over red boiling sunsets. Rainbows over deep grey seas. Rainbows over cemeteries and rooftops. Time and again she re-assembled those images from her black tunnel, searching for that memory and always failing. It was gone, lost over the rainbow. Somewhere she would never find it. Not in this life.

She even painted him, occasionally. She didn't need to try remembering his face, because he came to see her . . . when no one was there. Mostly he came to peer through the window, smiling that crooked smile, and mouthing words she could never quite hear. Sometimes he followed Becki when she came to visit and stood behind her; watching and grinning.

'He's there Becki. I tell the Doctors, but they won't believe me and now nor do you.'

'No, of course not. Why would we?' Becki patted Russ's arm. 'He's dead, after all . . . Aren't you dear? I know, because I saw. I saw what you did.'

Jan Edwards is a writer with more than 30 published stories, plus articles, poetry and reviews. She is an editor at the award-winning Alchemy Press. She has a degree in English Literature with Creative Writing and is Co-chair of the Renegade Writers group. But you might also know her as a Reiki Master.

PLAY TIME
by Marie O'Regan

Tommy stood still, head cocked to one side, listening to the night-time noises of the playground. By day these places were full of the sounds of children squealing with delight, maybe crying at some mishap—a fall, or a bang to the head or knee, perhaps an argument with a friend or a tussle with a bully. But overall playgrounds were happy places, full of joy. Even their name showed that to be true.

Night-time was different. By night the only sound was the wind moaning through the creak of the swing's chains and the whispering of the leaves on the trees—the slow sigh of the night's chill as the playground waited for morning to come and banish the darkness. That was all the noises could be, he decided. He'd listened to, and catalogued, each of these sounds, one by one, until he was satisfied, huddled as small as he could make himself: a small dark shadow on the last swing on the row.

He sighed, wishing it was earlier. There was no-one left to play with—all had gone home for their dinner, full of the day's adventures and ready for sleep to claim them; only to release them in the morning, eager for more. Their mothers had come for them, reducing their number by degrees until he was the only one left. He eased his weight back and kicked off with his feet, letting the swing carry him gently backward—he wasn't sure where his mother was; and it was late. *Shouldn't she be here by now?*, his mind whispered, and he told it to shush. *She'll be here. She'll come.*

He tilted his head at a new sound—one unexpected at this hour. There it was again, the high-pitched tinkling of a girl's laughter. He craned his neck to look behind him into the bushes, then scanned the rest of the playground, but could see no-one. Digging his heels into the earth below him, he brought the swing to a standstill, quieting the creak of the chain against the crossbar. A sudden gust of wind whispered through the trees, and errant leaves danced in the air before him. *Tommy* . . . Now he knew he was imagining things, because the wind couldn't know his name. Footsteps skittered off to his left, and he whirled around to see what was there. The sodium light guttered fitfully, barely illuminating a small circle around it, but it was enough. A shadow was cutting off part of the lit circle—a girl-shaped shadow, from what he could see. Boys didn't have pigtails. *Maybe it's not pigtails,* his mind whispered again. *Maybe it's horns!* He whimpered, and this time the laughter wasn't just in his head. It rang throughout the playground, and Tommy saw a light come on in a house behind the park.

'Silly, girls don't have horns.'

Tommy gasped—and felt icy fingers play his spine. The voice—and the pigtails, apparently—belonged to the girl standing at the edge of the light, staring at him as if he'd said something stupid. He hadn't, had he? He was only thinking.

The girl grinned at him, then, and he knew, he just knew, that she could hear what he was thinking—even if she said nothing about it.

He took a deep breath before asking, 'Who are you?'

'Who do you think I am?'

Tommy frowned. 'That's kind of a stupid question,' he said. 'How am I supposed to know that?'

The girl moved back a little, so that all he could see was her eyes. The rest of her stood in darkness, but her eyes glowed with yellow light, and oh, how they danced.

'I guess that's true.' She moved a step closer to him, and the wind screamed. 'My name's Mary.'

'You're out kind of late, Mary.'

'So are you,' she retorted, and she inched a step closer, twisting the cloth of her dress in her fists. 'Shouldn't your mother have come for you by now?' Her skin was pale, her mouth pinched—she looked so *cold*.

Tommy looked around at the gate on the far side of the playground, and sighed. No one was there. 'Yeah, she should.' He looked at Mary once more, his face hopeful. 'Maybe she got delayed, met someone . . . you know, got talking.' It wouldn't be the first time his mother had been a little late, delayed by another mother who wanted to chat; but it was never more than a few minutes, and she always ran so *fast* to get to him, so he wouldn't worry. He looked towards the gate once more, hoping he'd see her racing towards him, her red hair flying back in the wind, showing him her relieved smile when she saw him waiting. There was nothing.

'Kinda late, though,' Mary offered. Her voice shook, and Tommy wondered just how long she'd been waiting here. 'I mean, it's *dark*.'

'Yeah, it is,' he replied. He took a closer look at the girl; her eyes were huge with fear. 'You're not scared . . . are you?'

'Who, me?' She laughed, but he wasn't convinced. 'Nah, not scared.' She looked around, seemingly bored, and when her gaze came to rest on Tommy again there was something there that hadn't been before. 'You get used to it.' Yep, it was there, all right—it was anger, bleeding into her voice more with every second.

'How long have you been here?'

'I don't know.' She wouldn't look at him now. 'Long time, I guess.'

Tommy tried to think if she went to his school. She really didn't look familiar, and it wasn't that big a town. He should know her, if she lived nearby. 'Where did you say you live?'

She grinned at him, then; her small teeth almost too white in the darkness. 'I didn't.' She moved a step closer. 'What's the matter, Tommy? Scared?'

'No, I just wonder where she is, that's all.' He inched back from her, wary of allowing her too close even while calling himself stupid for letting a girl rattle him like this. 'It *is* late.'

Mary stood back suddenly, turned and walked towards the roundabout at the edge of the playground. 'You're going to freeze if you sit still like that.' She started the roundabout turning, pushing at the ground with her foot as if she were on a scooter. 'You might as well play while you wait, it'll keep you warm.'

Tommy hesitated. His mother would see him clearly while he sat on the swing, he knew . . . but the roundabout wasn't that far away, was it? She should still see him . . . and he'd definitely see her. The roundabout squeaked as it turned, and Mary giggled. That decided it. At least if he played with Mary for a while he'd be warm, and—more importantly—he wouldn't be alone any more. He cast one more glance at the gate and then ran to Mary, yelling: 'Wait up! I want to play!' The two children laughed as they played, and the darkness crept up and wrapped them up in its embrace.

Sarah Warner stood impatiently at the playground gate, trying to stop her hair from getting too messy in the wind. This wasn't the kind of day she'd have picked to go to the park but then her sister wasn't her—that much was painfully obvious. Sarah checked her watch yet again, as if catching the minute hand in the act of moving would magic Lauren into existence.

'What are you doing?'

The voice was unfamiliar, and it took Sarah a moment to realise the words were meant for her. Looking down, she saw a small girl, maybe eight or nine years old, wrapped in a shabby coat and with her socks rolled down around her ankles. One knee was scuffed, but she didn't seem to mind. The girl waited patiently, and Sarah forced herself to be polite. 'I'm waiting for my sister.'

'Is she coming here to play?'

Sarah suppressed a grin. 'No, honey, she's not. We're going shopping.'

The girl frowned, thinking hard. Her question, when it came, was so obvious Sarah could have kissed her. 'Then why meet here? Is she leaving her kids here to play?'

'No.' Sarah didn't want to talk about that. 'No, she isn't. She just likes to see kids having fun, I guess.' No need to involve this child in the misery of her sister's life; the emptiness.

The child said nothing, just stared at her, and Sarah found herself getting nervous. Why, for God's sake? This was just a kid! Someone called Sarah's name, and both of them looked down the hill—Lauren was bustling towards them, her dark hair unruly and a big smile plastered across her thin face.

'Hi! Who do we have here?'

Sarah didn't know what to say. The little girl looked Lauren up and down, her face serious—Sarah stifled the urge to laugh. Then she grinned, and her face lit up.

'I'm Mary. I was just saying hi.' She looked from Lauren to Sarah, and then back to Lauren. 'You two don't look much like sisters.'

Sarah took Lauren by the arm, not wanting to prolong the hurt for her sister. 'No, we don't, but we are.' She grinned at Lauren. 'Sometimes we even act like it. Come on, hon, time to shop.'

Lauren followed her, then turned and waved at the little girl, who grinned and waved back before disappearing into the crowd of children. 'Cute kid, huh?'

Sarah searched the playground, but saw no sign of her—she'd melted from view completely. 'Yeah, she was great. You hungry?' She urged her sister forward when she nodded, and tried to listen to the prattle—ignoring the feeling that the little girl was still watching them.

The clatter of cups on saucers and plates on trays in the heat of the café was almost painful after the quiet of the park in the cold. Sarah felt her face flush in the heat, and managed to get herself out of her coat without having to stand up, which was a relief in this small space. Lauren looked as pale as ever, and Sarah envied the way she never flushed. She took after their mother, pale and dark; while Sarah favoured their father, a man of far ruddier complexion and chestnut hair. She even had his freckles.

The waitress pushed mugs of hot chocolate in front of them, then trudged over to the next customer, already gesturing impatiently. Sarah took a sip of her drink, wiped the foam off her lip, and looked up to see her sister staring at her, deadly serious.

'What's the matter?'

Lauren had the good grace to look abashed. 'Another kid went missing last week.'

'Another one? Really?'

Lauren nodded, her enthusiasm escaping now she knew she had her sister's ear. 'From that playground.'

'The one I met you at this morning?'

Another nod.

Sarah sighed. 'Is that why you were so keen to meet there?' Lauren's face fell, and Sarah fought hard to stay kind. She didn't want to frighten her off. 'Honey, this isn't healthy.'

'What do you mean?'

Exasperated, Sarah blew her fringe out of her way, a habit Lauren knew only too well. Her chin set, as she grew stubborn in return. Sarah sighed. How long was this merry-go-round going to keep running? How many times were they going to end up right back here? 'You can't keep obsessing about kids that go missing.'

'I'm not obsessing!'

'You're scoping out the playgrounds where they disappear! How is that not obsessed?'

Lauren stared into her mug, her face solemn. A single tear spilled over onto her cheek and cut a track in her make up as it fell. 'It's not fair.'

Sarah reached for her hand. 'No, it's not. And I'm sorry, honey, really I am.' She squeezed her sister's hand and handed across a tissue. Lauren ignored her, wiping her eyes and focussing on her cup. 'Lauren, kids go missing. All the time. Sad but true.'

Lauren glared at her. 'That doesn't make it right!'

'No, it doesn't. But it doesn't make them yours, either.'

Lauren flinched at that, but Sarah pressed on, hating herself—and hating Lauren for making her do it. 'There are ways, Lauren, we've talked about this. Adoption, fostering . . .'

Lauren was shaking her head, vehement in her refusal to listen. Sarah grew exasperated. 'Why on earth would you think hanging around playgrounds is a way to get a kid? It's creepy!'

'I don't know.' Lauren's voice was low, choked with grief and self-loathing. 'I just like being near them, okay? It makes me feel less . . .'

'Less what?'

'Redundant. Alone.' She glared at her sister now, fierce in her contempt. 'I know how that sounds, you don't need to tell me.' She wiped her eyes, stared out of the window at the people wandering by with no idea how hollow her life was. 'It just helps.'

There was nothing to say, thought Sarah. There were no words that could help here; it was just sad, and raw, and hurtful. And that wouldn't stop anytime soon. She joined her sister in gazing at the world as it passed, blurry in the steamed windows; and perhaps better for it.

Lauren sat staring out of her living room later that night, watching the first snow of the winter. The flakes danced out of the sky as if they were bestowing a gift upon the earth—and Lauren thought maybe they were. All the usual ugliness that surrounded them was buried under a pristine, white blanket. Everything was clean and new, just for a little while. She raised her fingers to the glass and traced the shape of a heart, touched her lips to it and smiled.

The smile died, nascent, as tiny, unseen fingers echoed her movements on the outside of the window; leaving icy trails around the outlined heart, setting it hard.

The playground looked different tonight. It was colder, thought Tommy, but that wasn't it. The place looked deserted, forlorn—as if kids had stopped coming here. The chains on the swings screamed, and Tommy realised that was because they were rusty. How long had they been here, anyway?

As if called into being, Mary ambled past him into the middle of the playground, her gaze disinterested. 'Don't worry about it, they'll come back.'

'They will?'

'Sure, they always come back.'

Tommy didn't like this. 'Why did they leave?'

Mary smiled at him, then, and Tommy cringed. He'd learned to be wary of that smile—the real Mary came out when she smiled, and she wasn't the same. Tommy wasn't even sure if she was a real little girl, when she smiled. He thought that she might be some *thing* that just wanted to play the part of a girl, or even lived inside her. But if there was a thing inside her, where was the real Mary?

The girl scowled, her voice rougher this time. Deeper. 'I've told you. Best not to worry about that. It's not for you to know.' She cuffed him, and he stumbled. 'Let's play.' He followed her, too scared to say no—wondering, not for the first time, where his mother had gone. And why hadn't she looked for him?

Lauren stumbled in the snow, her breath coming in harsh gasps, her lungs burning with the cold. As she trudged up the hill, she searched for the child that must surely be out here. Who else had drawn on her window? Such tiny fingers, they'd die out here if they didn't get warm. Such thoughts buzzed in her head as she homed in on the playground, sure that whoever was lost would find their way here—in the hope that their mother would find them. She hoped that Sarah would find her soon, would help her find whoever was lost. What would she think, when she heard her sister rambling about lost children and icy fingers on her answer phone? She almost laughed, then realised she'd probably given Sarah enough ammunition to make a doctor listen. And then what would she do?

128

She realised she didn't care. Throughout her life, all she'd wanted was a child—and the one time that had been imminent, her chance had been taken away in an instant: her unborn child crushed by the steering wheel of her car as she careened into a wall to avoid an accident. There would be no more chances, not after that. There'd been too much damage, they said. It hadn't taken Dan long to leave after that, although in all fairness a lot of the blame for that lay at her door. She couldn't look at him, knowing what she knew—and he grew tired of promising he didn't blame her and it didn't matter.

Too late now to worry about all that. A cry in the darkness energised her, and she moved forward more purposefully as the park's gate hove into view.

Mary turned her head as she pushed her heels into the ground and halted the swing. Tommy, still in mid-swing, followed her lead as soon as he was able. He'd learnt to listen to her, to do as she said. It was less painful that way.

'What is it?' His voice was shrill in the night, his breath plumed out in front of him like Morse code, staccato evidence of his fear.

'She's here.' Mary smiled, and stepped off the swing, her mood suddenly light.

'Who's here?'

'You'll see.' She was making for the gate, eager to find . . . what?

Tommy raced after her, not wanting to be left alone. Not here. 'Mary, wait!'

She took no notice, just skipped down the path, humming tunelessly as she went. She threw a glance over her shoulder, just once, 'Come on, Tommy,' and then she was gone. The lights went out suddenly, and he was alone in the dark.

The temperature dropped.

Lauren reached the gate, almost sobbing with pain as the cold air burned its way into her lungs. The sound had gone. Just for a moment, she'd thought she heard a cry—but then maybe she'd just wanted to. There was more light, suddenly—just by the gate, but

Lauren couldn't see where it came from. And there she was. A little girl had stepped into the light, and stood gazing solemnly at her. As Lauren ground to a halt, she smiled, and watched delighted as Lauren sank to her knees.

'You're real,' she sobbed.

The little girl nodded, her face wise. 'Of course I am. We both are.'

'Both?'

Again she nodded, and Lauren became aware of someone standing just behind the girl. A boy, this time. Hadn't she seen his face somewhere before? Recently? He edged forward, his face shy, hopeful. 'Do you know my mum?' he asked.

'I'm sorry, love, no. Are you lost?'

'No.' The boy grew mournful, and stepped back. He seemed to fade a little. 'She is, though. She never came.'

The boy's face clicked into place for Lauren then. Tommy Ryan. He'd gone missing from the playground only a week ago, and his mother's body had been found just outside the gates, her throat torn open.

The little girl broke in, cross at no longer being the centre of attention. 'She didn't want you, Tommy. Remember? She would have come if she did.'

'No, honey, I'm sure that's not true.'

'It is!' The girl stamped her foot, and the world darkened. Something grated underfoot and Lauren sat back, stunned. 'I told you, Tommy. No one wanted you, just like no one wanted me!'

Tommy's face fell, and as he stared at Lauren she felt her heart break. 'Tommy, it wasn't your fault. You have to know that.'

The boy shook his head. 'Mary's right. If she'd wanted me, she'd have come to find me.'

Lauren had to at least try to help him. 'Maybe something stopped her.'

Mary growled at her, and she recoiled. 'Careful, you'll frighten him.'

'I just want . . .'

'To what? Make Tommy think he belongs? He doesn't, anymore than I do.' Mary took a step closer, and a cruel smile twisted her child-like features. 'Any more than you do. You're alone, too, aren't you?'

130

Lauren nodded, bereft.

'They left you, didn't they?'

Again, Lauren nodded, dumb with grief.

Mary sidled closer, and Lauren felt a small hand worm its way into her own. She clasped her fingers around it, feeling a warmth grow inside her. 'We're alone too.'

Lauren looked up at that. 'You don't have anyone?'

'Just Tommy.' She looked back at him, and he attempted a smile. The effect was repulsive—he looked like he was facing Hell itself. Mary beckoned him closer, and he reluctantly took a step closer, then another. 'Tommy and me belong together.' She ruffled his hair, and he cringed. His eyes remained locked on Lauren. 'Don't we, Tommy?' Tommy said nothing for a moment, then nodded, all hope lost.

Lauren reached for his hand, took it into hers and squeezed. He moaned, and wrapped his arms around her in a hug. He whispered: 'Please stay with us. Don't leave me alone with her anymore.'

Lauren hugged him tight, tears blinding her. 'I won't, I promise.'

Lauren's mobile phone shrilled into life, breaking the spell. For a moment she saw Mary as she really was, wizened and old, and needing their warmth to survive. No child, this, rather a creature that might have been a child once, but had been corrupted into this parasitic monster, eager for warmth to keep her here, and for other lives to keep hers going for a little while longer. This creature was hungry, and was prepared to kill to keep her playmate, Lauren saw. The vision of Mary going to Tommy's mother for a hug floated into Lauren's mind, and she cringed as she saw the woman wiping her tears away, and holding her close. Close enough for little teeth to rip into her throat, and tear it wide open.

Mary laughed, softly. 'Aren't you going to answer it?'

Lauren stared at the display. It was Sarah. As she clicked the button to take the call, Sarah's voice rose into the night, frantic. 'Lauren! Thank God, where are you? Listen . . .' Lauren dropped the phone, and the tinny notes faded from her mind. She looked at Tommy, and she made up her mind. What did life hold for her, anyway? An empty house and an empty womb, for ever and ever, Amen.

The mobile phone dropped to the ground.

Lauren stood, and took both children's hands. She tried not to cringe from the touch of the little girl, but the child didn't seem to notice. Tommy hung on, pathetically grateful for her affection.

'Come on, kids. Time to go.'

Darkness fell, and when the lights came back on they revealed an empty playground, save for a red scarf puddled in the snow; cradling a mobile phone, its volume fading as the battery died.

The sound of children laughing rang in Sarah's ear, as her sister sang a nursery rhyme.

Then they were gone.

Marie O'Regan *is an award-nominated writer and editor of horror and dark fantasy fiction, and her short fiction has been published in such places as* The Alsiso Project, When Darkness Comes, Terror Tales 2, Midnight Street, *among others. Her first collection,* Mirror Mere, *was published in 2006, and she is also the editor of* Hellbound Hearts *(Pocket Books) and* The Mammoth Book of Body Horror *(Constable and Robinson), along with her husband, Paul Kane. Marie and Paul's non-fiction interview book,* Voices in the Dark, *was published early in 2011, and Marie's first solo editing project,* The Mammoth Book of Ghost Stories by Women, *is released in November this year.. Visit* marieoregan.net *for more information.*

LIFE-LIKE
by Paul Kane

Sam gripped the handle firmly.

Sam could grip really well, in fact his hands did little else but grip. He tugged on the metal and the door opened with a satisfying swish. He was inside the shop. Looking around, he saw every conceivable toy. Brightly coloured planes hung from the ceiling on wires, engaging in imaginary dog-fights; a castle rested on a raised incline, surrounded by a tinfoil moat, tiny soldiers attempting to storm the walls on ladders; all kinds of stuffed animals, including bears with red ribbons tied around their throats—their black, opal eyes staring back at him; and running the length of the shop was a track on which two racing cars, one black, one blue, were zipping round, faster and faster, neither one in the lead. Sam had never had the pleasure of playing with such things and they'd always fascinated him. He felt like he'd missed out on something crucial, but that wasn't going to be the case with Sally. He would make sure of that.

"Hello, sir, can I be of assistance?"

Sam turned, a little startled by the voice, and saw a man dressed in a dayglo orange top and cream slacks. His black hair swept across his head in swirls, the lights above picking out indigo highlights.

"Hi, yes. I'm looking for a toy."

The assistant nodded; his painted-on smile patronising in the extreme. Of course he was looking for a toy—it was a toy shop, wasn't it. "Any particular toy, sir?"

"I . . . I'm not really sure," said Sam, his eyes swivelling left and right again. "It's for my daughter, you see. I'd like to get her something special."

"Ah, a little girl. I see." The man came over to stand beside him, his arm snaking around behind. Without actually touching Sam, he ushered him to a section of the shop so pink it could have been made entirely from candyfloss, and had the same sickening effect. There were fluffy kittens scattered all around the floor, helium balloons with hearts painted on them tied to every shelf, and glitter plastered all over the walls. "This is our girls department, sir," the assistant told him. "Now what did you have in mind?"

"I'm not really sure—"

"An 'Easy-Peasy' Baker Oven perhaps, which bakes edible synthetic cakes, a 'Beautifullicious' make-up and hairdressing kit . . ."

"She's a little bit young for that," said Sam. "In fact, well, the toy is a gift to celebrate her moulding day."

The assistant jiggled his head up and down enthusiastically. "I understand. What age did you choose, sir?"

"Six, give or take."

"Splendid. All right, then . . . " The man moved over to one of the shelves and picked up a box. Through the transparent front Sam could see a doll inside. It had frizzy, curly hair and wide eyes that opened and closed when the man shook the container. "How about a 'Missy Daydream' doll, sir? Just like the real thing—very life-like."

A bit too life-like, thought Sam. It looked the spitting image of Sally, only a couple of years younger. *Too creepy.*

Sam shook his head. "I don't think so."

"Are you sure? They're quite popular these days. It's not real plastic, just a very clever imitation."

"All the same, it's still a bit . . . I don't know . . . weird. A good idea though," Sam offered. "Something along those lines, maybe, but less . . . I don't know . . . "

The assistant thought for a moment. "I think I know just the thing. Have you ever heard of a range of dolls called the 'skins', sir?"

Sam couldn't say that he had. "Are they new?"

"Not exactly. They've been around for a little while, but not that many have been . . . created. We have been known to import them from time to time."

"So they're unique?" *Special . . . ? He wanted something special . . .*

The man's smile remained in place. "Oh yes, quite."

"In what way?"

"They're grown, sir, not manufactured."

Sam had never heard of this. "How do you mean?"

"They're not mass-produced. They're . . . " The assistant looked around and lowered his voice. "They're made from something called flesh."

Sam frowned, his eyebrows creasing. "Flesh?"

"That's right, sir. Not many people of your generation will have heard of it. But it's a bouncy, springy material. Very durable, comes in various colours."

Sam looked down at his own, resin-coated hands; the fingers curled round in a gripping pose. *Flesh? It was a new one on him . . . whatever would they think of next?*

"I don't suppose I could see one of these . . . 'skin dolls', could I?"

"You're in luck," said the assistant. "We have one left in the basement. If you'd care to follow me." He walked stiffly off towards a set of stairs; Sam followed him, knee joints creaking with every step he took. He'd have to remember to lube them when he had a minute or two to spare.

The basement was extremely dark. A flip of the light-switch revealed rows and rows of untouched stock, hidden away from the world. Boxes of every size and shape. Sam hurried to keep pace with the assistant, walking alongside him down the first aisle.

"So why is it none of these dolls are displayed upstairs?" he asked the man.

The reply was considered carefully. "They're not to everyone's . . . taste. Only someone like yourself, looking for that very extraordinary gift might appreciate its qualities."

Sam wasn't sure at all about this. But before he had time to say anything else, they'd arrived. The box was one of the biggest down here and the assistant opened up the cardboard flaps on the front. The inside was shadowy, and Sam bent down to peer into the gloom.

Something moved.

Sam jumped back, alarmed. "What the hell was that?" he shouted.

"Please don't worry," said the assistant. "It's just reacting to the light. Happens every time we come down to feed it too."

"Feed?" *This was getting stranger by the minute.*

"Yes, sir. In order to remain active, the doll must be fed organically. There's a certain amount of maintenance as well."

Sam had recovered his composure and was bending once again. "Maintenance? What, you mean like changing the batteries?"

The assistant laughed. "Why, goodness me no; it doesn't require batteries. I mean cutting hair, washing from time to time . . . that sort of thing."

Sam noticed that there were bars across the front of the box. The assistant followed his line of vision. "Ah, yes, it comes with its own . . . playpen. Where you can store it when not in use."

"Can you get it to come out a little bit further?" said Sam. "I'd like to see it."

"Naturally." The man reached into his pocket and took out a crumbling piece of biscuit. It wasn't plastic or synthetic, Sam could tell, it was made from something he'd never come across before. "Come here!"

At first nothing happened, so the assistant rattled the box. "Come on. Food!" he snapped. "That's right . . . .come on . . . "

Sam watched in amazement as a hand reached out into the half-light. It was small and peculiar, it had lumps where it should be smooth—and nails that didn't look like they were an extension of the hand at all, but rather individual things in their own right, perhaps glued on? The assistant continued with his coaxing, bringing the doll out to the front of the box, to the bars of the playpen. For the first time Sam could see it properly, crawling

136

and shuffling towards him. It was completely bare, pink—but a dull pink compared to his own colouring—apart from patches of red here and there, at the lips and cheeks especially. Its hair was long and brown and flowed over its shoulders. It didn't just hang there straight down, it seemed to have a life of its own; it was doing its own thing entirely. When it looked back at Sam it was with large, brown eyes; it blinked once or twice but there was no snapping sound. In fact there was no sound at all. He couldn't take his eyes off this thing, and if it hadn't shifted its own gaze from Sam back to the biscuit, they might have remained like that, locked in each other's sight forever.

The doll snatched the biscuit and shoved it greedily into the wet hole in its face. "Dadda," it said with its mouth full.

"It can talk?" said Sam, a little alarmed.

"Of course. It's been trained to say the following words: 'Dadda', 'Mamma', 'potty', and 'thank you'. "

"Tanku," repeated the doll.

"Amazing. There's no cord or anything," whispered Sam. Though it was hard to tell without seeing it standing up, the doll looked to be about Sally's size and age. It would certainly make a unique companion for his daughter.

"Am I to take it that sir is interested?" the assistant asked.

Sam didn't answer quite yet. He was too busy staring at the doll again. The man took this as a good sign and continued to smile his painted-on smile.

"Hi honey, I'm home," shouted Sam as he gripped the handle on the front door and pushed. He was so proud of that grip; it was such a fantastic grip.

"Hi Sam," shouted his wife from the kitchen area. "I'm just doing some ironing."

Sam followed her tinny voice through the hall and into the kitchen. There she was: Suzie, curly blonde hair in ringlets that framed her face perfectly, sunlight from the window reflecting off her shiny forehead, black eyelashes batting so fast they almost created a draft. Her tall, statuesque frame was complemented by a patterned gypsy-style top and a pair of tight jeans cut off just below the knee. Her white rubber shoes had little straps that curved over her delicate feet. God how he loved her.

The pair embraced and he gripped her shoulders, as he often did, pulling her in closer to him. Sam and Suzie kissed, heads clacking together, mouths meeting but never opening; Suzie running her fingers over his felt-covered head. When they were finished, Sam pulled away and said. "Well, I've managed to find a very special present for little Sally's moulding day."

"Really," said Suzie, beaming. "What?"

"You'll never guess in a thousand years, Suzie."

"Not another pet, Sam. We have a hard enough time keeping an eye on Ginge and Tinkerbell." As if on cue, the two cats appeared in the kitchen—one through the flap in the back door, the other from behind Sam. Both were 'meowing' electronically as they brushed up against Suzie and Sam.

"No, not a pet as such," said Sam. "I've got her a toy."

"Oh, Sam, I thought we'd discussed this already . . . "

Sam gripped one of her dangling ringlets and wound it around his hand playfully. "I know, honey. But, well, this is different. This doll is so—"

"A doll?" said Suzie.

"Baby, it's not like anything you've ever seen before . . . "

"Sam, you're so easily led. How much did it cost?"

"That's not important. I just know Sally's going to love it."

"It's not one of those creepy 'almost real' ones is it?"

Sam shook his head. "Look, it's probably better if you see for yourself." He took Suzie outside by the hand, gripping it firmly all the way. Sam led her to the bright red Ford Escape SUV on the drive. He put his hand through one of the windows—none of which contained any glass—reached into the cream-coloured interior and flipped the switch for the boot. There was a *snick* as it opened and Suzie walked around the back.

"It's inside the box?"

"Yep," said Sam. "But we'll get it inside first before I open it. Oh boy, are you in for a treat!"

Sally's moulding day arrived, and Sam and Suzie snuck the box—now covered in wrapping paper and a bow—into the upstairs bedroom for her to discover first thing in the morning. Suzie had taken some convincing about the present at first, even though she admitted she had never seen anything like it before; it was certainly not what she'd been imagining. But as soon as the doll uttered the word 'Mamma' and looked pleadingly up at her, she relented. Sam was right: Sally was going to adore this unusual gift.

As soon as they heard Sally stirring, and then whooping with joy, Sam and Suzie burst in and shouted. "Happy Moulding Day!" Both stood there proudly watching their daughter, strawberry hair in pigtails, eyes the size of small plates, remembering the day when they'd donated their own plastic to form her. It had been a major decision, but they had always talked about starting a family since the moment they met. And neither had regretted it for a second.

"What is it? What is it?" screamed Sally, jumping up and down.

"Why don't you open it and see?" suggested Sam, giving nothing away.

Sally tried to undo the bow with her stubby fingers, but couldn't find a purchase. Suzie patted Sam on the arm, and he was more than happy to help—grabbing hold of the ribbon from his side and tugging gently. It wasn't long before the box was open, and the pen exposed. Inside was the doll, cringing slightly in the corner. It was dressed in a purple outfit with frills—just one of an assortment the man from the shop had given Sam.

"Wow!" said Sally, hardly able to believe it. "A dolly!"

"Do you like it?" asked Suzie.

Sally nodded enthusiastically; she'd never seen anything

139

like this either, and was desperate to start playing. "Can I? Can I?" She was looking for the opening to the pen.

"Sure," said Sam. "She's yours, after all. Any idea what you're going to call her, Sally?"

His daughter stopped and thought about this, then said. "Clara." She opened the pen and tried to pull on Clara's arm, but again couldn't get a proper hold. Sam wished sometimes he'd insisted on gripping hands like his own.

"Here, try this," he said, giving Sally a piece of bread.

"What is it?"

"It's what the doll . . . it's what *Clara* eats."

Sally held it in her podgy palm. "Come on out, Clarabel. You and me are going to be friends."

Still hesitant, the doll crawled towards her and took the bread. "Tanku," it said. "Tanku."

Sally played with the Clara doll all that morning, having an imaginary tea party, dancing to the latest bopping beats, then dressing it up in a variety of garbs. Sam had to remember to change the doll's undergarment around dinnertime though—as the assistant had said, that's what keeps it going: in one end, out the other. There were no batteries required with this little beauty.

At her Moulding Day celebrations later on, Sally showed Clara off to everyone. All the other girls her age were very jealous— even the ones with Missy Daydreams, which their parents had never really cared for anyway. And Sam had to go through the mechanics of the doll with curious mothers and fathers as they watched the children play. *It's called what? Flesh?*

Only during a game of swings out in the back garden was there a small problem, when the Clara doll fell off onto the ground. Sally came running over to fetch Sam, yelling that there was something strange and red coming out of Clara's mouth. Puzzled, Sam dabbed at Clara's lip with a piece of rag, finally holding it there until the liquid seemed to dry up. He shrugged when Suzie joined him, as puzzled as she was.

"Tanku," the doll said quietly.

All Sam could think was it must be something to do with the 'growing' process that the assistant had been talking about; unique to these so-called flesh dolls. Whatever the case, Clara was soon dragged off for the children to play with until it was time for them to leave.

As the days went by, Sally seemed to lose interest in the Clara doll. Sam tried to get her to play with it, but just as quickly as the novelty had taken hold, it wore off in about the same time. A week later and Suzie was starting to get a bit annoyed at being the only one who fed and changed the doll; that's when she remembered to do so—usually reminded by a mewling noise the doll had started to make. Often hours would go by and no one would even think about Clara in her pen. Sally was too busy watching the paper screen TV or chasing the cats.

When she did take Clara out, it was only to make her the butt of jokes and games. Sam was a little shocked to walk into the bedroom and find Clara taped to a chair, with Sally throwing hard rubber balls at her. Where the projectiles had connected with its skin, the doll had turned a purple colour—obviously to match her dress, which hadn't been changed since that first day out of the box.

"Mamma," Clara was crying with each thud of the ball. "Mamma."

"Sally, stop that right now," Sam had shouted, then ordered her downstairs. He'd untied the doll, grasping the sticky tape firmly and unravelling it—and their eyes had locked again. Sam paused for a moment when he saw her leaking again, when he saw the wetness in the corners of her big, brown eyes.

"Tanku, Dadda."

Sam placed her back in the pen and turned off the lights.

On Clara's last day in the house, Sally went too far.

141

She thought it would be a good idea to see what would happen when you overfed the doll. Ramming biscuit after biscuit into its mouth, Sally laughed when Clara tried to cough it up again. "You're the one who *has* to eat," said Sally. "not me."

It was as she shoved another piece of bread into Clara's mouth that the doll clamped down on Sally's stumpy fingers. She bit through them almost up to the palm. Sally cried out in shock and alarm, swinging her other arm round to strike Clara.

It was then that the arm came off at the socket.

When Suzie raced upstairs, she saw the scene: Clara with Sally's hand in her mouth, the arm waving about in the air; and her daughter—her precious daughter!—on the floor screaming, dismembered by this foreign 'toy' Sam had thought it was so clever to bring into the house . . .

Clara spat out the arm. "Mamma."

Suzie went into a rage, lunging for the doll. She struck it and it fell to the floor with a bump. "Potty," it said, then leaked all over the floor because nobody had remembered to change her in a week. The puddle spread and Clara just sat there shivering. As Suzie approached again, the doll made a dash for the bedroom door—clambering over the bed and racing for safety.

Sam was at the open doorway. He let out a painful groan when he saw his baby lying on the floor, then a startled grunt as Clara crawled between his legs and onto the landing.

"Come back. Come here!" he shouted, turning and grabbing. He gripped her dress, ripping it at the shoulder, but Clara didn't stop. She spun around, backing off as Sam followed her.

"Dadda . . . Dadda . . . " she repeated. Then she said. "Sorry."

Her foot slipped on the top step of the stairs and Sam reached out. But his gripping hands, the ones he was always so proud of, failed him at just the wrong moment. The doll fell down the flight, toppling over and over, accompanied by a crunching sound that somehow managed to drive a spike through Sam. He looked down at Clara near the bottom. She wasn't moving.

142

He descended, noticing even before he got there that more of the red liquid had been spilt, and was flowing out of Clara. Crouching down, he dabbed at the doll's mouth, at its shoulder, but the liquid didn't stop this time. And Clara's head flopped on a neck that could no longer support it.

Sam wished that he was able to leak too . . .

The assistant didn't seem very surprised to see Sam return with the box a day or so later.

"You remember me? I bought a 'skin doll' a few weeks ago . . . "

The man said that he did. "What seems to be the trouble, sir?"

"There was an . . . accident. My daughter was injured."

The assistant continued to smile his painted-on smile, but it had suddenly lost some of its spark. "Oh dear. I do hope she's all right?"

"Her arm came off," Sam said bluntly.

The man remained silent.

"She's had to have a new one."

"And this was caused by the doll, sir?"

Sam nodded.

"Where is it now?"

"In the box. I've brought it back. It's broken; not moving. You might be able to repair it, but it's no use to us anymore."

The assistant opened the box and looked inside. "No," he said, bowing his head but still smiling. "I'm afraid it will be impossible to mend."

It was Sam's turn to say nothing. He opened and closed his gripping hands.

"In view of what's happened I think the very least we can do is offer our apologies and your money back . . . " The man raised his head. "That is, unless you would like to pick something else from the shop."

Sam opened his mouth to speak, then closed it again. Sally

143

had been very shaken up by the whole experience, and he doubted whether Suzie would ever speak to him again. Perhaps there was something he could bring back to make amends.

"Another doll, for instance?"

Sam shook his head. "No way. Not again."

The assistant smiled. "No, no, you misunderstand me. I don't mean another one the same—we don't have any 'skins' left in stock at the moment anyway. No, I was thinking, this time you might be better off with something a little more . . . "

"Life-like?" Sam said.

"Exactly," said the assistant, and smiled. Then guided him once more in the direction of the Missy Daydream selection.

Paul Kane is the award-winning author of numerous horror/dark fantasy stories, and books like Alone (In the Dark), Touching the Flame, FunnyBones, Signs of Life, The Lazarus Condition, Peripheral Visions, The Hellraiser Films and Their Legacy, RED, Of Darkness and Light, The Gemini Factor *and the bestselling* Arrowhead *trilogy (*Arrowhead, Broken Arrow *and* Arrowland*). He is also the co-editor of* Hellbound Hearts, The Mammoth Book of Body Horror *and the forthcoming* Beyond Rue Morgue *from Titan. To find out more about him and his work visit* shadow-writer.co.uk.

TRANSMOGRIFY
by Richard Thomas

In order to live I have to die.

I close my eyes for a second and her hot mouth is on my nipples, her hands cupping my breasts as our pale limbs writhe on the bed. A shock of air and my eyes flick open. I run my tongue over porcelain teeth, breathing in the crisp November air, and exhaling strawberry frost. Still, the remorse. When will I learn?

Numb to the bone I stand in the empty graveyard as the sun creeps over the horizon, limping home, drenched in a bloodmist that constantly frames my vision. The acid-rain will soon eat through the screeners I've put on. At this time of year AR50 may not be enough. As much as things have changed some traditions stay the same. I come back to the rituals. The burial.

In the distance leaves burn, wet and moldy. A dense cloud of dirty smoke drifts over the skeletal forest that rings the iron fence, chipped and forgotten. I am alone, as expected. The obituary was a formality but I'm a stickler for details. Long slender fingers push deep into the cashmere overcoat abyss that drapes to my knees and hugs my empty shell. The sharp wind rapes me again and again. I play a game in the flayed tresses that flit about my face. They are as black as my heart and I hide from the very surroundings I set out to embrace today.

Footsteps. I glance around, picking up the motion of a lone figure, head down, treading towards me. Dark and tall, it must be Remy. Who else would show? Who else was left? I shiver but not from the cold. I fed last night and am still full of the sustenance of her lifeforce. She had been expecting something akin to a gothic romance but was sorely mistaken.

The evolution didn't happen all at once. It took time. Years. Lifetimes. But I have plenty of time. I have eternity.

I rub the port at the base of my skull, a nasty habit like twirling my hair. I have to see DocAught soon. Time for a tune-up. A little nanotech and a full viral upgrade and nobody will be the wiser.

A thousand voices whisper and my eyes shoot to the dead branches. A Starling catapults up into the fading light, fluttering its wings. Panic stricken eyes gaze my way as it drops from the sky, twitching for but a moment, then still. Rigid.

He is closer now. There is nowhere to run. Not that I could have. I miss him. When he finally looks up his eyes go wide and his brow furrows, stopping in his tracks. A heat flushes my skin and for a moment I hesitate. The longing blurs my vision as the heat flows to a million points of skin that weep beneath my clothes.

"Excuse me, miss," he says.

"You must be Remy," I say.

"Um . . . well, yes, but . . . " his eyes are on my face like a magnifying glass - inspecting, doubting.

"I'm Cinder. But you can call me Cindy," I offer.

"OH, right. Wow. Finally we meet. It's just . . . "

"I know. I look just like her."

"Well, twenty years ago, right . . . the same blue eyes, uncanny."

"Consider it an homage. I had them dyed to the same Tiffany blue a couple of years ago. Mine had always been such a boring brown."

"Right." He turns to the grave and stares at the headstone. "Old school."

"It's mostly symbolic, you know, with the organ laws and all . . . "

"Yes. She's not in there. I know."

"You ok, Remy?"

"I didn't think there'd be anybody here, especially not you. I thought you were a myth, something that she talked about at night, a phantom that didn't really exist."

"Long story. Nothing you need to know about. Pedestrian."

"Right."

"I was just leaving anyway, it's getting late. Curfew."

"Yes." He stands close to me, a massive presence, more grey at the temples than I remember.

"Here, Remy, she wanted me to give you this."

I walk over to him, every bit of silk rubbing against my flesh, screaming out. I wrap my arms around him and press my head against his chest. The pounding. His hands are on my back and I find myself turning feline. I purr into his grey woolen coat and rub my face in his musky scent. Wormwood and formaldehyde burn my nostrils as I brush up against his legs. My knees are like a cricket making music as they rub together.

For a second he lets down his guard. Remorse and anguish float to the surface like a bloated corpse wrapped in black trash bags. Against my own wishes I take a sip. Just a bit of him for posterity. A quick inhale and he coughs. I lick my lips, rubbing out a bitter coat of wax that I'd pasted on earlier. Ruby Woo. The casing is new, but the inhabitant, ancient.

I push away and step back. For a moment we are knee deep in snow, the Celtic crosses and cracked stones dusted with powder, as his breath exhales in a cloud, eyes dimming to dull ashes. He staggers, barely able to raise his hands from his sides. A crack over the horizon as the sound barrier breaks. The 6:42 to Los Angeles. Always on time.

"It's ok, baby. Everything is going to be fine."

Remy falls over on his side, glancing up at me, his eyes empty.

"You won't remember this moment, for I've taken it. Forget me. Forget her. We're gone, and won't be back. It's better this way. Consider it a bullet dodged Remy and move on with your life. Let it go."

"Ok."

"Down the street from you, that blonde with the synthetics, the skin job on a leash she calls a dog, that one. She's a good catch for you. Don't come here again."

"Ok."

I need to go home and jack in. Now. My hunger has been awakened. He'll be ok. He'll be alive. It's the least I can do for him after all of these years. Samantha is dead now. Long live Cinder. Half of the time I'm gone anyway. It doesn't matter.

I'll always be alone.

Standing at the grocery checkout the young girl with the blonde ponytail can't look at me enough. Her face flushes red every fifteen seconds. She scans the bizarre selections that I've grabbed in a frenzy as the ache washes over me in waves. Six blood oranges. A 24 oz.

147

bottle of Intrigue K-Y Jelly. 1 gallon of compressed nitrogen.

"Are you, like . . . I mean, do . . . . " she sputters.

"No."

"Oh, ok."

12 razor blades. A six-pack of Frost Gatorade. 8 cellular protein cutlets.

"Are you sure? I mean, didn't I see . . . "

"No, sweetheart, you didn't."

12 feet of Tripp Lite U042-036 High-Speed USB 2.0 cable. A tube of black cherry lip balm. A 6.8 oz. Red Currant Votivo candle. A 50-count bottle of Vitamin B12-H_SharkOil.

"I mean, I don't like girls or anything, that's not what I'm trying . . . "

"Honey, look at me."

The high school cheerleader with the punk rock fantasies pauses for a moment with a can of Vienna Sausages in her left hand, the other wandering up to her shirt collar, fiddling with the tab, running behind her neck to massage the only acceptable exposed flesh.

A flash of light and french doors fly open. An empty bed rests in the middle of the room as pale blue moonlight fills the space with stardust. A cigarette smolders in an ashtray on the nightstand as the dull patter of a shower running seeps from beneath the bathroom door. There is an indentation in the mattress. Lace trim edges the sheets, wrinkled ivory bunched in piles. It is quiet in the room but for the echo of a gasp, the exhale of air, and the sigh of completion.

"You couldn't handle it . . . " squinting at her name tag. " . . . Jennifer."

I extend my wrist to the scanner, and run the bar-code over it. BEEP. Cinder Bathory. $426,384. Transaction ok? $1,235.45. Accessing account. APPROVED.

Welcome to Facebook. Facebook helps you connect and share with the entities in your life.

I try to pry the plastic off of the new USB cable. These damn things are so hard to open. My hair is pulled back and to the side for easy access to my port. My skin is pink and splotchy from the blistering hot shower and the obsidian silk robe clings to my damp body like tape.

My hands shake and drop the package to the floor. The third one I've burnt out this month. Nothing has any depth anymore, nothing satisfies. Everything is manufactured, and that makes it farther from the truth, the core of it all, the purity. Soon the snacking will not be enough.

I pause for a second to gaze around my sparse studio apartment. I live like an eccentric millionaire, eating cans of cat food and fearing my own demise while my checking account stands at $400,000. There is nothing but Glacier water and a hexagrid of hemoglobin cubes in the fridge. The grocery bag stands on the counter forgotten for the moment. A king size four-post bed covered with 1000-thread count sheets fills the room. It was hand carved by Buddhist monks four thousand years ago. A blinking 36" monitor sits next to a hybrid computer that I found in Chinatown. Resting on the beaten Salvation Army desk, it waits for me, the leather desk chair eager for my supplication. It has Intel guts, Mac OS XX_Cheetah, a terabyte of hard drive space, and enough security to route whatever happens back to the very brown coats that might be tracking me.

I should move to the desert and leave it all. I've evolved beyond my needs, and my life is more complicated for it. The itching of the nanodrones is in my head, DocAught says. It isn't possible for me to feel them. But I do. They crash around the inside of my veins and the siren songs, the rapture, makes me double over and crash to my knees. I tear open the plastic, slicing my index finger in the process. By the dull glow of the monitor I suck at the broken skin, as my eyes slide into whiteness. My history will be my undoing, but it is not the crimson shot I want tonight. They wait for me, a bunch of addicts, scratching at the scabs, ready to tear them open again. And I'm coming. I'm coming.

I unravel the cord and jam it into the side of the computer. Sliding into the small leatherbound swivel chair I fumble around at the base of my skull and plug it in. My eyes flutter and a gasp escapes my lips. Fingers fly to the keyboard as I login. I have 432 friends. I have 23 new messages. I've been poked 12 times. I skip it all and head to a special private chat room. There are others like me. Others that think they are like me. But they aren't.

Tomorrow they'll be weak, fatigued, with headaches or

migraines, depressed over something they can't quite figure out. Their immune systems will plummet and regardless of the hypodermics they shove into their thighs or the bots they have infiltrating their systems, my tech is better. They plug in just like I do, seeking something to fill the void.

PRIVATE CHAT - Room 2112.0101
Bloodrunners
[2] members present
Ashestoashes has entered the room

cureforpain: hey ash, wassup
breakingthebroken: so i didn't think that was fair, you know?
cureforpain: nk, lb
breakingthebroken: sistersister, where have you been?
ashestoashes: oh you know, same old stuff, stupid job, stupid boyfriend, blech
breakingthebroken: we were just talking about that crap
cureforpain: ask her, she'll tell you
ashestoashes: what?
breakingthebroken: oh, nothing, stupid boy i think is working me
ashestoashes: what do you mean?
breakingthebroken: i'm just being paranoid that's all
ashestoashes: what happened
cureforpain: come on, spill it or i will
ashestoashes: you can tell me
breakingthebroken: <sigh> i text him, and it's always real fast and short, brb, or he won't take my calls, and when i ask him what he's doing he never tells me, i try to hook up, and can't find him, you know, stupid shit but then . . .

I lean back in the chair and close my eyes. The flow is slow but unmistakable. Fear, bits of anxiety, regret, remorse. Even Cureforpain is letting it out. He's been trying to get Broken in the real world for months now. Anger, frustration.

ashestoashes: let just tell you something, and you just listen,

150

ok?
breakingthebroken: ok
cureforpain: here it comes, preach baby :-)
ashestoashes: if he never returns your calls, if he never has sex with you, if he blows you off for his boys, if he's always working late, never wants to see the movies you do, never wants to eat the food you like, basically, he just doesn't care about you, move on . . .

The rig has been filled and the air tapped out. Leaning forward I'm blinded by a shroud of white as memories cut in and out. Mountains and a cabin, AUF WIEDERSEHEN! gunfire and the pounding of horses hooves thundering by. The cold stone of an empty hallway lost deep in the bowels of some ancient castle. Snow and the soft rub of animal fur on my naked flesh.

My fingers fly over the keyboard, lecturing the kids once again.

> . . . if he won't let you look at his phone sadness, frustration, anger, betrayal that means there are calls on there or texts he doesn't want you to see, numbers, and if his phone rings fury, despair, failure, remorse, exhaustion, nausea at his apartment and the voicemail starts to pick up and you hear a female voice, and he purrs in your ear, hold on a sec baby abandonment, suicide, desperation, failure, anger, anger, anger, stupidity, loss while he jumps up to answer it and you hear the words nothing or nobody or later, then he is screwing you over he is using you loneliness, rage, fury, emptiness, anxiety . . .

breakingthebroken: omg i'm gonna barf
breakingthebroken has left the room
ashestoashes: too much?
cureforpain: naw, she needed to hear it
ashestoashes: so what's up with you?

The sun peeks under the edge of the velvet drapes. Exhausted, I breathe in and out, my skin heating up, tightening. I've turned back the clock three years tonight. I'm five pounds lighter. Sweat glistens on my exposed throat, and I lean back in the chair as my hand slides down the front of my robe. My eyes close as I embrace this mortal coil.

There are predators and there are prey. Donors and recipients.

I have to move around a lot. I have a Xenon AmTran card. I have five million frequent flier miles. Conway, Arkansas. Rolla, Missouri. Peoria, Illinois. Off the beaten path. The security is too dangerous in the metropolitan factions. You can only nibble on the second shift of the Dell computer parts factory for so long. The Caterpillar assembly line. The AT&T Global telemarketing center. They start to get sick. People stop showing up, and glances dart my way. They think it's sex. When the whispers at the vending machines start, it's time for me to disappear into the night.

The places where emotions are raw and on the surface, that's where I linger. But in time I find that no matter how depressing the job, how dismal the future, how anxious my friends become, it has its limits. People leave, people get a bad vibe about you, and they stop opening up. The funeral homes call the police. The hospitals ask for ID. The AA meetings start questioning your steps. Their hackles go up, and their senses heighten. Online it's easier to sip. And the body of water that I surf with reckless abandon is much larger and better stocked.

I'm tired of writing pablum for the broken hearted wrist slashing nation. I need to reinvent myself. I need a new home.

DocAught is coming tonight. A house call. Like he does every hundred years or so. Something has to go in the casket where Samantha should be. They may harvest every organ for the good of the people, every bloodshot eyeball and broken digit. But there is always something left. You'd be surprised how many useless parts we have. The vomeronasal organ, a tiny pit on each side of the septum. A set of cervical ribs left over from our reptilian days. The male uterus. A fifth toe. It isn't pretty.

I need to get ready, prepare myself for the transition.

Silence has expanded to fill my tiny apartment. A section of candlelight throbs from the window ledge. A pair of forlorn window frames blast the studio with a foul chill. I am rotting from the inside out and have waited much too long. The door hangs open wide, a forlorn shriek that swallows the light. I will not be disturbed for this space does not exist. Not tonight.

My pasty skin is a moonglow in the center of a collapsing star. Eyes closed, my face is buried in the lavender scent of the downy pillows. A thin sheen of icy sweat coats my body as my soul fights to escape. Any other night and my head would be filled with visions of fingertips and razor blades, bloodletting and rope burns, tongues shoved into every eager crevice. There is no room for that tonight. Shoulders twitch, my hands grasping and releasing the bedsheets, and I repeat one word over and over again.

Transmogrify.

I have lost myself again. Torches burn at the river's edge. There is the sharp snapping of canine teeth and the grumbling of angry peasants.

"No . . . no."

Convulsions and my neck snaps back, eyes rolling up into my skull, my tongue darting for moisture in every corner of my mouth.

Forward, back. Forward, back. Flying sideways, a hard turn to the right, pulled around a corner, and gravity pulls my stomach down, pressure on my face, a great rush of wind.

He's here.

I don't need to see him to picture him clearly. So many times we've done this. My keeper. So many times we've hunted together. My lover. His hand is on my bare back, the size of a stingray. His weight crushes the bed and it cries out in resistance. Not a sound from him, not a word. I can't remember the last thing he said to me. Yes. Yes, I can.

"Go."

A tingle races over the surface of my skin as he runs his massive paw up the small of my back, stopping just short of my port. A sigh escapes my lips as a solitary bloody tear glides down my cheek.

I picture him the way I last saw him, in a back alley of New York City, 1908. A bowler hat atop his bald, gleaming dome. The dark wool suit stretched taut across his broad shoulders, his legs like tree stumps ending in squared off shoes. His prominent nose crowding out small, gleaming eyes, a fire burning inside, his full lips tight. The clink of a beer glass dropped on cobblestone, and his

153

patience had run out. Just like that.

He leans over me and presses his body against mine, his cold musculature like a marble sculpture. I am slowly being suffocated by a distant god and I don't care. A harp string vibrates and the clasp of a briefcase opens. Plastic unwraps and latex gloves snap on. The slow turning of a lid being removed fills my ears as a hint of birch mixed with sassafras drifts to me.

I am waiting for the cord, the cable, the life. He is not.

One hand is firm at the base of my neck and a device is shoved in the port. A leap drive. I struggle but cannot move. He holds me down with one giant palm as the toxic potion fills my nostrils, burning, and the drive comes to life with a hum.

"There are creatures far worse than you, my love," his baritone rumbles.

I am emptying, spilling, falling from a great height as my eyes gush a river. A soul I thought to be long gone, diseased and broken—breaks. Not a single utterance, only the spinning and whir-ring of the pod at my neck. Outside my window in the suicide of winter there is a void of life. A crackling of ice as a solitary branch fractures under the weight and shatters on the ground.

Richard Thomas was the winner of the ChiZine Publications 200. "Enter the World of Filaria" contest and Jotspeak. His debut novel, a neo-noir thriller entitled Transubstantiate *(Otherworld Publications), was released in July of 2010. His work is published or forthcoming in the* Shivers VI *anthology (Cemetery Dance) with Stephen King and Peter Straub, the* Warmed and Bound *anthology (Velvet Press), the* Noir at the Bar *anthology,* Speedloader *(Snubnose Press),* ChiZine, Gargoyle, Murky Depths, PANK, Pear Noir!, 3:AM Magazine, Word Riot, Dogmatika, Opium, Vain, Crime Factory, Metazen, Dirty Noir, Stepaway, Shotgun Honey, Cherry Bleeds, Rotten Leaves, We Are Vespertine, Blink-Ink, Leodegraunce, Eternal Night: A Vampire An-thology *(Living Dead Press),* Outsider Writers Collective, The Odd-ville Press, Colored Chalk, Cause and Effect, Gold Dust, Nefarious Muse, and* Troubadour 21.

He lives in the northwest suburbs of Chicago. He is currently pursuing a MFA at Murray State University in their low-residency program.

NINE TENTHS
by Jay Eales

Prologue

"But it's not my birthday for another week!" Sarah protested, though not *too* much at the prospect of an early present.

"I know," Marcus said. "I just wanted to surprise you." He had a lunatic grin as he grabbed both her hands and led her onwards, paying no attention to the street furniture strewn in his path as he backed up the pavement. From time to time, he would jig Sarah's arms up and down to encourage her using the medium of dance, enhanced by occasionally slipping on a discarded pizza box, or tripping over a chained up bike. Every so often, he would glance back over his shoulder, sizing up any substantial obstacles coming up. He particularly eyed up a battered old metal bin with '68' daubed on it in magnolia paint, rubbish overflowing its boundaries and leaving the lid parked atop it at a rakish angle.

"So . . . what have you got me?" Sarah could no longer hide her curiosity.

"Patience! It's just a token of my *luuuuuuurve*, baby!" Marcus suddenly let go of Sarah's hands and skipped around her, making her turn on the spot to keep facing him.

"Where'd you get all this energy from on a Sunday morning, anyway?"

"I'm just high on life. That and the three espressos I necked before I woke you."

"Ah, that explains why your pupils are spinning," Sarah said. "Anyway, don't change the subject. You were about to spill the beans about my prezzie?"

Marcus looked down the road again. "Nearly there," he said. He continued to cajole her along the path with a succession of hit and run kisses wherever he could find some exposed skin. Sarah continued to make mock protestations at her boyfriend's hyper behaviour, but her eyes were gleaming. They passed number 66, and Marcus spotted the bicycle chained to the street light outside the front door, and could not resist giving the bell a quick pump. A couple of curtains twitched at the nearby houses where the residents were already up and about, but nobody was looking for a confrontation, even with a mostly harmless looking Tigger-like twenty-something who was nine stone nothing ringing wet.

"You're an idiot," Sarah said, as Marcus continued to caper around her like a court jester.

"Yeah, but I'm *your* idiot," Marcus shot her a camembert grin.

"Who else would have you?" Sarah ruffled his hair fiercely, before pushing back his unruly cowlick. It took three attempts before it would stay.

Marcus took the opportunity to swoop on her again, nibbling at her collar bone and across her bare shoulder to the nape of her neck, brushing aside her hair to better reach his target, and making a series of 'mmn-mmn-mmn' noises as he did so, until he was standing behind her. He put his hands over her eyes and nudged her forward again, as they approached 68.

"Careful!" she said, as she stumbled blindly on, and Marcus adjusted his grip so that he covered her blindfolded with just his left hand. Sarah heard Marcus rummaging around in 68's dustbin, dislodging and pushing aside bin bags in search of something. She caught the sour tang of spoiled foodstuffs from more than a few days earlier. Luckily, the weather had been pretty mild or they would have been able to smell it all the way down the road at their flat. Students, she assumed, surprised that they had put out the rubbish at all. Marcus gave a small triumphant grunt as he hauled something free from the bin. At such an early hour on the Sabbath, and without a triple-espresso stimulant to help, Sarah could not fathom what it was that Marcus was doing, until he took his hand away from her face and got her to turn around to face him. He had his right hand behind his back, still hiding something from her.

Before Sarah could comment, Marcus brought out his prize with a flourish, presenting it to Sarah with a courtly bow, and adopting a poor cod-Shakespearian accent. "For you, milady! Tis nought but a trifle, the merest token of my undying affection." Sarah automatically took the proffered gift, a bouquet of flowers, amazingly, still wrapped in protective cellophane and with an attached message card, slightly crumpled from their extended stay in the dustbin. It would have been a lovely arrangement, had it been six or seven days earlier, when the flowers had been freshly cut and purchased. Whereas today, they were more tired than Sarah was, wilting and shedding petals at the merest movement of her hands. Any fragrance that the flowers might once have produced had long since been overpowered by the aroma of rotting fried chicken remains and cigarette ash from their proximity in the bin. Marcus had eyeballed the discarded flowers while passing on the way to the corner shop for milk the previous day, and the whole crazy plan was born fully formed by the time he had arrived back at the flat.

"I'm . . . overwhelmed," Sarah began to speak in Marcus' cod-Elizabethan manner before thinking better of it, and wrinkled her nose at the pungent odour instead. As she held the flowers up for closer examination, she read the message card. "Who's Lizzie?" She raised an eyebrow in mock outrage. "Is that your . . . *strumpet?*" With a theatrical flourish, she tossed the bouquet into the road between two parked cars. "Here's what I think of your harlot's cast-offs!" She giggled as the flowers shed petal confetti as they arced through the air.

"Ah, that . . . " Marcus said, pausing for thought as he leant forward to retrieve the discarded gift. "Obviously . . . Well, *obviously* . . . it's my new pet name for you!" He held up one hand in supplication and he stretched between the cars into the road, and so did not even see the car that struck him.

One

"His eyes are open!"

Marcus blinked at the cold white light, feeling the detritus of sleepy dust in his eyes. He made to raise a hand to wipe it away, only to find tubes taped to his arm, and let out an involuntary yelp of alarm. In front of him, he could see a lot of movement, but his vision was blurred, and the women in front of him were strangers.

"Marcus?" One of the women, the one with a halo of blonde hair framing her face, leaned in to give him a cautious embrace. He accepted it. "Marcus? It's Sarah. You were in an accident."

Marcus pulled back against his pillow and looked around him, blinking rapidly as he tried to clear his vision, but recognising

157

the room he was in as a nursing ward, with pale green curtains instead of walls on two sides. At the mention of the word 'accident', the other woman, the one that Marcus now recognised as wearing the uniform of a nurse, put her hand on Sarah's arm.

"Sair . . . " he attempted to speak, but the dryness of his throat made it difficult to get the word out. "Ahh . . . Cuh huv . . . wor?"

Sarah turned to the nurse and sai. "Oh, could you get him some water, please?"

"Of course," the nurse said, but she squeezed Sarah's arm a little tighter. "Sarah, it's probably best if you don't tell him too much about the accident for a while, okay?"

"**'m noh fuk'n deff!**" Marcus spat at the nurse, his face flushed and veins pulsing at his temples.

Sarah stood open-mouthed at Marcus' outburst. She immediately felt the need to apologise. "I'm so sorry! He's not like this normally . . . "

"Don't be silly! He's been through a lot, Sarah," the nurse shrugged it off. "He's bound to have a lot of pent up emotion rattling around in that noggin! Better out than in."

"But still," Sarah continued. "I don't think I've ever heard him swear like that."

"We get a lot worse than that most weekends," the nurse laughed as she parted a curtain to go in search of a water jug, and to notify the duty station of the change in Marcus' condition.

"Back soon," she said with a smile through the gap in the curtain, before pulling it back across to maintain their privacy.

Sarah returned her attention to Marcus, taking his hand, and rubbing the back of it with her thumb sympathetically, while trying to avoid the needles taped in place, drip-feeding him with saline and glucose. Mistaking it for him returning her hand-holding gesture, Sarah did not see that Marcus had balled his hands into fists. But she did not miss his parting comment, his eyes firmly fixed on the curtain.

"Cunt."

Two

The doctor's office had an imposing amount of wood panelling on view. Enough to build a small ark. Sarah's expression was grimmer than ever, and she kept tugging at her sleeves, as though her cardigan had shrunk in the wash.

"What I'm trying to say, Miss Ford, is that Marcus has suffered an extremely serious head trauma, and it is astonishing that his physical recovery has been as accelerated as it has, in just a few months . . . " Doctor Rothkiss exhibited his most practiced sympathetic air, but he had never been terribly good at it, and it mostly came across to people as vagueness and barely-concealed irritation.

"It's not his physical health I'm worried about," Sarah butted in. "It's his personality! He doesn't remember anything from before the accident. Well, not *anything*, but he only seems to remember things after I remind him," Sarah was on the verge of tears, unconsciously stretching her cardigan completely out of shape. "He's not the man he used to be."

"Miss Ford. Take a moment to calm yourself, if you would. As I've tried to explain to you in our previous consultations, Mister Hales has had a life changing experience. It's not unusual for there to be some memory loss. I can't in good conscience promise you that it will return in time, though it is not unheard of." Rothkiss shifted uncomfortably in his seat, as Sarah continued to sniff. He nudged his tissue box forward, encouraging her to take one.

"He's so *angry* all the time. I don't know what to do for him," Sarah finally took a tissue, if only to stop Rothkiss from pushing them at her in lieu of anything more helpful.

"While it is more common to find hostility coming out in patients coping with a physical injury—perfectly normal behaviour when frustrated by limited mobility issues—I imagine that not being able to remember your childhood can also be a burden. Personally, I get into a right old tizzy just trying to recall where I left my car keys! Perfectly normal." The Doctor attempted a warm smile, not entirely successfully.

"Is this *normal*, Doctor?" Sarah stuck out her left arm and rolled up her sleeve at him, so that he was confronted with her bruises. And the scabbed over rings where Marcus had stubbed out his cigarettes on her. "Before the accident, he didn't even smoke!"

"Good grief!" Rothkiss said, for the first time properly looking at Sarah, and showing genuine emotion. "He did this to

159

you? Have you spoken to the authorities?"

"No!" Sarah said. "I don't want him arrested! I just want him back. Back as he was . . . "

"Miss Ford—*Sarah*, you are endangering yourself if you remain in the home with him, if he's capable of doing this to you."

"You told me there was no reason why he shouldn't make a full recovery, Doctor! I thought that if . . . . if I could just hold on, he'd come back to me."

"Sarah! I never promised he'd be *exactly* as he was. I could never do that. I can only give a diagnosis based on past case histories. In some cases with similar injuries, similar degrees of brain damage, the patients achieve full mobility and life returns to more or less as before, but there are always examples where the results are less favourable." Rothkiss stood up and moved around to Sarah's side of the great oak desk, as Sarah pulled down her cardigan to cover the accusatory weals on her skin, the point made well enough.

"You've heard of Foreign Accent Syndrome? It's where a head injury or other trigger can cause an otherwise healthy individual to completely lose their native accent, sounding as though they have become French, or Japanese, or some other nationality. Just one tiny part of the brain, starved of oxygen just so," he pinched thumb and forefinger together to demonstrate. "and it can cause a catastrophic change. We're still learning all the time, but as much as we know today, it can still sometimes feel as though we're blindly thrashing about in the dark."

"It's like living with a completely different person. Sometimes, he doesn't even look like Marcus any more. I keep thinking it's a nightmare, and that I'll wake up, and he'll be Marcus again. It's my fault. If only I hadn't thrown those bloody flowers into the road."

"You can't think like that, Sarah. If Marcus hadn't gone to pick them up. If the driver hadn't been using your road as a rat-run shortcut. If, if, if. You're not to blame. Nobody is. Not for that. But *these*," Rothkiss pulled back Sarah's cardigan sleeve, bringing her injuries back into the light again. "*these* are down to Marcus, and nobody else."

"They're not the worst of it," Sarah said, and Rothkiss took a sharp breath.

"He didn't . . . " His words trailed off into silence, not wanting to anticipate Sarah's next words.

"Oh, nothing physical. It's all his mind-games. He'll sometimes start talking like Marcus, the *real* Marcus, and it gives me hope. I think it's over at last, and then I see him sneer. It starts in his eyes before it reaches his mouth. That's when he laughs. He gives me hope, then he snatches it away, and I fall for it. *Every. Single. Time.* I don't know who he is, but he isn't Marcus."

"Sarah, I'm not your GP, but I really think you should let me refer you to one of my colleagues."

"You think it's me? That *I* have the problem?" Sarah pushed Rothkiss away and stepped back from him.

Rothkiss cut off her retreat. "I think that Marcus needs help, but you need it too. It's a lot of pressure that you've put yourself under, but you don't need to do it alone."

"It's not him. Why won't you believe me? He looks like Marcus, and talks like him, except when he thinks I'm not watching. But it's not. *He's* not."

"Sarah! Will you listen to yourself? If we were living in the Middle Ages, you'd be burning him as a witch. Or possessed by the Devil! This is not rational thinking!"

"Rational? He went to sleep Marcus Hales and woke up . . . I don't know who."

Three

He never touched her again. Not physically, anyway. But her mind, on the other hand . . . He had ways of getting into her head that no psychologist could untangle, no matter how many referrals she took up. He had her conditioned, and played her guilt like a Stratocaster. Guilt over her part in making him the man he had become. For his own amusement, he started to bring other women back to the flat when Sarah was home. For the most part, once he got them inside the door, one look at Sarah sitting there, and they were away again. A bit of no-strings attached infidelity was one thing, but most lost the taste for it when the injured party was standing in front of them. Most. He would email her links to XXXTube videos of him fucking other women in their bed, but they did not achieve the desired effect he was looking for. After the first one, she stopped opening them. So he sent them to her friends. Bingo. Isolated from any relationships

161

outside of the flat, Sarah had no respite from it.

One thing that Sarah did pick up from her sessions with the headshrinker, was that she stopped thinking about him in ways that set alarm bells ringing with the medical professionals. Or at least, she stopped talking about it. She found coping mechanisms. She never called him by name. She did nothing to anger him, but no longer rose to his baiting. Like a toy he'd grown bored with, he dropped her, and mostly found his pleasures outside. Mostly.

He had done such a good job on her, whispering poisonously in the night, that she was still tied to him, unable to just pack her things and leave. It was nothing to do with fear that he might come after her. She had always had a stubborn streak, and would not give up when she set her mind to a task. As a girl, she nursed a duck with a broken wing back to health. Sarah's father told her he would put it to sleep humanely. It would not suffer, he promised. But she set her jaw, and even then, he knew better than to argue with her. So it was he who went to the vet and browbeat them into giving him antibiotics for the bird, and Sarah made Quakers her pet project. In some altogether creepier symbiotic manner, 'Marcus' was her new pet project. Like the duck's wing, the car accident had broken Sarah and Marcus, and she would knit them together again, no matter who tried to get between them. Or who made any attempt to offer help.

And then one day, like many a bully, he took it too far. He crossed the line that must not be crossed, and something ignited in Sarah. A purifying flame. A moment of clarity. The scar tissue that had formed around her under the barrage of mental torture was now her armour against his forked tongue. His barbed accusations could not penetrate her chainmail. The guilt he had traded as currency was spent. There was no more to be had. Lying prone in their formerly shared bed, with her kitchen knife to his throat, he looked into Sarah's eyes, and she into his. Something passed between them; some moment of revelation, and then they were free. Without a single word passing between them, or any form of protest—the blade remained in Sarah's hand, but it was unnecessary—he quickly threw on jeans, boots and a zip-up hoodie, and left.

Sarah watched through the venetian blinds at the bedroom window. He did not even slam the door as a parting 'fuck you' gesture, but as he stood under the street light, he looked up at the window,

162

right through her. Nothing of Marcus remained. Sarah drew back into the shadows, but saw him pull up his hood, shrouding his face within the night. And then from somewhere within, he summoned up an unnatural wail. It was the urgent yelp of a mating urban vixen, the hiss of steam escaping from a pipe, a crying polecat struggling with razor wire, the drone of an insistent car alarm; it was all of these things and none of them. It bounced around the houses for a minute, causing Sarah to shudder involuntarily. As the last echoes faded away, another voice picked up the refrain. And more. And yet more, both nearby and distant. As he loped off into the darkness, he was not alone.

Epilogue

Sunday morning. Just after eight o'clock. Sarah counted off the street lights, one every other house. She clutched an envelope in one hand and a single white rose in the other. A fresh one, this time, kept overnight in some water. As she approached number 68, she noticed that the new tenants had retired the old metal bin in favour of a wheelie-bin and a regimented set of different coloured recycling bags. Going up to the next street light, Sarah rifled through the pocket of her coat, and withdrew a couple of plastic gardening ties, which she used to affix the flower to the lamp at her eye-level. When she was sure it was firmly attached, she opened the envelope and brought out a photograph of Marcus with her in happier times. Both of them were making bunny ears behind the other's head. She lost herself in memories for a few seconds, letting the emotion well up in her, and then took out the remaining item from the envelope, a prewritten Sherwood Florist message card, and fixed them both to the flower with ribbon through punch-holes she had prepared earlier. She admired her handiwork, sniffed back the tears as she kissed her forefinger before touching it to Marcus' image in the photograph. Job done, she turned and went home, without looking back.

'Lost to me now, but I'll remember you always. "Lizzie" xxx'

Jay Eales is the editor of Violent! *and the publisher of* The Girly Comic *for Factor Fiction. His comics have also appeared in* Negative Burn, The Mammoth Book of Best New Manga *and* The British Fantasy Society Journal. *He was News Features Editor for the award-winning* Borderline – The Comics Magazine, *and his fiction published in* Drabble Who? *(Beccon Publishing),* Murky Depths *(House of Murky Depths) and* Faction Paradox: A Romance in Twelve Parts *(Obverse Press). Forthcoming in 2012:* Alt Zombie *(Hersham Horror) (contributor) and* Faction Paradox: Burning with Optimism's Flames *(Obverse Books) (editor). Forthcoming in 2013:* Dark Adapted Eyes *(editor/contributor) from Factor Fiction. Website:* factorfictionpress. co.uk.

MISTER DEATH
by Paul Bradshaw

It was almost dark when the dead came knocking at the door. They always came at that time, although Glade was puzzled by it. After all, no-one could see them except him.

Glade opened the door hesitantly, and came face to face with two of them, a tall one and a short one, both male. He knew at once that they were the dead. An eerie coldness emanated from them. He felt it wafting his way like an icy invisible cloud.

'What do you want?' he asked them.

'Are you him?' asked the tall one. His eyes were so dark, and seemed to dig right into Glade's like strange daggers.

'Am I who?' Glade replied, acting dumb.

'You know,' urged the tall man. '*The one.*'

'I can't help you,' Glade said, and began to close the door.

The tall one placed his large foot in front of the door, preventing Glade from closing it.

'We know you're him,' the short one said. 'Mister Death.'

'We want you to do it,' the tall one said. 'We're desperate!'

'Everyone is desperate,' said Glade. 'I can't go around helping *everyone.*'

'We don't want you to help everyone,' said the short one. 'Just us. *Please.*'

Glade had no intention of helping them. He wished that he had never acquired the gift he had. He wished that he had never become Mister Death, or whatever it was they called him.

'I'm not the one you want,' he told the dead men finally. 'I can't help you, I'm afraid. I just can't.'

He looked the tall one directly in the eye, defiant that he would not help them. The coldness about them was intimidating, and caused him to shiver slightly.

After a few seconds the tall man reluctantly removed his foot from in front of the door, not taking his gaze away from Glade's. This enabled Glade to close the door at last, which he did. He watched the pair slowly walk down the pathway to the gate, and disappear, as if into thin air.

Glade's heart was beating swiftly. He staggered into the lounge and flopped on to the settee. He knew the dead could not harm him, but still the encounter had been quite scary. He always found the dead to be scary.

He closed his eyes, as suddenly he felt very tired. A disturbing exhaustion had been creeping up on him the last few months. He knew the cause, and wished to God that he had never become the monster they referred to as Mister Death.

The next morning Glade made his way to the tea shop. He had enjoyed a long night's sleep and was feeling utterly refreshed. It was a cool day, and he hugged his greatcoat tightly to his body as he strolled across the pavement.

The bell tingled as he entered the shop, and he ventured over to the table by the window that he always sat at. The middle-aged waitress smiled at him as he caught her eye, and he smiled back. Shortly she came over to him and he ordered the usual pot of tea.

It wasn't long before Susan arrived. Glade saw her approaching from across the road, and lingered on her form as she finally came into the tea shop. She joined him at the table by the window and they exchanged greetings, a kiss upon the cheek and a big hug.

Glade was so happy to see her. It seemed so long since they last met, even though it had just been a couple of days. She ordered tea, as Glade had, and settled down for a morning chat and a catch up.

'I see the Germans are advancing,' she said grimly.

'Yes,' said Glade. 'Denmark and Norway, according to the radio.'

He did not wish to discuss the war. He merely wished to enjoy her company, admire her beauty, gaze into her eyes, and hold her up close.

He watched as she sipped tea. She had removed her long coat to reveal a fetching pink and white dress. Glade reckoned she was the loveliest girl in the world.

'Something's troubling you,' he said at last.

She smiled awkwardly. 'You know me so well,' she replied.

'Yes I do,' said Glade. 'Please tell me.'

166

She placed her teacup on to her saucer, and reached over to grab a hold of Glade's hands, which she gripped in hers.

'It's Amelia,' she told him, staring him directly in the yes.

Amelia; Susan's younger sister. Glade had spotted her several times when he had been at their house.

'What about her?' Glade enquired.

Susan bit her lip slightly. 'She is going to die,' she said. 'Tomorrow. She'll be hit by a tram.'

Glade shuddered. Of course he was aware of Susan's gift, which was more of a curse than a gift at times. It was part of the reason they had been drawn together, the both of them being unique to the world.

'That's terrible!' said Glade. 'You saw a vision?'

It was a silly question. It was obvious that she had seen a vision. Glade was so shocked that he was becoming confused in his head. All he could picture was Amelia. an image inside his brain of that sweet young girl.

Seconds later, when he had recovered from the shock, he noticed a young man had approached their table and was standing right beside him and Susan. Glade was startled. He knew at once that this was one of the dead.

'You are Mister Death, aren't you?' the man asked.

Glade saw that the man was in a soldier's uniform, and an awful iciness surrounded him as with all the dead. He seemed to have appeared from nowhere at all.

'I'm sorry,' Glade whispered. 'I can't help you.'

Susan was staring across the table, and Glade knew that she realised what was taking place. She had known him for so long. She herself was not able to actually see dead people, only him.

The young soldier appeared to accept Glade's response immediately. He initially glared at Glade before turning his back and wandering away toward the exit to the tea shop. As he did so Glade spotted that the back of his head had been blown away, and that what was left of his brain was clotted thick with dried blood.

'He's gone,' Glade told Susan.

'Who was it?' she asked.

Glade told her. She seemed somewhat disturbed, yet Glade was not concerned about the soldier, he was thinking of young Amelia.

'How old is Amelia?' he asked Susan.

'Thirteen,' she told him. 'I saw it clearly. The tram hits her full on. She dies almost instantly.'

'When did you receive the vision?'

'This morning,' Susan said. 'It was just before I awoke. That's normally when I get them. It was horrible, Peter.'

Glade grabbed her hand again, holding it tightly under his.

'Don't worry,' he assured her. 'It's going to be alright. I promise.'

Susan nodded, tears arriving to her eyes.

'What time does it happen?' asked Glade.

'Just before three in the afternoon.'

'Ok, well don't worry. I'll be there.'

'Promise?'

'I promise.'

Susan reached for a handkerchief and began to dab at her eyes, wiping off the wetness around them.

'You're my hero,' she told him.

'Not a hero at all. I love you.'

Glade slept soundly that night. The dead had come knocking again but he had ignored it. He required a good night's sleep so that he could be refreshed for the next day.

He awoke as light dawned, and as he lay between the sheets he thought of his gift, and the time he had first discovered he had it. He was like a young boy in a sweet shop then; he just wanted to use it as much as he was able to. When the dead came knocking he had never refused. Then the more he helped them the more people found out about it, and there was no stopping them, and no stopping him. He helped them all the more, dozens of them, hundreds of them. He thought he could use the gift as often as he wanted to.

Until that day he looked into the mirror; the day he noticed what was happening to him. He was supposed to be a young man, but resembled someone much older. Each time he helped the dead a little bit of his own life was squeezed out of him. He had shrunk away from that mirror in horror.

He had learnt the error of his ways; the lesson that with his gift there came a price.

Presently he arose, and got ready for the day. He sat on the settee, and watched the grandfather clock in the corner of the room as it ticked by. The radio was playing quietly. He listened to reports of Hitler's abominations. He did not take his eyes away from the clock though, and shortly before three in the afternoon he arose from the settee, snatched his greatcoat from the hall, and left the house to head into town.

When he got to the trams in the town centre he immediately spotted the commotion that was taking place there. A group of citizens was gathered at the tram-lines, and much shouting and wailing was going on. He ran up to the crowd, and pushed to the front.

'I'm a doctor!' he lied. 'Move away, I'm a doctor!'

The group dispersed slightly, so that he was able to see what was occurring. He began to tremble when he saw the prone form of young Amelia lying beside the tracks. He knew at once that she was dead.

He knelt down, and reached out for her.

'What are you doing?' he heard someone cry out.

'She's dead! She's dead!' someone else shouted.

'Quiet!' yelled Glade. 'I'm a doctor. She's not dead. She's going to be alright.'

He gathered her cold body in his arms, and as he held her close he placed his warm palm upon her forehead. He could feel the death in her; it was icy cold and horrendous.

'Sssshhh,' he assured her. 'You're going to be alright. You're going to be alright.'

He felt the gift working inside him. It was lurching right through him, building up through his guts, and causing him to retch a little. It was like an absurd thrill, swimming through him, like a bizarre rollercoaster ride. He could see a strange glow arrive to the top of Amelia's head, as the gift coursed through him, transferring over to the lifeless form of the young girl, a lifeless form that was quickly becoming a form filled with life once more.

He felt weak and faint, but still held her close, as voices rang around him, voices that were intermingling, not making any sense.

'It wasn't my fault!' he heard someone say. 'She just stepped right in front! It wasn't my fault!'

Then Glade saw Amelia's eyes snap right open, and she

169

gasped loudly. Her body had become warm in his arms, and as he continued to hold her right up to his bosom he suddenly felt quaintly nauseous, and collapsed unconscious to the ground, noises reverberating around him.

When Glade woke up he was in some bed in a strange place that he didn't know. The sheets were all white, so were the walls, and a weird surgical smell pervaded. He then realised that he was in a hospital; and when he glanced up he spotted six ghostly forms standing by the bed, all of them without clothing.

He was immediately taken aback.

One of the forms reached out to him, an old female with bulging eyes.

'Help us,' she pleaded. 'We know who you are. Mister Death. *Please help us.'*

Glade then understood that they were the dead, and they had come up all the way from the morgue.

'I can't help you,' he said weakly. 'Please go away.'

He shivered at the accumulation of coldness that came from the group of dead people. It was so cold that a migraine began to arrive to his head. Then he noticed a young nurse arrive from the ward entrance, and at once the dead all vanished, as if in panic.

'Ah, you've woken up, Mr Glade,' the nurse remarked. 'How are you feeling?'

'Tired,' said Glade, rubbing at his eyes.'How long have I been here?'

'Not long. The ambulance fetched you. Some girl was hit by a tram. Someone says you saved her?'

Glade paused. He had to be careful how he responded to that one.

'Sort of,' he said. 'I did nothing really. Some kind of miracle I think.'

'Must have been,' the nurse said. 'Now you take it easy. You'll be able to go home when you're ready. I'll be back soon.'

She turned and trotted off to some other patient, and as she did so Glade noticed that Susan was standing in the doorway to the ward. When the nurse left she came over to him and sat on the chair next to the bed.

She placed her arms around him and delivered an enormous hug.

'You're my hero,' she told him. 'I really love you.'

With that she gave him a passionate kiss upon the lips.

'You know I'll do anything for you,' said Glade, when the embrace was over.

'That was more than enough. You don't know how grateful I am.'

'How is she now?' asked Glade.

'She's doing well. In shock, but doing well. Thanks to you.'

They held hands, and there was a silence around them for a few seconds. Glade welcomed it. Sometimes it was good to just wallow in each other's company.

'How are you feeling?' Susan asked finally.

'Exhausted. It took a lot out of me.'

'I appreciate it. You know I do.'

'How do you think it happened then?' asked Glade.

'I'm not sure. Haven't had chance to ask her. She was just crossing the road and got hit.'

'A bit scary.'

'Yes, scary.'

'Only the tram driver was saying she just stepped out into the front of the tram. Are you sure she's alright?'

Susan went quiet for a short while. Glade studied her. She appeared to be thinking hard, trying to get her head around it all. Eventually she responded.

'You know it's difficult right now,' said Susan. 'After mother died, and then father was killed in action. We are both finding it hard to cope.'

Glade recalled what had happened with Susan's parents. Not long after her mother had died of tubercolosis her father was killed in action somewhere in France. This had been hard to take, especially for someone as young as Amelia. Glade wished there was something he could do to help.

He had already offered to bring her father back, but that wasn't possible with his body being overseas. This was one dead person that was unable to contact him for help. He stared at Susan, who seemed lost in her own little world.

'Susan?' he asked.

171

She snapped out of her trance. 'Sorry, I was miles away,' she replied.

'Will you stay with me tonight?'

Susan reached over and kissed him again. 'Of course I will,' she said.

The following morning Glade awoke sharply to find Susan sobbing heavily into the pillow. Still half-asleep, he was not aware of the reason, and was instantly perturbed to find his love in such a state.

'Susan?' he pleaded, placing his arm around her. 'What is it? What's wrong?'

At first she could not speak, such was her heavy weeping, but eventually she was able to tell him the cause of the misery.

'It's Amelia,' she said. 'I had another vision.'

'Another vision?'

'Yes. It was horrible.'

'What was in the vision?'

She could not answer right away. Glade was patient, gazing at her face as the morning sunlight beamed into the room. After some seconds she spoke.

'Amelia was dead,' she sobbed. 'She had hung herself in the old barn she sometimes goes to. Peter, what am I going to do?'

'I can save her!' Glade reassured her. 'Try not to worry. Let me know the time and I'll be there.'

'Peter, don't you get it? She had hung herself. *She had taken her own life!*'

Glade took a moment to reflect. He reckoned she was right. Susan had a big problem there, and more to the point, Amelia's problem was even bigger. After all that had happened to that family recently it was no wonder that the poor girl was suicidal.

'I think I was right about yesterday,' said Glade, as he held his love up close. 'Amelia definitely stepped in front of that tram on purpose. She wanted to kill herself.'

'You're right,' said Susan. 'Now she is trying again. Peter, will you save her *please?*'

'You know I will,' said Glade. 'I will always save her, you know that. But let me put this to you. If I save her today, who's to say she won't try again tomorrow? And if I save her then again she

172

might try the day after. And so on and so on. I could be saving her forever. And every time I do save her my own life will wilt away just a little. Each time I bring her back I will be killing myself. What do you think about that, Susan?'

She went silent for a long time. Glade reckoned he had said the wrong thing. He was afraid that he may lose her if she did not help with Amelia. He *wanted* to help the girl, but thinking practically it would be detrimental to himself. It was indeed a dilemma.

'I don't know what to do,' said Susan. 'I don't want to lose you and I don't want to lose Amelia. I shouldn't expect you to save her each time, but if you don't then I will lose her. But then I will lose you! Oh, what am I going to do?'

Glade could not answer. He had no idea what she could do. It was her choice to make.

Then Susan began to climb out of bed, and he allowed her to do so.

'I must go,' she said. 'I have to see Amelia. I left her with Aunt Annie again. I have to be with her more. To keep an eye on her.'

Glade tended to agree with what she said, as he watched her leave and go to the bathroom. It was a delicate situation. Only Susan was able to choose how to resolve it.

He knew what he had to do. He waited all day for the moment when Amelia killed herself. He spent the day on the settee again, listening to the radio and psyching himself up for the task ahead.

His thoughts were filled with notions of his life as Mister Death. He could not understand why they called him by that name. After all, he gave *life,* and not death. So according to him the name was incorrect. Yet he still had to live with it; *Mister Death.*

The time arrived, and he got up, grabbing his coat before leaving the house. A hazy drizzle of rain was in the air as he walked up to where the secluded barns were located. It was a good spot that Amelia had chosen, he thought. A good spot to get away from it all.

He was hesitant in entering the barn when he got there. He knew he was going to come across a horrid sight. Although he was used to confronting the dead when they pleaded with him for life,

173

this was entirely different. So he took a deep breath and walked into the barn.

He gasped when he looked inside, and his heart lurched greatly. He had expected to witness the sight of Amelia, which he did now see, the young girl dangling from a rope attached to one of the high beams of the barn. A grotesque expression was upon her face, and her head was tilted to one side, her eyes glaring, and yet a bizarre twisted smile also, her lips pulled horizontally taut into an insane grin of pleasure.

However, he did not expect to see a second body, someone older, also hanging from the beam, a thick rope tight around the neck, obviously dead.

It was Susan. She had made her choice.

'No!' yelled Glade, and he dashed forward to free the both of them, as though his swiftness would make them less dead than they were at that moment.

He climbed the haystacks and set them both free of the ropes that held them, laying them both across the hay. He was in panic. He did not wish for either of them to be gone from the world. So he went to work.

He grabbed the cold form of the young girl first, placing his hand upon her forehead. Holding her up close and tight, he coaxed life into her, squeezing her to him, feeling the strain once more, the unpleasant sickness that occurred on such occasions, making him queasy and churning his stomach. He gagged horribly, and he was shivering as if in a weird fever, as the pulse of life transferred from his body to hers.

In less than half a minute it was over. Amelia had come to life; yet Glade realised that she was not happy.

'You again!' she screamed. 'You did it again! Leave me alone! Leave me alone!'

With that, she turned and fled from the barn, her legs buckling under her at first, until her strength returned, and she ran off quickly into the rain.

Glade did not have time to mull over all of that, he had a more pressing matter to attend to. He scrambled over to where Susan lay, and held her in his arms, his palm upon her head, which was cold to the touch. He urged life into her, his insides stirring up and causing him to vomit slightly, as he started to tremble and quiver, the fever coming to him again.

'Come on, Susan!' he urged.

He squeezed her close to him, but nothing was happening, she showed no signs of living, no pulse returning. She remained as cold as ever, as dead as she had been when he had entered the barn. She was resisting!

'Susan, Susan, come on!' he cried. 'Come back to me!'

She did not come back to him. She was relentless in her refusal to be revived, and the more Glade tried to bring her back the more useless it became. She was resisting so hard that he began to sob, tears streaming down his cheeks, and a terrible feeling of nausea arrived. She wasn't coming back.

Glade was unable to bring her back, especially when he succumbed to an unwelcome unconsciousness, falling down in a heap upon the hay.

Glade did not like funerals. He did not think that he was different from anyone else in that. Yet now he had two funerals to face; one of his love Susan, and the other of her sister Amelia, who had leapt from the top of the church tower and died just one day following the episode at the barn.

He had been correct all along. Amelia would find a way out in the end no matter what he or Susan did. Now Glade was attending that double funeral, standing some distance from the actual proceedings, a lone figure on the periphery.

It was a sunny day, but a sad one. He had tried many times to revive Susan since that initial attempt in the barn, but all had been futile, and it had taken a lot out of him. He had fainted each time, as she resisted his efforts to bring her back. Her choice had been made and there was no changing that. Glade just felt utterly helpless.

Eventually he watched the end of the funeral, as the small group of mourners slowly walked out of the cemetery, white handkerchiefs evident, all held to wipe away tears. He was going to miss Susan, there was no doubt about that.

He just felt that life was not worth living any more, as he surveyed the cemetery, now silent following the funeral. Silent, yet filled with the lonesome figures of the dead, all standing next to their graves, staring his way. Hundreds of them, all eager for him to help them back into the land of the living. They were not calling out to him this time, merely pleading with their eyes, begging him to use his magic on them.

So he began, striding past each grave, placing his magical palm upon each forehead, hugging each cold, dead figure up close, then moving on to the next. He did not miss any of them out; he made sure not to. He gave life to them all, and at the same time he lost a little of his own.

Weaker and weaker he became, as he transferred life to those hundreds, until finally he came to the last one, and after the dreaded feeling of queasiness and nausea he lurched over and started to vomit violently on to the grass, after which he collapsed to the earth, and a smile came to his face as his last breath of life ebbed away, and he fell dead upon the cold, dank soil.

Paul Bradshaw used to publish the small press magazine The Dream Zone *from 1999 to 2003. He has had over 80 stories accepted for publication in various small press magazines and anthologies, and his short story collection* The Reservoir of Dreams *was published by BJM Press. He has been a Terror Scribe for over ten years.*

A VISION OF CARCOSA
by John B. Ford
& Steve Lines

I sat at the edge of the mist shrouded lake watching the slow fall of dusk. The grey ghosts of daylight faded steadily to shadow and, as I enjoyed the solitude, my mind turned to thoughts of dark infinity as I softly whispere. "Goodbye, Day." Many were the evenings I had spent in this silent seclusion, with strange dreams and phantasies filling my head. It seemed to me that this time of twilight was created for me alone, (for I preferred the light of other suns to that of our own).

As the twilight deepened a fathomless darkness filled the void above, until, one by one, the stars appeared; each twinkling light taking up its own preordained place in the majestic heavens. Seated by the lake I saw the swirling whirlpool of crystal tears which was the Milky Way reflected in its cold, dark waters and it seemed to me as if I floated alone in a limitless expanse of shimmering stars and eternal darkness, and, as I meditated thus, I experienced a longing; a craving for ultimate knowledge and this thought I uttered:

"Forces of the infinite universe I challenge thee, enlighten me! Enrapture me with the gift of the knowledge of all. I seek understanding. I seek enlightenment. I seek truth!"

Immediately I grew troubled, for perchance it was not meant that mankind should know all. Mayhap we are denied knowledge of the nature of all things to preserve our very sanity!

The silence of those following seconds seemed as dark and deep as the silent lake before me. Then came a stirring of the breeze in the twisted branches of the nearby trees and a mist began to rise from the surface of the water and it was as if the rolling vapours danced to an evil, unheard threnody. A moment later, high within the mist above the gloomy water, there came a movement of clouds and beams of tainted moonlight fell upon the pallid fog, causing me to start with surprise, my reverie broken. For a second I laughed aloud in relief at the realisation that it was nothing but the moon and the mist—then I saw that the moonlight was illuminating a vague figure, a figure that seemed to be walking on, or above, the lake.

A feeling of utter apprehension filled my heart as the figure began to move slowly towards me. I made to get to my feet, but unaccountably found myself unable to do so. As the uncanny figure approached, I beheld a death-white visage and realised it was a featureless mask of bleached bone. Two orbs of absolute darkness peered at me through the eye sockets and it seemed as if my very soul was very carefully and cruelly scrutinised. At length the figure, which was swathed in folds of pale yellow silk, reached the shore and stood above me.

Then the figure spoke. "A million mysteries haunt your mind; black veils fall across your sight, silhouettes show against the light—yet still you know nothing! But soon the veils will lift, and you shall pass through measureless black lagoons of emptiness to the Place Where the Black Stars Hang and there you shall find what you seek."

"Who are you?" I asked.

"I am—Truth," replied the stranger.

"But what is your name?" I questioned.

"I am Truth," came his reply.

"Truth?" I asked

"Can you not accept the truth?" asked the stranger.

"Truth is what I seek," I replied, somewhat puzzled.

"I am Truth."

I stared in awed wonderment at the blank, white visage of the stranger. Again he spoke. "You have all the mists of Hali in your brains. Did you not call to me? Summoned, I came. Do you not you hear the Hyades singing in the evening of the world? Dusk is dusk and the shadows of men's thoughts grow long in the evening. Soon you shall know more than any mortal living for the Hour of Truth is at hand."

"You will grant my desire?" I asked with barely concealed excitement. Then I knew doubt. "Do you speak the truth?" I asked.

"It is the shadow of a truth," was his enigmatic response. "I am the catalyst for all that was foreseen; I am the herald for all

178

that shall be . . . " His voice grew faint as he recited this litany and I realised his body was fading also, melting into the rolling clouds of mist. Soon his words became inaudible, his form merging with the night like the secret dreams of a cat. As he faded into the darkness so my consciousness ebbed away.

When awareness returned to me I imagined that I still lay where I had swooned, by the shore of that misty lake, but as I got to my feet I realised that this was not so. I stood by a lake wreathed in rolling mist, it was true, but this was not the familiar mere: location of my nightly ponderings, but a far more sinister body of water. For a moment I gazed into its black, silent depths as the clouds of mist rolled about me. Then I gazed upwards at the heavens, hoping to achieve comfort in the knowledge that the stars still hung in their familiar patterns, but even this was denied me. In crimson skies shot with darkness hung alien stars, black and cold as the fathomless void: and they radiated nothing but the night. Unfamiliar moons wheeled across these skies of insanity and for a moment it seemed as if I stood alone at the centre of a kaleidoscopic maelstrom of chaos and entropy. I tore my eyes from this vision of madness and once more looked toward the brooding lake. Then, attempting to ignore the uncanny skies above, I turned away from the ominous lake and made my way towards the gates of a nearby city, a city unlike any other I had ever before seen. Ah, but then it came to me that resolution awaited within the walls of that strange metropolis; there I would find the solution to my burning desire for knowledge and truth, and to every question that Mankind has ever sought to answer.

I entered the city.

In time I came to a winding street of cobbled stones where the houses leered above me and towered drunkenly as though gathering together for comfort beneath those strange skies. Feeling suddenly fatigued, I looked about for any place of rest. With observation came a curious fact to my notice, for the entire street was lit by gas-lamps, yet the light from every lamp seemed to hardly penetrate the gloom. With still greater surprise I saw the houses of the street held not one sign of light or life. But this impression of lifelessness I soon knew to be false, for with a start, I heard the door of the house nearest me creak slowly open.

179

Cautiously I walked over to this house, all the time trying to peer inside, but my eyes met only with a barrier of blackness—and this darkness I dare not enter. So instead I stood upon the threshold, calling my greetings loudly into that shrouded unknown. But in response came an abrupt shuffling and my eyes seemed to perceive vaguely a rapid movement, as finally there came a voice in reply. The words I heard were spoken with a kind of throaty, almost inhuman quality.

"Leave, leave now! Never before has a stranger been foolish enough to walk the abandoned streets of Ythill. Return—while you still can."

But only perplexity filled me.

"Why do you insist on living in the dark?" I asked. "What do you have to fear?"

This time his reply came quickly.

"I fear not for myself, it is much too late for that, for we have found the Yellow Sign . . . It is for you that I fear."

By now my eyes had picked out the vague outline of a body stood before me, but still the features of the face remained indistinguishable. Meaning to reassure the man against his childish fears, I suddenly lifted up my hand to place it upon his shoulder. But at once came a muffled cry to my ears and immediately the door was slammed shut. Then fearful was my realisation, and clinging to me the essence of death—for my hand had travelled right through the body of the man!

For a moment I stood recollecting my wits. I shivered deeply at the thought of being almost beyond the threshold of darkness when the door had closed. But in the following seconds came a blessing like a beacon in the night, for I beheld a splendid palace at the heart of this city of despair and from every gilded window spilled warm and comforting light.

How foolish I had been! For everyone knows that darkness is the dwelling place of evil, but light; light is only of goodness, light is the very essence of Truth, for it dispels the uncertainty of darkness and naught can hide from the purity of light. But every light casts a shadow . . .

I stood before the illuminated edifice and smiled to see the door

180

stood open—as though in welcome. But as I entered within that palace of light, two men, dressed in the accoutrements of war, and obviously guards of some kind, appeared at either side of me.

"So Bremchas, what have we here?" Asked the guard on my left.

"A stranger in Ythill, friend Bicree. We must take him to Cassilda, for it is said she knows all the faces in Ythill." Said the guard on my right.

"Yet this one has no face."

"I seek Truth", I told them perplexed, as they herded me from the entrance toward an ascending flight of steps. The guards spoke no further as they led me up the stairway and into a hall. As I entered, they left, presumably to return to their posts.

I gazed at my surroundings. At the further end of this sparsely furnished room stood a throne of roughly hewn stone, flanked by tapestries depicting the Hyades, though they were threadbare and worn. There was an archway to the right and to the left a doorway leading to a balcony that overlooked the lake. Through this opening I could just perceive the sky beyond, which was violent pink as two glowering suns set into the lake.

Upon the throne sat the figure of a woman. She was wearing a simple, elegant dress of emerald green. As I drew closer I was surprised to hear a gentle sobbing emanating from her. As she wept she toyed with a silver diadem which she turned unceasingly with her delicate, pale hands.

At the sound of my entrance she looked up—and her face was the greatest vision of beauty my eyes had ever met with. Her skin, so pale, seemed somehow frozen in youthful adornment; radiant blonde hair fell in loose curls, splaying outward over her shoulders like the unravelled heart of a golden sun. And when, with her eyes of indigo, she gazed deeply into my own, I knew she held the answer to my every question.

I spoke softly. "Why do you weep?"

And when she replied, her whispered voice held the sparkling teardrops of a thousand stars as she softly sang:

The cloud waves surge with Hali's tides
The twin suns drop from uncanny skies
Darkness weaves its spell in Carcosa

Black are the stars strange in the night
And strange moons shine in their ebon light
But not as strange as dim Carcosa

The Hyades will praise the King
With melodies that none shall sing
In the silent streets of cold Carcosa

I cannot sing, my song unsung
Shall die on my lips: a tear will run
But who shall care in lost Carcosa?

I stood in silence as the song ended. At length the woman spoke. "I am Queen Cassilda. I know all the faces in Ythill and not one of them is new to me. Are you a spy from Alar? Or perchance you have come for the Yellow Sign?" When Cassilda spoke, her voice was a thing of great beauty to me; her wondrous tones seemed to soothe my soul.

"The Yellow Sign? I replied. "I have heard such a thing mentioned."

"I have not found the Yellow Sign, so why do you come?" asked Cassilda.

"Truth." I told her.

At this her face went white. "You are Truth? . . . The Phantom of Truth?"

"I am not He, though I have knowledge of such a one."

"But only ghosts go about dressed in white."

At these words I glanced at my clothing, only to see that I indeed wore white robes.

Cassilda continued. "I am but a queen, a pale sad queen. It seems that the world is finally coming undone; the End Days are here." As she spoke the silver diadem dropped from her hands and fell to the floor. Will you unmask, Phantom?"

"But I wear no mask." Confusion tainted my voice.

"No mask! No mask!" Cassilda was visibly distressed and this in turn upset me greatly, for I felt great empathy for this unhappy creature.

"Why don't you leave me alone? She asked, almost

pleadingly.

"But I seek truth." I answered, not knowing what else to say or do.

Cassilda gazed at me with her deep, sad eyes and, taking a hand-mirror from the folds of her dress, held it momentarily in her lap.

"You seek Truth. Then behold the Face of Truth," she said as she passed the mirror to me.

I held the reflective glass to my face and gazed within, and I saw Truth. For the visage that gazed out from those silvered depths was white as bleached bone and featureless. It was the visage of the Phantom!

Cassilda rose up from the throne and began to walk from the room, but as she passed by me her soft voice spoke once more. "Come with me and I will show you a vision."

Leaving the hallway, I followed Cassilda and became surprised by a coldness that seemed to radiate from her very body. We passed out onto the balcony, and, stepping onto it, gazed out upon the vast, brooding lake.

"Below is the lake of Hali. It swallows so many suns." Said Cassilda mournfully.

I gazed down at the still, silent lake, as the cloud waves rolled and poured about the walls of Ythill. Then I stared in wonderment as a city shimmered into existence upon the horizon. It was difficult to tell whether it stood beyond the shores of this sombre lake or rested upon its very waters. Black domes and monoliths and strangely twisted spires of black pierced the crimson sky and reflected the ebon light of the vile stars and, as I watched, a moon began to rise and it seemed as if the towers of the black city stood *behind* it.

Cassilda spoke. "And can you see? Beyond Hali—the city of Lost . . .

"Carcosa." I finished. For as soon as I had laid eyes upon that distant edifice I knew its name.

"Carcosa, indeed." Her voice was hushed, reverent.

"Does the Truth lie in Carcosa?" I asked.

"There are no truths in Carcosa," she replied. "only that all truth is a lie. Nothing human dwells in Carcosa. . ."

183

As I stood and gazed at the twisting spires of far Carcosa I heard Cassilda gasp in absolute terror.

"The Yellow Sign!" she cried. "The Yellow Sign!" You have it!" I turned in surprise and saw that the Cassilda was pointing to my chest, her eyes wide with horror. I looked down and there, embroidered upon the front of my robes was a sign in golden thread, a sign in no earthly language.

"I have found the Yellow Sign", she cried.

At this I heard the crashing of a gong and the lights about the hall and upon the balcony flickered and turned to vermilion. The banners about the throne room fell, to reveal banners emblazoned with the Yellow Sign. I turned to Cassilda, but she had left the balcony. I gazed out towards that city of death and as I did so a darkness descended, and in my ears I heard the mocking laughter of the King. Then I heard the sound of mighty pinions beating and from far, cold Carcosa, he came . . .

I awoke chilled to the bone and stiff with cold and with the mocking laughter still ringing in my mind. I realised I was once again by the familiar lake of my nightly sojourns. Above me the familiar stars twinkled whitely. Had it all been a dream; some fever induced vision? I got to my feet and was much relieved to see my own face gazing back at me from the waters of the lake. Bemused I turned to make my way homeward, when, upon the grass, a glint of reflected starlight caught my eye. I bent to investigate and perceived a black, lozenge-shaped stone of polished jet lying upon the damp grass. Picking it up, I noticed that upon one flat side it was embellished with a peculiar pale sigil . . .

*'A Vision of Carcosa' is the work of **John B. Ford** and **Steve Lines**.*

John is quite a well known author/editor/publisher, who established his own BJM Press in the 1990s and was widely published in the many small press magazines of the period. He has had three collections of short stories published and collaborated with such authors as Ramsey Campbell, Simon Clark, and Thomas Ligotti.

Steve is a well known artist, editor, and musician, now also becoming recognised as a very talented author. He has been running

Rainfall Books virtually solo since 2007 while John has gone about caring for terminally ill family members. Steve's first novel (in collaboration with John B. Ford) is titled The Night Eternal *and will be released on 5th May in Bristol at the first Terror Scribes meeting of 2012.*

A SELECTION OF FLASH FICTION
by Christy Leigh Stewart

Waiting For Daddy

My older sister, Elizabeth, and I have to stay in our room while mommy meets her boyfriends.

Elizabeth keeps me company while we wait and she distracts me from the noise coming from outside our door. Sometimes it's too loud, though, and that's when we listen to music with our head phones.

Mommy said it wasn't that she was trying to hide us from them, but them from us. She said that sometimes the boyfriends weren't good men, like our daddy had been. I never knew him, because he left when I was a baby. Elizabeth tells me he and mommy used to fight a lot and mommy says he'll come back to us one day.

Once she's done with her boyfriends.

Tonight she's done earlier than I thought she would be so I make sure to hug her extra tight so she knows how happy I am, and maybe next time she will be as quick as she was this time.

"Did you two have fun?" She asks us both but is looking only at me.

"Ya, we played games."

"Good. That's good." She kisses me on the top of my head and smiles gently at Elizabeth who seems sad for some reason.

I think maybe she's happy we got let out early and is worried about next time. "How long do your boyfriends have to keep coming over, mommy?" I ask for the both of us.

My mommy gives me the gentle smile now and rubs her stomach. "I think it'll be very soon, but I can't take the test just yet."

Mommy promised us this was the last time she would need

186

to make a baby. She thought so last time too, but changed her mind afterward. I think she's done now though. I think she looks like a princess.

She doesn't think so though. She says she has to be just a bit more pretty for daddy, and then he'll want her back. She says if she can eat just another one of her babies she'll be young and pretty enough for him.

I hope she's not lying this time. I'd like to meet daddy.

The Player

I have my fair share of women.

They come in and out of my life all the time, but I wouldn't consider myself a player, and don't think anyone else does either. I don't demean these women, not at all. I care about each one in their own way, even if we're together only a night.

It's not just sex for me, which is a misconception. It's much more than that, but it's hard to explain. It's the companionship, if even for that short time, and it's the excitement, and perhaps danger. It's the unknown. Really, that must be the most enticing part.

When I'm with these women, I am face to face with one of the essential parts of life, and exploring it is intriguing, erotic. I am at awe each moment, with each touch and each taste. Truly, this can't be just sex. There must be another word to describe this type of melding and intimate act.

Necrophilia doesn't cut it either. It seems like such a nasty word, used by people who don't understand. And my heart goes out to those people, and I wish them luck in life, because it can't be easy to live, not knowing what it is to die.

But I do, because I've been up close to it. Smelled it, tasted it, fucked it. Been inside and outside of it at the same time. Known it for it's stark truth, both grotesque and beautiful.

OMG u guyz

I'm one of those people you've heard about on TV.

I'm that angry and disgruntled teenager that goes to school and shoots everyone.

Well, I will be. Very soon.

As we speak I'm making my plans. Making a list. Checking it twice. All that shit.

My problem is, though, that there has been SO many school shootings that people know what to look for. Dark clothes, rock/metal/goth/whatever music, psychopathic drawings on text books, dark poetry, and on and on and on.

I've got it figured out though. I know how to make everyone unsuspecting. They might not even see it coming when I'm standing in front of them, shooting them like fish in a fucking barrel.

My first advantage, I'm a girl.

No one expects this kind of shit out of us because we're . . . I don't know. Nurturing? Because we have babies? But what about all those chicks who get abortions or kill their babies or abandon their kids or leave their kids or rape their kids or sell their kids or . . . Whatever, no one will see it coming, in any case. If I have my vagina to thank for that, then thanks a lot vagina.

The second advantage, I'm a girl.

I'm not some dumb fucking boy with a gun fetish. I've thought this out.

Rock music may be good and all, but if listening to it will give anyone ANY inclination I'm going to murder them, then I'll go without. I listen to Justin Timberlake. I have posters of him on my wall. I have his image as my desktop wallpaper. I masturbate to Googled pictures of him. There are no holes in my façade.

I may feel moody but I don't need to wear black or dye my hair black or wear black make up. I have no undergarments that aren't thongs. I don't have any top that doesn't show at least one areola. I don't have skirts that don't expose my genitals. I don't have pants that don't display my thongs. No one would see me and say 'That's someone that's planning to shoot me in the face'. Hell, they probably wouldn't even expect me to run in this shit. But I can. I've been practising.

I have a lot of pent up rage I need to get out, sure, but I don't need to get it out through poetry or journals or something else someone can figure me out with. I'll wait and let out my rage when I'm killing everyone, what could be more relaxing?

188

I do have my lists though, of people I don't want to miss. People I wont let escape. The girls, I have listed in my notebook under 'Best Friends' and the guys names I write everywhere. I write them after my name with a plus sign or in a heart. I've even given some of these guys blow jobs in the school bathrooms.

They'll never see this coming.

Christy Leigh Stewart knows your dad and thinks you need a haircut. christyleighstewart.com

But She Looked Above and Nothing was There

by Wendy Jane Muzlanova

I.

Caroline played in the sunny garden of her happy house. The house was happy because her elder sister was largely absent these days—the little one couldn't remember exactly why, although she suspected from the straining-to-hear-them arguments that Moira had been going about with . "very unsuitable type." Mum and Dad looked worried most of the time. Caroline felt sorry for them and tried to be extra good in order to help. Why did Moira have to be like this? She had stuck two fingers up at Dad just the other day and had told him t. "Fuck off!" Dad didn't deserve that. All he did was work hard and get worried when the auditors were due.

When Caroline's parents were out one afternoon, her elder sister had lain on their parent's bed and called her boyfriend on the telephone. Caroline sat on the stairs, hidden and curious.

Moira said things like. "I love you . . . I can't wait until you're inside me again."

Caroline didn't really understand, but felt sick all the same, at the sound of her sister's voice, husky and honeyed. Moira had never sounded that way before. Her normal tones were sly and vicious or shrill and threatening. Caroline had been thoroughly indoctrinated by her elder sister and regretted being born fat, stupid and not at all pretty. She hated Moira and frequently prayed for her sibling's death. Caroline did not care to whom she prayed, as long as she thought that the deity might have half a chance of getting the job done for her.

Caroline saw the unsuitable type one day and realised that he wasn't a boy. He was a man—a skinny, dirty-looking man with a droopy moustache. Caroline thought that he was really ugly. She had a sudden intrusive image of the man being inside her. Her mind flashed secretly-glimpsed sci-fi horror moments at her and images of parasites gleaned from the science programmes she watched constantly on the television. Her parents were proud that she was such a studious and serious little girl.

She put Moira and her horrible boyfriend out of her head and began to collect lime-coloured caterpillars. She knew that this species of caterpillar grew up to be Cabbage Whites and she knew that they would flit around all over her garden in the summer.

She would lie in wait for the butterflies. When one rested, finally, she would catch it and put it in a jar. Caroline was bewitched by the tongues of butterflies. They protruded long from their mouths and ended in a neat little spiral curl. She had once caught the end of a butterfly's tongue and held it between her small fingers. The butterfly made no protest. What could it do, after all? The same as the flies. What could they do, once their wings had been plucked?

Grown-ups never spoke of insects feeling pain, so Caroline had always assumed that they did not. The way that the denuded flies had buzzed madly on the table in the garage seemed to suggest otherwise, however, and Caroline felt ashamed of her experiment. Still, she had a restless, insatiable need to know, to investigate life— and death. She arranged the caterpillars, all wriggly on the paving slabs, and cut them in half, with her pink nail scissors. She wasn't a bad little girl and no-one would ever have said that she was cruel. She was, however, an inquisitive little girl.

She had heard some rumour about worms, that when they were cut in half, they would become two new worms. Caroline wanted to see if that was true, and would the two new caterpillars be friends and be happy to see each other? Would the two halves recognise each other for who they were?

When this didn't happen, she was distraught. Even though the caterpillars were mute—to her ears at least—she could hear a silent yet deafening agony emitting from their desperate writhing. She felt appalled at her own actions and quickly made tiny tissue paper bandages. She placed the bisected pieces of caterpillar together

191

again and carefully wrapped them, trying to bind the severed pieces. It didn't work. The caterpillars bled dark green and died quickly. Her sadness immediately forgotten, Caroline became instead fascinated and surprised. She knew that humans bled red. This was one of the many lessons which her sister had taught so proficiently.

Years later and for the rest of her life, Caroline dreamed about men who would hurt her. They would hurt her and then heal her, make her feel special.

She found exactly who she needed when she met her empty-eyed monster in a usually safe bar. Dmitry was a professional, but enjoyed his work to such an extent that he didn't mind bringing it home every night. Caroline needed to feel pain. The bruises and the raw areas made her feel grounded. Most of the time, Caroline was frightened that she might just disappear from the face of the earth, even before the eyes of whoever happened to be around at the time. Dmitry made everything real for her. He was her god. She worshipped at his feet, where she fell. When she was alone, when her beast was elsewhere, she could not help the way her mind sometimes drifted backwards.

II.

It's a stretching-for-ever walk-way, over the river. It's a frighteningly narrow bridge, even to me, just a little girl. I look down. I should never look down. Mum tells me this. I look down and see all of the gaps in the fragile wood, underneath my feet. The river rushes below. It wants me. I can feel it. It wants me to jump. It wants me to fall through the rotting boards so that it can get me.

I look back towards the abattoir. I see metallic walls, the spill of dark blood, washing the floor and running down to the river. The stink wakes me. It lets me know. Something is not right.

So many times I cross this bridge in nightmares, the old boards falling away beneath my feet, my heart leaping upwards, the death plunge, the freezing, hugging water and the pounding, gasping awakening.

III.

I knew that Caroline was sick when I met her. She's not right in the head. I don't think she ever has been. She tells me about her childhood sometimes, when we are both drunk, before I hit her, before I restrain her. She trusts me. She knows that I love her and, anyway, the pain I offer her is nothing compared to what she suffered at the hands of her elder sister. I'm certain that she is the reason why Caroline is in torment. She is the reason why Caroline needs vodka. She is the reason why Caroline needs my fists and the hard, relentless punishment I give her when I fuck her. Caroline needs to have her life filled right to the brim with whatever I can inflict upon her, because the pain blots out her thoughts. Caroline wants to feel nothing. She does not want to think.

I've seen photographs of her when she was young. She was a happy, smiling baby, sat in the lap of a scowling, hateful sibling. What could she do?

Yes, Caroline has grown up to be quite a hard woman, at least when she's out of the house. She always attacks long before there is any need for defence. I feel sorry for her. Sometimes, she shocks people with her callous brutality. She needs to keep her mouth shut a bit more. She doesn't seem to care what is acceptable and what is not.

Her work-mates keep a sensible distance from her. Work is work. Work is not the problem. Life is the challenging stuff. Have you seen what I've seen? No. I didn't think so. I can tell that you don't know. Get right up in my face. You'll see. No reaction. I stand my ground, always. You're the one in danger. In fact, I'm always hoping for attack. It's the perfect excuse for self-defence. Perhaps I could argue reasonable force, if it came to that. I would just have to be careful that they didn't realise how much I had enjoyed it. Be my recreation. Be my vent. Venting is healthy. I know that. I read it somewhere once, in a magazine, I think. Come on. Take me on. Take me on and I'll do you harm. I'm asking for it. Don't stand too close to me in a queue. Don't ever disrespect me. Don't make me smell your breath in my nose. Don't touch me without my express permission. Don't even fucking think about it . . .

IV.

In truth, Caroline often felt unhappy and persecuted at work. Before she left the house in the morning, she liked to give Dmitry a really thorough and lovingly-executed blow-job. When the boss was a bitch to her and she had to reply, she replied to her using the lips that had been around her beloved brute's formidable cock. It did make her feel vastly superior—and she relished that. She needed all the help she could get. It was a comfort to know that, whenever she spoke, she could feel the memory of Dmitry in her mouth. She loved the feel and the taste of him. She knew, without a shadow of a doubt, that the sex-life of her fat and lazy manager did not include such delights.

One day, she gave gleeful and certain self-defence advice to one of her colleagues.

"If you're walking somewhere you're not sure of . . . SWAGGER!" she told her. "I always fucking swagger and no cunt ever bothers me. Keep your house keys in the palm of your hand, but have the sharp points protruding from your balled-up fist. That way, when you hit the fucker, you're going to do some serious damage. And if you don't have your keys on you—or if you don't have a home at all—hit the fucker on the nose, but upwards, with the heel of your hand. At the very least, he—or she—will suffer excruciating pain. At best, you'll drive shards of bone right through the front of your attacker's brain. Well, they have it coming, right? That's what the heel of your hand is for, driving home a point."

V.

Caroline had a dream last night. She was holding the blade of a kitchen knife and she had it positioned just at the entrance to that fucking bitch's decrepit, stinking vagina. And using the heel of her hand, she drove the point home. She kept replaying the moment over and over in her mind, during the day. It was one of the nicest dreams she had ever had.

Caroline says to me. "Take me to the river. Take me to the river, walk me by the burn. Walk me through the woods and hear the twittering birds. See the unknown walkers and imagine. Imagine serial killers and rapists in the den. Imagine the drama. Imagine the reconstruction of my very last walk, on the television. Take me by the river. Take me in the park. But only if I want you to, only if I pretend that I really don't want it."

Caroline has one close friend whom I tolerate. I know he's not going to fuck her. He doesn't think of women in that way. He gives her

194

all of the tenderness which she does not want from me. If I were to be kind to her, her mind would shatter, once and for all. I wouldn't do that to her. I love her. She goes to her friend's house sometimes and they drink. Sometimes they go out dancing. He loves her as much as I do, but he's not going to fuck her. She worships me. She's my little acolyte.

"Remember the Rape Park? We arrived home, late at night, from Glasgow, drunk. We heard the pig-squeal of the victim, the voices of the men. We saw the standing circle through the trees and we thought, Get into the house. Lock the door quickly, behind us. *We were sure that they didn't want any witnesses. Once inside, we laughed and gasped and drank again and we never thought to call the police. We sometimes speak of the Rape Park and I suppose we should have been traumatised, at least by our indifference, but we're not. Perhaps that's the most frightening thing about the whole event, for an onlooker now. We just didn't care about the person on the ground.*"

Caroline is really beautiful, you know? If you like that kind of pale, haunted look, anyway. She would never believe me if I told her how beautiful she is, so I don't. I fucking love her and I love fucking her. It always reminds me of a fight to the death. Don't believe her if she tells you that she's the only one who comes out of it injured. Sometimes she bites. She says she likes the taste of me after the bite.

Why is she so hard on the outside? I'll tell you why. She's completely and utterly consumed by hatred, by rage. She told us this, years ago. She has forgotten those childhood prayers to her gods. Caroline doesn't know that her words were heard then and are not forgotten now, by those who listened. Caroline has no concept of mercy at this time. We don't advocate forgiveness. It's not part of our creed.

VI.

She watched a film on her laptop. Men in robes stripped themselves naked and beat themselves with knotted ropes until their backs were bloody. Caroline thought about religion and she wondered about penance. She thought about forgiveness and dismissed it.

A woman's body had been found early that morning. The papers hinted at dreadful injury, but it was not until much later that the extent of the victim's torture was made public. A serrated kitchen knife, a frenzied attack, some kind of sex offender, no doubt. She hadn't stood a chance. Caroline knew all of the details, of course.

195

The dead woman had been her sister. The police were very kind to her. Anyone could see that Caroline was in shock. She looked pale and haunted. She hadn't been in contact with her sister for years, but when it comes down to it, family is family, right?

Caroline was relieved that she had never shared her dream with anyone except Dmitry.

She was devastated that he was gone. She had returned from work and there was no trace of him at all. None of his clothes in the wardrobe, none of his food in the cupboards, no gags, no handcuffs in the bedroom they had shared. She pulled open a drawer in her dressing table and brought out a little photo album. She had to see his face.

As a child, she often didn't understand their words. "I think it's over her head," they would say. But she looked above and nothing was there.

Caroline wondered all over again about what they could have meant.

She knelt at the side of her single bed and began to pray.

"Take me by the river . . . "

Wendy Jane Muzlanova has led a checkered life. She has had many different jobs, ranging from tomato picker to teacher, and many different husbands, ranging from Egyptian to Russian. She is, she says, a foul-mouthed polyglot. In addition to writing nasty stories and poetry, she also creates rather good visual art. In her free time, she destroys reputations, especially her own. When she grows up, she wants to be a spy. Her writing has featured in Women Writing the Weird *(edited by Deb Hoag) and* Bite Me, Robot Boy *(edited by Adam Lowe). For more on Wendy's amazing adventures, visit her at* soutarwriters.co.uk/wendymuzlanova.

CRY BABY CREEK
by David Price

The rain is pouring down, shattering the surface of the water. For those who dare to listen, restless spiritual voices can be heard; it is a cry of anguish from the victims of Cry Baby Creek.

The hostel had a comfortable lounge and the weather wasn't too good, so Kelly Barbiero was happy to relax with a good book and a cup of coffee. There was just one other guest in the lounge that evening; a rather studious young lady called Alison, who tended to keep herself to herself.

Alison was tucking into a chicken salad and keeping an eye on the weather. It was supposed to clear up later. She hoped so. Like Kelly, she would soon be making her way home.

"Lousy weather, huh," Kelly said.

Alison peered at her through a rather large pair of glasses that gave her a somewhat owlish appearance.

"I'm sure it will clear up," she replied.

"Hope so."

Alison glanced out of the window.

"My name's Kelly."

"As in Ned?"

"Barbiero."

"Ah. Well I'm Alison White. I suppose you want to know what I'm doing."

"Well . . . "

Kelly blushed and looked to the floor.

"I'm studying the paranormal," Alison told her. "And there's a place around here that interests me. They say there are ghosts hanging around it. I'm going to try and contact them."

"Right."

Kelly was intrigued, obviously, and it was a very quiet evening; and like most teenagers, Kelly was always up for an adventure.

"So you're going ghost hunting?"

"Just beyond that ridge over there," Alison replied, pointing through the window at a distant hill. "there is a stream called Cry Baby Creek. It has a rather dark history." She glanced at Kelly, and there was a mischievous glint in her eye. "Maybe you'd like to hear about it?"

"Sure."

Alison placed her empty plate to one side and smiled at her.

"There was a series of unsolved murders around here back in the '60's," she began. "No one knows who was responsible, but whoever it was, he dumped the bodies in that creek. They say . . . if you listen real careful . . . you can hear the dead crying out for justice. I'm going to try and record their voices."

Kelly's eyes were almost popping out of her head. "Gosh," she said. "you can do that?"

"I can try." Again, Alison smiled. "So what do you say, Kelly Barbiero—would you like to come ghost hunting with me?"

Oh Lord, no, Kelly thought, *I wouldn't like that at all; I'd be scared to death.*

But of course, the only word she said was *'yes'.*

Alison nodded. "Half an hour, then; it should have stopped raining by then."

As soon as the weather cleared they set off, Alison's equipment crammed into their backpacks.

Kelly was nervous, and in truth, so was Alison; but with the bravado of youth they marched on.

After the rain, the air felt cleansed and the walk was quite pleasant; even if they *were* trudging through mud!

In a little over twenty minutes they arrived at Cry Baby Creek (which, according to a rather dilapidated sign, was actually called Bentley's Creek).

"You really think the dead are going to talk?" asked Kelly.

"Here's hoping, kid. We're listening, and these ghosts want to be heard."

Alison began setting up her equipment (which was quite elaborate), and talked about *EVP* and *clairaudience,* all of which went right over Kelly's head. Still, it was a lark.

In less than ten minutes, Alison had set everything up; now

198

it was time to play a waiting game.

"They'll talk when they're ready," she said. "We just have to give them time."

So they waited. At length, a wind picked up and shadows started flitting about. Occasionally, Kelly fancied that she could hear a voice, or the sound of weeping. But of course, it was getting dark and they were in a secluded spot; this was bound to play on their imagination.

Yet the sounds continued until, finally, Alison ventured a question.

"Is there anybody there, and do you wish to speak to us?"

Was that a mumble, a word? Surely not! But Alison knew that her equipment would pick up far more than the human ear.

"Tell me your name."

A machine clicked, a little like a Geiger counter.

"How long have you been here?"

It was surely just the wind, but Kelly was certain she could hear an excited babbling; yet as the wind died, so did the (apparent) sound of voices.

The dead don't talk, really they don't.

For the next few minutes, Kelly comforted herself with this thought.

After a while, Alison started picking up her equipment. "Alright," she said. "Let's see what we've got."

Back in Alison's room, the equipment was set up and ready to be studied. Kelly was fine with that. Now that she was back in the sanctuary of the hostel, she was a little happier.

"Here goes", Alison said, pressing a button on a recorder.

They listened; at first to the wind.

Then Alison's voice came on—*Is there anybody there, and do you wish to speak to us?*

Was that an answer?

Alison stopped the tape, played it back, and then slowed it down.

Wrr irrr, wrr irrr.

"Does that sound like 'we're here' to you?"

Kelly shrugged; that was an obvious interpretation, and it

199

certainly did sound like a feminine voice. Alison wrote '*We're here*' in a notebook, and switched the tape back on.

Does anybody here know the identity of the Cry Baby Creek killer?

There was a sound, but nothing that made sense. *Digs tsssst . . . Duss sssst . . . toes ettt.*

Alison rewound the tape, but it still sounded like gibberish. *Dug . . . dug . . . toes.*

Frustrated, Alison just scribbled away in her notebook. *Diggles toes—Duggles toes . . . digs toes et . . . Dugs less . . .*

"Douglas!"

Kelly nearly jumped out of her seat.

"Alison!!!"

"Douglas. The killer's name was Douglas."

She rewound the tape and played it back.

Yes, they could have been saying Douglas (they could have been telling them to dig less and mind their own blooming business, too, but Alison now had the bit between her teeth). She wrote '*Douglas???*' in her book and switched the tape back on.

"Let's hear this thing to the end," she said.

An hour later, Alison had made the following notes in her book.

'*Cry Baby Creek—*

7 (?) Victims—

Killer's name . . . Douglas --- (Thomas? Thomson? Thoms?)'

It wasn't much, but Alison considered it a good night's work. "We can ask around tomorrow," she said. "See if some of the older folk remember a Douglas T."

Kelly was, to say the least, a little sceptical. "A bit of a long shot after all this time, isn't it?"

Alison smiled, and patted her arm. "We live in hope, kiddo. We live in hope"

That evening, they were alone in the hostel with the proprietor; a large and rather weathered lady called Elaine. Outside, the wind howled, and so they pulled their chairs up close to a roaring log fire. After that night's events, Kelly could well imagine that they were surrounded by a hoard of screaming banshees. "What a night," she said.

"Well, *we're* in the right place," Alison replied, resting her head back against the chair and closing her eyes.

Kelly looked into the fire.

If asked to describe this location, she would have said it was *sleepy;* and yet—sparsely populated as it was—a serial killer had been at large for years. How on earth had his crimes gone undetected for so long? More to the point, was he still alive and in the vicinity? Kelly couldn't see herself getting a lot of sleep on *that* night.

"Who do you think this *Douglas* was?" she finally asked.

"Oh, some weird loner; who knows? He probably kept himself to himself. Or lived with his mother, they usually do."

"And no one knew what he was doing?"

Alison just shrugged.

"This is a place that people pass through. Most of the victims were doing just that, Kell. They could have vanished anywhere; and if those remains hadn't floated to the surface, those murders might never have been discovered. I suppose there is a chance he's still alive. Mind you, I hope not."

Kelly was thinking the same thing. *If* he was, and *if* he caught wind of the fact that two young girls were investigating the murders . . .

Kelly Barbiero, you should be ashamed of yourself. What would your mother say?

Her mother, a police officer, would have told her to keep out of it and leave this kind of thing to the professionals; but her mother was on the other side of the world.

So fine, see this thing through.

It was, she supposed, as good a way as any to pass her last few days in Australia; and she was as liable as anyone to get caught up in the thrill of a chase.

Her chores finished, Elaine came over to join them.

"So what have you two been up to," she asked, in that unashamedly nosy way that Australian's have.

"Well, you know," Alison replied. "Trying to find out a little local history."

"Whizz. You know about the murders?"

"Sure do."

Elaine wiped her hands on a towel and threw another log on the fire.

"All word of mouth now, of course. Only real old folk actually remember that far back." And as she had done many times before, Elaine told the story; and was quite engaging, even if she did have a tendency to exaggerate.

"It all happened years before I was born," she concluded. "but it gives folks around here something to talk about."

"And what about the older folks?" Kelly asked. "The one's who'd remember?"

"Ain't too many of them, now. There's old Douglas, of course."

Alison had to strongly resist the urge to jump out of her seat and shout *who?*

Douglas!

"Don't think I've met him," she said, in as calm a voice as she could manage.

"Old guy; lives in a shack about a mile from here. Douglas Toast."

"Toast?"

"That's not his real name, of course; it's what they call him."

Alison and Kelly exchanged glances.

"Why would they do that?" Kelly asked.

Elaine laughed and clapped her hands, making Alison jump. "Why indeed. Something that happened years ago; and folks still talk about it."

Alison nodded in encouragement.

"Douglas was the town lush, always in his cups. They say that's what caused it to happen. He was in a bar one day, really knocking back the booze, when suddenly he jumps to his feet, knocking over the table and screaming blue murder. *Douglas, you stop yer messin'* the barman says; but old Douglas, he keeps hopping around and cussin'. Next thing anyone knows, his strides catch fire—or, rather, his legs did. Spontaneous Human Combustion; that's what the Doc says, never seen anything like it. Well, old Douglas became quite a celebrity after that. Pretty much keeps himself to himself these days, mind; probably got sick of all the jokes."

202

Douglas Toast. Oh yes, that was so right.
"And you say that this Douglas lives nearby?" Alison asked.
"Not far. But I don't think he'd welcome visitors."
Then we'll just have to keep out of sight, Kelly thought.
"More coffee?" Elaine asked.

The two girls were awake early the next morning, and enjoyed a good breakfast as they talked about the previous night's events. They agreed that old Douglas was 'quite probably' innocent . . . that it was old news . . . and that they 'really should' leave it at that . . . no point in going out to old Douglas's place, really . . . even if he *was* the killer, what could *they* do?

Still, it was a nice morning after the night's deluge, and a good long walk should be quite pleasant.

Breakfast finished, they set off, happily trudging through the mud. This holiday was turning into quite an adventure.

"Where to?" Kelly asked.

"Old Douglas's place, of course," Alison replied.

Topping a ridge, they looked down on a ramshackle lean-to that was, they assumed, home to Douglas Toast. It was quite dilapidated, and had a couple of rickety wicker chairs outside the front door.

They crouched behind some bushes, as though getting ready to begin a long vigil. Kelly thought that all this creeping around was ridiculous; but at the same time, it *was* exciting.

Reaching into her coat pocket, Alison pulled out a pair of binoculars and looked through them. She had certainly come prepared, Kelly thought.

A look at the hut, and then she scanned the surrounding area.

The door to the hut suddenly opened and the two girls ducked out of sight as an old man stepped out and emptied a pot of water onto the ground. He was as thin as a scarecrow and just as well dressed; wizened, too, after years of exposure to the sun; to Kelly, he looked about a hundred.

He walked stiffly, no doubt a result of the burns to his legs. Oh yes; this was their man, alright.

203

"Douglas Toast, gotta be," Kelly said.

Alison looked at the man again. She couldn't see his face properly, but the hairs on the back of her neck were standing on end. *Just imagination,* she told herself; but it was a feeling she couldn't shake off.

"What do we do?" Kelly asked.

"Wait 'till he leaves, and then take a look inside."

"Take a look . . . are you out of your mind? What do you think we're going to find in there?"

"I don't know; evidence?"

"Evidence?"

Alison put the binoculars down and turned to face her. "It won't hurt to take a look. I'll go in; you can stay here and make sure the coast is clear. I'll give you my 'phone number, and you can warn me if he comes back."

Kelly shook her head. "This is crazy."

"I'll be in and out in a flash; you'll see."

"Ooh!"

Kelly glanced around, as though looking for an escape. This was lunacy, to say nothing of illegal; they couldn't just break into a man's home, even if it was an old hut that looked on the point of collapse.

Kelly chewed her lower lip, but Alison had a determined look on her face.

"This is dangerous," Kelly finally said.

"I intend to finish what I started, Kell. You can go back to the hostel if you like, but I'm staying right here. I've *got* to see this through."

Kelly looked around, but there was no getting out of this; Alison was committed to seeing this adventure out, and Kelly wasn't about to let her go it alone.

"Alright," she said at last; and hoped she wouldn't regret it.

After about an hour, Old Douglas left his hut and set off into the woods with his rifle. Kelly didn't like the look of that at all.

"Are you sure about this," she asked.

"Sure I am," Alison replied. "You've got my number. Just give me a bell if you see him coming back."

204

They waited for a good five minutes, then Alison got to her feet and set off down the hill. *This girl is 'way' too reckless*, Kelly thought.

Alison got to the door of the hut, gave it a push, and it opened without resistance. A quick glance around, and then she stepped inside.

Don't be too long, Kelly thought, her thumb resting against the redial button on her mobile 'phone.

Alison was inside for less than five minutes, although it seemed a lot longer to Kelly. Finally she emerged, her jacket bulging.

Damn it, Alison, you never said you were going to burgle the place! Kelly had a dark vision of being arrested in Australia.

Alison scrambled back up the hill as fast as her legs would carry her and then sank down next to Kelly, unzipping her jacket.

"I knew it, he's our killer!" she said, as a number of items fell to the ground.

"You got proof, then."

"Oh yes."

Alison picked up a bracelet. Inscribed on it was the name *Melissa*.

"Melissa Groome, vanished in 1969 while out walking her dog."

"And he hung onto that piece of evidence?"

"Sure; ain't you ever heard of a killer trophy-taking?"

The other items had no inscriptions, but they were obviously very old; a Brownie box camera, which looked positively ancient, and a silk scarf. Alison had done quite well, Kelly thought; but under the circumstances, they could hardly go to the police.

Using her mobile 'phone, Alison took a picture of the objects, and then scooped them back up.

"Right then," she said. "There's a need for a plan B." She stood up. "So I'm going to put these things back where I found them. Then we can go back to Cry Baby Creek and try to contact the victims. One way or another, old Douglas is going to get what's coming to him!" And she set off back down the hill. "Shan't be long."

Kelly felt that Alison might be the death of her!

Later that day they called into a diner for a meal, and then returned to the hostel to pick up Alison's equipment. Maybe the spiritual voices would be stronger this time (not that a few ghostly recordings would make for very convincing evidence, but they were making this up as they went along!).Whatever the next few hours had in store, at least they could say they tried.

When they got to the creek, the sky was an inky black and no stars could penetrate the clouds. Alison felt that a storm was on the way, and hastily set up her equipment.

"Okay, let's do this," she said, and switched on her tape recorder.

Kelly glanced around, completely unnerved.

Oh get a grip, Kelly; there's no ghosts around here.

There was a light breeze, and nothing beyond that gentle whisper; she could live with that. As a comfort, she told herself that the voices had only ever existed in Alison's fevered imagination, and that old Douglas 'really was' nothing more than a harmless old recluse.

"Last recording," Alison said, after a while. "And I am calling out to all the lost souls of Bentley Creek." She glanced around, a little nervous. "We have been investigating a series of murders that took place around here back in the 1960's," she continued. "and I am convinced that we have found a reasonable suspect. He is known, locally, as Douglas Toast . . . and he still lives around here."

She paused, giving the spirits time to answer.

"Does this name mean anything to you, or even the name Douglas?"

The two girls listened, but there was nothing more than the insistent whisper of the wind.

A twig snapped and both girls jumped. "Who's there?" Alison cried, with more than a hint of panic in her voice.

"Oh for goodness sake, it's probably just a squirrel," Kelly said. "Can't we just go back to the hostel?"

"If we do that . . . "

The wind suddenly picked up, and this time the voices really did call out to them, loud and clear this time.

Dugss Waaarn us.

Alison just said, 'Oh!'

Just then, a blue light seemed to manifest itself below the surface of the water, a glow that started to intensify and coalesce into something vaguely human.

Then, as they watched, this spectral figure began to rise to the surface; thin, seemingly naked and smooth as marble.

Warned us . . . run . . . danger coming . . . run . . .

It rose out of the water and hovered before them, a shimmering blue entity with tortured eyes.

Rrrrrrun!

Then it vanished, like a popped balloon.

"What on earth?" Kelly said, and turned to Alison.

"Did we just . . . "

A buzzing sound could then be heard, getting louder and louder, the sound of a large insect; far larger than anything they had ever seen.

The buzzing continued; and then the sound of breaking foliage told them it was on the move, and heading in their direction.

"Alison, let's go."

The foliage was suddenly ripped apart; and then a huge, almost human-shaped figure came crashing through the bushes and into the clearing.

"Oh God!"

This creature resembled a giant locust with a huge black body, flapping wings and a heart-shaped head. *This* was The Cry Baby Creek Killer; not a man, but a monster!

It hovered before them; red eyes blazing like fire, arms raised to display fierce-looking talons that could rip apart human flesh. Nothing like this should ever have been seen outside of the very depths of Hell!

Alison grabbed Kelly's arm and they ran; but the creature was swift and set off after them, skimming over the water like a dragonfly, its shadow growing in the periphery of their vision like a descending storm.

Up into the air it rose, as though getting ready to dive on its prey; but the trees impeded its attack, buying them a few precious seconds.

Yet it wasn't enough, for the road back to the hostel was a mile of wide open countryside . . . this was the urban legend that no-one lived to tell about, and now it was chasing its next victims.

Alison was suddenly wrenched out of Kelly's grasp and lifted up into the air, but she struggled for all she was worth and in seconds the creature had dropped her. Without even thinking, Kelly grabbed a fallen branch and started batting away at it.

"Go away, damn you!" she cried.

The creature made a grab for her, but Alison threw a rock and struck it on the side of the head. The distraction wasn't much, but the two girls were up and running again, hoping against hope to evade this woodland sprite.

"Split up," Alison cried; but before they could act the bushes in front of them parted and Douglas Toast stepped out in front of them.

"Down," he shouted, and the two girls hit the ground as he raised his rifle and fired.

The loud and shocking report echoed through the clearing, sending a flock of birds into a panicked flight; then came a scream of anguish that they would never forget, followed by a hefty thud as the creature's lifeless body hit the ground. The mystery had been solved: The Cry Baby Creek Killer was now dead.

After a time, Kelly dared to look. The creature lay spread-eagled on the ground, but there was only a spreading red stain where its head should have been.

"Damn sonofabitch!"

Douglas Toast walked up to the creature and stood over its body. Strangely, he seemed a little regretful.

The two girls got to their feet . . . and of course, Kelly had to utter a line straight out of a bad horror movie. "What on earth was that?" she said.

"A creature," Douglas replied. "And if folks had known about it, I daresay he would have been given some fancy pants Latin name. I called it the bloodsucker. Murderous little critter, weren't he?"

The old man cracked open his gun and smiled at them.

"So you two Sheila's thought old Douglas was a serial killer, did you? Well you were wrong; I tried to warn people; 'stay away from here', I said; but who'd listen to a crazy old buzzard like me? I knew I'd have to kill this here fellah one day. Came close a few times, too, but he was dab hand at dodging bullets."

He slung the rifle over his shoulder.

"Reckon I'll dump him in the creek. What do you say?"

And with that, he grabbed one of the creature's legs and dragged it towards the water.

And all Kelly and Alison could do, was look at each other; bewildered, shaken.

"Did that just happen?" Kelly asked.

Alison smiled.

"It sure did, you daft Pom," she replied, and went back to the creek to collect her equipment.

It was almost five minutes before Kelly thought to say. "Who are you calling a daft Pom?"

Later that evening, in Alison's room, the tape came to an end. Only this time, there was nothing to be gleaned from the recordings; no words, or screams; just Alison's questions and the wind. It seemed the spirits were now at peace.

"That's it, then," Kelly said.

"I reckon." Alison switched off the tape. "There's nothing more to be done here."

Kelly nodded; in any case, she'd had quite enough excitement for one day. "How about a coffee," she suggested.

"Coffee Hell, I need a drink!"

Alison jumped off the bed and grabbed her coat. "Come on, Kell; let's go and find ourselves a bar. We can drink a little toast to the dead of Cry Baby Creek." And linking her arm through Kelly's, she led her out of the room. "I think it's time we girls had a little fun, don't you?"

Kelly thought that they'd had quite enough 'fun' for one day; all the same, a nerve-calming drink wouldn't go amiss.

"But what are we going to say?" she asked.

"About the creature?"

"Yes."

"Nothing, hon; they'd lock the pair of us up!"

"So we keep our mouths shut?"

"Absolutely; I think it's for the best, don't you?"

"Well .."

"Come on, let's go for that drink."

So they went to a bar, let the story die and left the locals to their tales; some stones, Kelly knew, were better left unturned.

And she certainly wasn't about to start telling a tale about the night she was chased by a Mothman-like creature in the Australian Outback . . . they'd probably think she'd had a touch of the sun!

David Price has been a published writer since 1996. He edited a magazine called Tales of the Grotesque and Arabesque *between 1997 and 1999, and had a collection of stories called* Evil Eye *published back in 2001. For more details, you can check out his website at* daiprice. weebly.com.

BASTARDISING
METAPHORS IN
BANCHORY
by Chris Kelso

I look at Deborah in her frock, standing awkwardly with both feet crushed into tight stilettos. Her hair cascading in ringlets, eyes gaping like looking fish, blood smeared all over her crooked little mouth like treacle . . .

You know the story . . . you're walking into your local newsagents for some Winegums and a packet of Golden Wonder crisps, when **BOOM**—an unknown virus hits your town turning everyone around you into slobbering, brain hungry reanimated corpses . . .

I know, I know, we've all been there, but how did *you* cope? If you—

A)   headed towards your nearest rooftop/government army quarantine base and held out until the virus was properly contained

B)   obtained an extra 40-round magazine for your Glock handgun

OR

C)   killed yourself

—Then chances are you dealt with the zombie holocaust as effectively as possible and maintained some glimmer of your precious humanity in the process(for a while at least). If you do fall into this category of people then I must congratulate you (congratulations!). But if you're one of those rare people like me who tried reasoning with your recently infected loved ones, then chances are you wound up in the same situation that I've found myself in . . . shuffling through the streets as a bloody zombie yourself!

First thing's first though—I don't want you to think this is a Romero-style epidemic here. By this I mean that I'm not using zombies as a metaphor for the repression of bourgeois American society or as nuanced symbolism pertaining to the Cold War or even as a flimsy social commentary regarding consumerism. No, no . . .

This is me writing about my life living amongst the brain-dead AS one of them.

For someone as well-educated as I am, you'd think I'd take no time in rising to the top of the un-dead hierarchy, but quite the opposite has transpired.

(Insert formidable silence here.)

In fact, I'm considered somewhat of an outcast in today's society. When you think about it, I guess this all does kind of sound like a metaphor, doesn't it? Sorry.

At present I'm standing in a queue of zombies outside a truck sat on its axles. Inside are a number of humanoid morsels crying and praying for mercy. There's a kid who looks like he's relishing it all and there's a middle aged man dumb with fright. How has it come to this? My future seemed so bright you know!

So low is my stock these days that even my girlfriend Deborah has left me for a superior specimen curiously nickname. "Skull Smasher Zombie" by his living dead compatriots.

They're inseparable. It's disgusting.

My mother continues to smear her reflection with Windolene.

My father continues to eat with his mouth open.

My old brown Cinquecento remains unblemished. It was never a great car but it got me from A to B and served me well during my time among the living—nothing too ostentatious.

My girlfriend continues to be a bitch.

To think, if I hadn't caught them both eating each other I'd have been none the wiser. Yes, these are changed times. If you have a single functioning particle in your juicy, delicious brain then prepare for a life of isolation and constant ridicule. This damn metaphor seems to be surfacing at an uncanny rate.

Metaphor . . . bubbling up . . . foaming around me . . . a-a-n-n-d-d . . . there it is.

I keep expecting to wake up . . .

. . . Slide out of bed on a trail of my own sweat . . .

. . . Grope around for a light switch to beat away the hideous shadow that's been cast across the face of the world . . .

But I never do wake up.

(Pause for dramatic effect.)

We have these morsels cornered—two unpopular teachers from my school.

Mr Garitty and Mr Phelps.

Well, I sa. "we". I'M not really doing anything besides watching. I've been relegated to the back of the group, not that I have any desire to be at the vanguard. I've yet to completely abandon my dignity and sense of moral self.

Yes, I think now's as good a time as any to seize the ethical high ground!

There are 3 primary desires of the recently undead—nourishment, sex and television. The casual zombie has no other hidden layer, no buried facet where all their sensitive, vulnerable and knowledge-thirsty components are situated . . . only surface aspiration.

They've all lunged at the human feast, knocking over garbage cans and making some of the most obscene chewing noises I think I've ever heard. I can only see a bare human leg sticking out, calf flexed, ankle drawn tight.

I'm feeling a little left out. My strongest social response is to succumb to crowd politics.

Before I know what's what, we're eating them both alive.

Their screams are awful *and* arousing.

Garitty and Phelps both taste a lot like failure.

Mmhmmm . . .

My mother still finds time to fret when I don't chew properly—you can't spel. "smother" withou. "mother", I suppose. In a way it's

213

comforting to know that some things never change . . . rather like women in some respects.

Now wait just a sec here!

I'm not a misogynist; I don't hate all women. In fact, you could say with a certain confidence that I *love* most women. But given that my experiences with the opposite sex have proved gratuitously bloodier than an early David Cronenberg film, and as complicated as an Egyptian Sudoku puzzle, you can perhaps forgive these apprehensions of mine.

It should be noted for posterity that zombies have no sense of decency either. So you can probably imagine the foul hybrid that is . . .

. . . FEMALE ZOMBIE!

As indecisive as she is cruel and blood thirsty . . . shrill, moody and in possession of an alluring beauty . . . loving, maternal . . . hateful and twisted . . .

Casting my eye over the wasted town, I catch sight of Deborah and Skull Smasher Zombie acting out an elaborate oral sex routine. They've wrapped themselves in a lotus position, naked in semi-foetal glory for all to see.

Deborah is sluiced in sweat and viscera. Skull Smasher Zombie kneads all her bony contours with his fingertips.

Then, true to his title, Skull Smasher punches Deborah's head clean off.

It's all very sudden, very unnecessary, and I'm sure if my moral centre hadn't been so dulled of late, it would be a thoroughly shocking scene to behold. But as it happens my moral centre *has* been dulled. I'm an abomination remember, just like everyone else. Debs is dead (again) . . .

Oh well.

A teardrop of semen bled from the eye of Skull Smasher's penis as he gazed down at Deborah's twitching, headless body.

Bet she wishes she'd stayed with me now, eh?

When I was among the living I had no propensity for violence. But in the past two days since the holocaust I've hunted and killed—

5 disliked teachers

3 accountants
A tax man
A local politician
Several individuals of ethnic minority
A doughy faced policeman
A man parking in a disabled space
A supermarket cashier
2 innocent lovers warm in each other's embrace
An entire Buddhist men's club
An old man we thought looked shady
A woman who dressed too revealingly
A man with a book in his hand
2 Smiths fans
A vegetarian (guess that's 3 Smiths fans?)
A group of loitering teenagers
And countless others

You wouldn't know it to look at me.

I'm the killer with the kind eyes.

If I think rationally, I know a person's life has no meaning beyond the arbitrary importance they themselves give it.

But this doesn't excuse my behaviour.

I'm watching the TV or staring through a window frame.

I can't decide which.

I don't bother to blink. My eyes are burning on the vista, my brain melted and rotted to mulch in my skull.

Nothing pleases me anymore.

I feel bored and tired.

The burning eye of the sun covers everything in a sort of radioactive yellow. Stink lines from the junkyard start to steam up the glass portal in front of me—a TV, a window, whatever . . .

Two rusty oil sentinels dominate the landscape here—Brutalized Aberdonian architecture. To my left there's a busted up old warehouse with kids inside playing around with chemical drums and shards of broken glass—seem happy enough. The rippling surface of the see looks serene. It's too distant to be real. Nothing pleases me anyway.

I'm stuck in this crumbling city. Rather in here than out there among the street-smart living dead.

I miss Deborah.

Debs and I made passionate love. Passionate might be pushing it a tad. We sought union in beds and on floors, against walls, in the cramped spaces of Cinquecento's and in the deepest crook of beach coves—we'd fuck anywhere on offer

I remember the first time we ever kissed. It was in the height of summer 96 where the sounds of lawns being mowed and spitting sprinklers were heard down every block. We'd always been friends she and I. But that summer our relationship sparked into life, something new and unexpected and wonderful. I was as surprised as anyone when she tried it on with me!

She stabbed me with a stiff tongue—my first kiss.

I'm certain I was lousy at it.

Now I'm looking at her decapitated skull rolling down a warm tarmac road being chased by the starving undead.

If I'm to experience intimacy again, will I need to finagle a zombie?

Hmmm . . .

There's a kid with a backward baseball cap and parachute pants on. He's gaping idly at a television through a store-front window—new *Two and a Half Men*'s on—I can't tell if he's a zombie or not, but he's blending in nicely.

This loneliness is going to push me over the edge, I'm sure of it. Even when I choose to walk amongst them I feel isolated. No-one really connects anymore.

I hate every single one of them.

I hate the way they shuffle through life, leaching off of civilised society, eating the brains of the living, moaning and groaning and moaning and groaning . . .

God it's just occurred to me the way I've been behaving. I'm no better than they are.

God Deborah . . .

Light of my life, fire in my soul, sad beauty I'll miss you're soft touch . . .

Oooh . . . new *Two and a Half Men*'s on . . .

216

Chris Kelso *is an author, editor and occasional literary agent. He enjoys the work of Trocci, Samuel R Delaney, Burroughs, Bukowski, Alasdair Gray, Octavia Butler, Stahl, Sartre, Phillip K. Dick, Samuel Shem, James Baldwin, McInerney, J.M Coetzee, Hubert Selby Jr. and others. He has worked for Eraserhead Press, Chomu Press, and now Dog Horn Publishing. Dog Horn Publishing will be releasing both his debut short story collection,* Schadenfreude, *and his novella* The Best Years of Your Life.

BAIT
by Derek M. Fox

If you wanna know what came out the river in July '99 read on . . .

Locals, what few remain, never stop talking about it, not even after they've upped and gone I daresay. If ever you're out this way I guarantee you won't stop talking about Cal Winters either.

I'm Nate, and I got this notion to write it down afore somethin' happens. O' course all you writers out there 'preciate how easy it is to jot down notes when you know a locale; sort of pull on the atmosphere, ensure places are described, add a few finer points.

Fact is details lessen over time, but I'll do m'best.

See, there I was fishin', my line bobbed once, in fact several times, the rod bent nearly double, so far over in fact that whatever had grabbed t'other end—nigh on pulled me in.

Snagged on a drowned branch I guessed.

Aw hell, I'm ahead o' myself. Tell you what, let's slip back to the Fall of '98.

Any of you know Calvin Winters? No? Big feller in height and girth, most of it muscle. Most aim to steer clear of him. Times he went fishin' any others around gave him distance. If Cal chose the east shore, locals settled on the west.

Illusion or what, that there river would bubble and froth whenever it caught that guy's reflection.

Allus used big, barbed hooks too. Pike man to the bone Cal. Had a liking for big fish wi' big teeth. Predators. Like him I reckon. He was one mean sonofabitch.

And don't that about sum it up?

During '98, up till and including Christmas, most of us gathered in the bar at the *Hook an' Tackle*—the place to be no matter what day in the season, time o' year. Had us a high old time, but maybe not Cal Winters.

Where he came from hell knows; just ambled in to our section o' New England one November evenin' a little over a year

218

back. Rented Seb Cowley's place adjacent to what used to be *Cowley's Boats*—rowing boats, pedalos, nothin' big. Hardly suited our big river. Guess Seb did all right 'til the stroke got him. Lasted a coupla weeks. Heck, we gave him a good send-off.

Gotta say everything went fine for a while with Cal. Always gossip o' course. Out this way small town folk like to know a-l-l there is to know 'bout incomers—usually store and pub jawing, like it fills in the down time. As for talkin' to Cal, he kept pretty much to hisself. Few went by the boat yard 'cept Jenny Travers.

That Christmas they were having a one to one jaw in the corner by the fireplace. Flames dusted Jenny's face like a warm caress, twinkled in smoky blue eyes, loveliest eyes this side of any river; gorgeous smile too with a laugh that sounded like fairy bells. That saying's tacked over the bar, writ and left there by a wanderin' poet.

You'll guess male blood roared every time Jen came by, meaning whenever she walked in any place our heads swivelled like a bunch o' fairground clowns, us guys admirin', sort of undressin' 'er, doing things . . . In our dreams. I mean come on!

Sure you might ask why a gal like her would want to tie in with a bear like Calvin. No finesse, diction proved any lack of real education. That guy'd spit on the fire and fall in raptures over a bottle of rye at least twice a week. And he sure could take his rye well enough.

He'd walk in straight, an' walk out the same way, back as rigid as the rod he used for fishin', drained bottle and fumes lingering. Fit an' all, like he never *looked* boozy, no bags under them mean, agate hard eyes, no slack jowls, slurring of words. Nothing like that. Cal was THE MAN whose look stated *ask no questions*. And yeah, odd times he'd chat about fishin' whenever he felt like it. 'Bout how he could make that rod sing, how he'd flick them pike out the river as easy as we might pick strawberries. Used barbed hooks. Wily as them fish are, Mr Pike never swam free of Cal's hook.

Lookin' back I reckon not many did.

Odd thing, Cal did share his catch. Drop a quantity off at our butcher cum fishmonger, left 'em for folk that liked the taste you understand. Flavour's too earthy for me, more an acquired taste.

Jenny was an acquired taste. Eighteen goin' on twenty five, that female could run rings around her old gran. Old lady took her in when Jen's parents died.

Hey, we got ourselves some shock that New Year's Eve when Jenny disappeared. Quick as anyone can snap their fingers she'd gone. No note, nothin'. Gran was at a loss. Neither me nor the neighbours dare say anything to the old woman. Going on eighty five, folk made a book on how long she'd last.

Speculation regardin' Jenny's whereabouts was rife, bottom o' the lake being most likely. Some of us knew she an' Cal argued some. I mean Jenny did give as good as she got.

I'm sayin' we're a suspicious lot, fingers levelled at Cal. A gang of males checked patches o' river almost daily, anxious to suss its secrets.

Long, meandering, and deep, our river held all manner o' things. Kids had drowned in it; over time tourists who hired row boats came croppers. Yep, a fair few cadavers surfaced from her secret pools. *The disappeared* we call 'em . . . suicides mainly.

In mid-January, ice floes thick enough to walk on, a dog dragged out what was left of the floral dress Jen wore on Christmas Eve. Most saw her leave with Cal, a wiggle of her cute little ass, the way she blew us a Christmas kiss, well it made our day. O'course Cal's scowl, his I-got-what-you-ain't smirk emphasised an underlying *don't dare touch.*

Right. Like would anybody want to come up against a feller that used barbed hooks?

Lemme say that a hook like that piercing a fish's lip ain't pretty. A hook of that ilk piercing anywhere ain't pretty!

You'll have guessed small community folk are close knit, allus on the lookout for each other. Given it was the butcher's dog found Jenny's dress, I told the others we'd never report her missing to the law. Mind, law didn't work from here, nossir. Law was housed eight mile down river by the bridge where the main highway slips into the next county.

There's a world-wide sayin' states, *Never take the law into your own hands.*

Come on, I mean why'd we wanna do that?

Time slid into March. Two months on, an' Jenny's loss a real puzzler to folks.

I'd go my usual walk through woods, trees like cathedral pillars close by where the old miner's shack still stood after twenty years. Walkin' back I'd drop by Gran, sure the old gal had survived.

220

We'd drink coffee and chew the fat, mostly 'bout Jen.

Calvin you ask? He dropped from our corner a mite quick. Rented cottage stood empty, his attempts to own us with a look, a threat, a hook, all gone.

Some thought it unsettling to be honest that he should go like that. Come fishin' season, fellers on the west bank checked Cal's spot expecting to see him. They didn't.

River went kinda comatose too. Sunlight sparked off of her ripples, flow caught our next Fall's leaves, a million or so tiny boats, carried to the sea, or drowned deep when the rains came. For certain our river remained a permanent threat.

Take one from here, I take you—the river's threat and I guess our community motto. Had a ring to it.

As I recall Sam Baker hooked the first bite that July. His last cast of the day.

An arm—a left arm, all fish bit. No tattoo like the one Calvin wore—would you believe a pike's mouth, razor teeth? The same we'd see whenever he strutted around shirtless.

Mentioned the river threw out unsettling stuff so not easy to know what might wash up. What's more, water does things to corpses after they been submerged a while.

Over time more bits surfaced—a left leg, then up came a right. Left foot next, strips of purple black flesh. Kids found that one in the shallows.

If it was Cal, we liked to believe we were well rid.

By the way, I told nobody nothin' 'bout how Jenny said she'd done a fine job luring Cal. But even so, she weren't too sure that what kept surfacin' was him, it being pike ripped.

You should understand that me an' Jenny started out childhood sweethearts. Can you imagine the look across the school playin' field? A stolen kiss close by where the willows curtained the river banks—our reflections drowned in the matt surface o' summer days.

Only me and Gran knew Jen hadn't really disappeared. Bein' honest I have t'say it was her and me thought up the scheme to get rid of you-know-who and give us all a chance. See most were scared Cal would do bad things, Jenny mightily so after she'd done . . . Well like lured him into the water. Scared silly that he might not be . . . y'know . . . properly dead.

221

The dress was a neat touch of hers. I watched her wrap it around a stone and throw it in. Reason we never told the cops.

Things died down yet it wasn't the same, townsfolk trying to justify the fact that no stranger had better think he could own us. Then attemptin' to face up to what did surface. We were made more skittish wonderin' where the arm wearin' a pike head tattoo WAS?

Keep faith in m'neighbours, I kept telling m'self.

We carried on looking (and hooking) seeking the one extra proof needed.

The bits already mentioned we stacked in the butcher's other freezer. Only a matter of time afore one smart ass came up with the idea we cook 'em come Thanksgiving. 'Yeah,' I said, 'and feed the fishes!'

A week on and every piece disappeared, the freezer empty. Not one toe nail.

A year older and here's me with a hook fastened around a windfall branch.

Twilight with little surface ripple can be a tad upsetting.

An' yeah it resembled a branch but the naked arm I did hook, what little skin clung to the flesh and the bone, wore the remains of a mean looking tattoo. Once seen it ain't easy to forget that vicious look in cold black eyes.

Blast it, the line wouldn't come free. And certainly not when a big rod surfaced in a big hand, and a custom made barbed hook whiplashed across surface swell.

I slammed against a tree, thank Christ avoiding the hook. Harder to avoid the giant who stepped out of the water lookin' like a well-scrubbed patchwork doll knotted with fishing line. He smiled, the look real dark. Rotten. Sayin' *don't ever mess with me.*

"Where's my Jenny?" Bubbles bubbled out of Calvin's blubbery mouth.

I gawked, I fish-mouthed, unable to raise a sound.

"Best tell me," he, *it,* said. "otherwise you're bait."

Rarely do tourists stop by to hear our tales.

Eleven years on, the place is all but deserted. Gran died.

Jenny and I are together—and reasonably safe.

Take heed though: If you do stop by best not walk down Main Street, or wander close to the river. Likely you'll catch sight of a dark bulk, the legend COWLEY'S BOATS writ on its bright orange slicker.

If you're conscious of a hand reaching, or find yourself caught by a barbed hook, don't fret too much, Cal Winters will ask one question:

"Where's Jenny?"

Just state you don't know. Odds are he'll release you.

If he does . . . RUN.

Feel free to stop by mine and Jen's place—the old miner's shack in the deep woods I mentioned—always assumin' you like pike to eat.

A matter of taste. But then none of us sussed how powerful Cal would be.

Yet he does have limits.

If you do bump into him don't let him read this story.

Hold up, he can't . . . when I saw him up close his eyes were all bitten out!

Maybe his hearin's okay . . .

Derek M. Fox *is an author, creative writing tutor from Derbyshire, in the UK. He has steered dozens of students into publication, and his own credits include countless short stories (his tale 'Porcelain' from F20 received an honorable mention from Ellen Datlow); two novels, the popular* Recluse *and* Demon; *two collections,* Treading on the Past *and* Through Dark Eyes *(the latter out now in trade paperback from Cosmos); plus* Heart of Shadows *and* Sinister Quartet, *both of which examine Lord Byron's association with the supernatural.*

LIGHT FINGERS
by Selina Lock

The car tyres crunched on the gravel lane that led into the graveyard. A middle aged woman got out and helped an elderly lady alight.

"Get out of the car, Sophia," the first woman said.

There was no movement from the car.

"Get out here now, young lady."

"Sophia Clare Butler! Out of the car now!" she shouted.

Finally, a grumpy looking twelve year old appeared and made her way slowly towards the two older women.

"Now, stay with Grandma Iris and help her with the flowers, while I nip to the shops."

"Do I have to?" Sophia asked.

Her mother gave her a hard stare, reached into the car and handed her a bunch of daffodils. Sophia stared back at her mother for a second before dropping her gaze and taking the flowers.

"C'mon Sophia, let's go see your Great Grandfather Eric," Iris said and started a slow shuffling walk towards the graveyard gate.

Sophia looked longingly after her mother's car reversing down the lane, before following her Grandma, kicking stones as she went.

The lane narrowed into a passage with the small village church one side and a high stone wall the other. An apple tree overhung the passage, its branches reaching down to brush the heads of the unwary. Sophia shivered as she left the light of the spring sun and entered the shadowed path.

Iris kept up a litany of remarks as they walked. About the last time she had seen her husband, what they had buried him in, how they were lucky to get a plot in the churchyard and that there was a space waiting for her above his coffin.

It was all a bit weird and morbid, Sophia thought. She was fond of her Great Grandmother, or Grandma Iris for short, but she did seem to be obsessed with death. Her own, or one of their many deceased relations, half of whom seemed to be buried in this churchyard.

The path narrowed further as it wound around the side of

the church and into the churchyard proper.

"May the Lord protect us from the Hanged Man," Iris said, while rubbing the gold cross she wore around her neck.

Sophia started. It had been ages since her last enforced visit to the graveyard and she had forgotten all about the Hanged Man. She remembered Iris relating the tale to her when she was younger. It was the tale of a man who lived in the village a hundred years ago. He had a young daughter who disappeared, and everyone in the village thought he had killed her. They hounded and taunted him until he hanged himself from the apple tree above them, right where Grandma Iris was relating the story. His spirit was supposed to haunt the spot, not able to rest until his daughter had been found. He stopped the villagers from resting easy in their graves as retribution for their treatment of him.

She grinned at how silly she had been to believe in the story. Also at the way that on previous visits, she had run as fast as she could down the path, fearful that tree branches would snatch at her. That they would mistake her for the Hanged Man's missing daughter and give her to him to keep.

Iris still seemed to believe something haunted the graveyard, but this was the twenty first century and Sophia knew it was superstitious nonsense. To prove it, she reached up and snapped a twig off the nearest branch. Nothing happened, of course. It was just an old apple tree, after all.

Iris had shuffled into the churchyard and found her husband's grave. She gestured for Sophia to bring the daffodils over and then sent her off to empty the vase of the old, dead flowers.

Sophia stomped over to the bin full of rotting bouquets and the old dishevelled plastic arrangements. Iris shouted after her.

"Don't walk over the graves. It's disrespectful."

It's not like the occupants were going to notice, Sophia thought; they were dead and buried quite a long way down. Still, she probably wouldn't like the idea of someone walking over her if she were down there, so she threaded her way between the graves on her way back.

Sophia left Iris muttering at the graveside, telling her dead husband the latest news while snipping flower stalks.

She wandered past the rows of drunken headstones; the area reserved for wealthier families. The ones who had big stone boxes above their graves, with statues and fancy carvings. This area had been weeded and neatly mown, probably where the wedding parties liked to take pictures, she thought.

Remembering her tedious stint as a bridesmaid, Sophia had been turned this way and that for photos. She tried not to squint at the sun and had to paste on a smile when the photographer told her off for sulking. All for the promise of a present at the end of the day, and what had it turned out to be? A gold cross, just like her grandma's. Not exactly fashionable.

One set of graves stood a little apart in their own plot. There was a large double grave and a smaller one beside it. She could only make out part of the inscription, as the headstones were worn and covered in moss.

What she could see was that they all shared the same date of death. She wondered what could have killed a whole family at once. Perhaps they were brutally murdered? She bet Iris would know the story if they had been.

The little and large graves each had a low fence around them. A raised stone wall with Fleurs-de-Lis wrought iron stakes embedded in it and each stake connected by a chain. The graves themselves were covered in what looked like precious stones, amethysts glinting in the sunlight. Or that was what she had thought the first time she had seen them, but apparently it was some kind of fancy glass gravel. I mean, who would put anything valuable on a grave? It would not last five minutes.

She sat down next to the little grave and let some of the glass pieces run through her fingers, watching the light dance around them as they fell. She glanced around, thinking someone might tell her off if they saw her, but they were the only ones around. Plus, there were no flowers on the graves or anything, so they must be too old for anyone to still be visiting them.

She leaned back against the gravestone, put her headphones on and flicked through her iPod. She wondered what track to play and whether she could convince her parents to get her an iPhone for her birthday in May.

Someone shaking her shoulder woke Sophia up and she wondered where she was. Then she saw her mother frowning down at her and felt the rough stone against her back.

"You were supposed to be helping Grandma Iris," her mother said. "Not having a nap."

"Sorry," Sophia mumbled.

Her mother sighed. "Let's just get home."

Sophia shot straight up to her bedroom and threw herself on the bed. Her mother's disappointed tones echoed in her head. She rolled over, placed her iPod in its dock and turned the volume up to try to blot them out.

By lunchtime, her mother seemed fine with her again, so Sophia dared to ask if she could go round to Jen's. Her mother pursed her lips for a moment before her face relaxed.

"Okay, but be back by four."

Sophia grinned. "Thanks Mum, I will be."

Ten minutes later, she was cycling the two streets to Jen's house. They spent the afternoon taking photos with Jen's phone, playing with effects and uploading the results to Facebook.

Sophia was only allowed on the family laptop for an hour a day, under supervision, unless it was for homework purposes.

She could not wait until she was allowed to have her own laptop and phone, like Jen. It was so unfair of her parents to keep the wireless password secret, so she could not even get online with her iPod. They also checked all the music she downloaded before letting her listen to it. Heaven forbid that they might trust her to talk to her friends online or have any fun at all.

Four o'clock came too quickly and she headed home. At least it was Saturday, which meant family film night. Pizza, popcorn and probably some kind of action film, as it was her brother's turn to pick.

She was halfway through a slice of pepperoni pizza when the phone rang. Her mother answered it and came back in holding the phone.

"It's Jen's mother. She wants to know if you remember where Jen had put her phone?" her mother asked.

"It was on her bed I think," Sophia replied.

"She says it was on her bed," her mother repeated into the phone as she wandered back out of the lounge.

A few minutes later, her mother returned. She had Sophia's Hello Kitty backpack in one hand and Jen's phone in the other. Her face was white and pinched.

"What's Jen's phone doing in your bag young lady?" her mother asked quietly.

"What are *you* doing going in my bag?" Sophia replied defensively.

"I didn't. I noticed it poking out of the side pocket as I walked past. Now, how did it get in there?"

"Don't ask me! Perhaps Jen put it in there as a joke?" Sophia said.

"I hardly think so. Her mother said she's very upset at losing it."

"I don't know what it's doing in there. Perhaps it fell in."

"Fell in?" Her mother's voice got quieter and sterner.

"I'm sure there's an explanation," her father commented. He was trying to keep the peace, as usual, while her brother grabbed another slice of pizza and settled in to watch the show. Sophia nodded and frantically tried to remember what had happened when she left Jen's that afternoon. She was sure the phone had been on Jen's bed when she went downstairs to get her bike. She had left her bag in the hall for a few minutes. Perhaps Jen's younger sister had slipped the phone into her bag then? It did not seem like the sort of thing she would do, but Sophia couldn't think how else it had got there and she certainly had not stolen it.

"I really hope there's an explanation," her mother said, throwing Sophia's bag to the floor.

The rest of the contents spilled out. Sophia's purse, glittery lip balm and notebook, but also a brand new lipstick, a black memory stick and a Top Gear DVD.

She stared at them in shock. How did any of that stuff get in her bag? Someone was messing with her.

The rest of her family also stared at the items scattered on the floor and the shouting began. Her mother had only bought that

228

lipstick that morning. Dad had important work on the memory stick, and her brother had been looking for that DVD all afternoon. The noisy demands for an explanation grew until her father roared at them all to shut up.

Sophia looked at him, her eyes wide. Her father hardly ever raised his voice. He looked back at her, with disappointment creasing his face.

"Why did you take all these things?" he asked.

"I didn't, Dad. I didn't." she replied.

"Don't lie. It only makes it worse. Just tell us why you did it."

Sophia just kept repeating that she did not take them. Why would she? She did not understand what was happening.

Her dad rubbed his face and pointed to the stairs.

"You'd better go to your room and think about what you've done. Your mother and I need to discuss what to do about this."

Sophia ran out of the lounge, tears pricking at her eyes.

The next hour passed in a blur, as her parents came up to lecture her about stealing. She wanted to protest, to shout out that she hadn't done anything wrong, but all she could do was sob. How could they believe she would do something like this?

They took her iPod and told her she was grounded for a month. She was going to go to school, do homework and her online computer time was on hold until she explained her actions. How could she explain when she had no idea what had happened?

Eventually the sobs subsided and she was left feeling exhausted. She opened her top middle drawer, looking for Mr Squiggles, her favourite teddy. She had put him away when starting secondary school, as she didn't want to look like a baby. Tonight she just wanted to curl up and hug him.

She lifted the pile of t-shirts he was usually under, but there was no sign of him. She started hunting through all her drawers, flinging her clothes on the floor, but she still could not find him. She moved on to her shelves and wardrobe, looking everywhere she could think of. She felt the tears starting again until it hit her. Marcus. Her brother must have taken him in retaliation.

She stormed into his room and found him Skyping friends.

229

"Where's Mr Squiggles?" she demanded.

Normally she would have been mortified at mentioning her teddy in front of Marcus' friends, but nothing seemed normal tonight.

"What? I don't have your stupid teddy," he replied.

Then he pointed his webcam at her and spoke to his friends.

"Behold, my sister, the thief."

"I'm not a thief, I didn't take anything."

"Yeah, right. Get out Soph, before I call Dad up here."

She hesitated for a second, but the thought of another confrontation with her father was just too much.

Back in her room, she hugged a pillow and thought about her day. What was happening? Why would someone want to make her look like a thief? Who had taken Mr Squiggles?

Was it only this morning that she was not really listening to her Grandma Iris at the graveyard? Rabbiting on about showing respect for the dead and not disturbing their spirits. It seemed like that had all happened days ago.

She dug her hand into the pocket of her jeans and pulled out five purple stones. The ones she had taken from the fancy grave of a child this morning. These were the only things she had taken today. She stared at the stones, looking dull in the glow of her bedside lamp. *These* were the only thing that *she* had taken.

A few minutes later, she walked carefully down the stairs and tip-toed past the lounge, where her parents were still watching TV and talking quietly. About her, she did not doubt. In the kitchen she paused, her hand hovering over her mother's house keys. They already thought she was a thief, so she may as well live up to their expectations. Sophia grabbed the keys and slipped out of the back door.

She had a few moments of panic trying to manoeuvre her bike out of the shed. Each step sounded like a thunderclap to her. Finally, she was through the back gate and wheeled her bike down the drive.

Then she peddled as fast as she could down the street.

She was panting when she arrived at the churchyard. She felt like she had never ridden so hard in her life. Pursued by the fear of her parents realising she was gone, of being out on the streets alone in the dark, but worst of all, of being wrong about what she was doing.

She leaned her bike against the church railings and peered into the gloom beyond. She thought the church would be lit by spotlights, like at Christmas, but they must have turned them off to save money. The street lamp she was under was the only light in the area. She was glad she had grabbed a torch from the shed on her way out.

She turned her flashlight on and picked out the group of graves she had been looking at that morning. They were further back from the street than she remembered. She went to open the front gate and found it only rattled rather than moving. The sound made her freeze and she looked at the gate more carefully. Locked.

Great. She couldn't climb over; the railings were too high and pointy. That only left the path from the lane at the back of the church, where it would be even darker.

Taking a deep breath, she walked around the back of the church, shining her torch a few steps ahead of her. She concentrated on where she was going, heart still thumping and her breathing slightly ragged.

Something scraped the top of her head, tangling in her hair, making her yelp. She started panting again and slowly reached a hand up to free herself. She had walked farther than she thought and realised she was caught on a branch of the Hanged Man's tree.

She kept repeating that it was just a story, and there was nothing to be afraid of, while she freed herself. Above the beating of her own heart, she heard the creaking of the branches above her. It sounded like the noise the tyre swing down by the stream made, the squeaking of rope against wood.

She yanked her head down, pulling strands of hair out, but escaping the tree's embrace. A breeze cooled her stinging scalp as she moved forward. It brought with it whispers. She imagined that she heard a voice pleading with her to stay.

Sophia started running towards the front graveyard, the torchlight bouncing before her. She misjudged the corner and careered into the church wall. The impact jolted the torch from her hand and knocked the breath from her lungs. She gasped, rubbed her shoulder and bent to pick up the light. Dizziness rushed through her head, blotting out her vision and she froze in place. Once she could see again she realised the torch bulb was smashed.

Her eyes adjusted to the dark and she could make out the slightly lighter grey of the path in the moonlight. The graves looked misshapen and seemed to loom out of the night at her. Sophia looked back at the darker patch beneath the apple tree, wondering if she should just go back home.

She could always come back tomorrow, when it was light. Surely she was just being stupid, coming here in the dark. She was already in serious trouble with her parents; this would just make things ten times worse. Plus, she was starting to ache all over and her head was really sore.

She took a couple of steps back the way she had come, paused and took a final look towards the family of ornate graves. There was something on the child's grave. It was the size of a small cat, with a patch of white in the middle. Sophia hoped it was a cat, but knew better as she squinted at it.

"Mr Squiggles," she whispered.

She moved towards the teddy bear on the grave like a moth to a flame. She had to get him back.

When she reached the knee-high wrought iron fence around the grave, a figure appeared from behind the headstone. It was a little girl, about half Sophia's age and height. She wore an ankle length nightie with long sleeves, and lace around the edges. The girl was the colour of moonlight and just as insubstantial, but Sophia's muscles trembled at the sight of her.

"I knew you would come," the girl said. Her face was calm, her head cocked to one side.

"You took a little bit of me with you. You stole from me, so I stole from you," the girl continued.

Sophia tried to speak, but her throat felt tight. Her body felt weighed down with guilt and trying to move was a huge effort. The girl held up a finger and wagged it at her.

"Thieves must pay," the girl carried on in a sing song voice.

"That's what the man said. Thieves must pay. Daddy stole

Mummy, so we all had to pay."

Sophia's throat started to feel very dry and sore as the girl continued.

"Daddy stole Mummy and he would burn in hell."

The girl's voice got harsher and her silver glow turned orange. Flames started flicking around her feet and Sophia started to feel hot.

"Daddy stole Mummy and he would burn in hell. But first we would all burn on earth."

Sophia started coughing and choking on invisible smoke, as the flames writhed up the girl's torso. Sophia smelt cooking meat as the girl's face started to melt. The flesh dripped from her skull and evaporated, leaving no trace.

Sophia's lungs started to burn as she gasped for breath.

"The man said thieves must pay. Daddy stole Mummy so we all burned for his crime!" the girl shouted.

"So shall you," she hissed as she moved closer to Sophia. The heat became more intense, and Sophia soon grew light-headed. She fought to gain control over her body, willed her legs to run, but could only manage a few steps backwards.

A wind swept through the graveyard, lessening the heat and smoke. Sophia sucked in a deep breath as she heard the creak of a swinging rope and a moaning noise.

The girl's head whipped towards the apple tree. The flames died down slightly as she did so.

While the girl was distracted, Sophia found she could move very slightly. She dug her hand into her jeans pocket and grasped the purple grave gravel.

"I'm here to return what I took," Sophia said and threw the stones at the girl's face.

The stones tore holes in the half melted visage, causing the girl to scream in rage. As each stone hit the grave behind the girl, her figure grew dimmer.

Sophia darted past her and grabbed Mr Squiggles. The girl reached for him at the same time, but missed. Instead her hand closed around Sophia's wrist, causing the skin to immediately blister. Sophia fell to her knees, crying in pain.

The girl clung on, even as she became more and more insubstantial. Another gust of wind blew the last trace of her away.

Sophia scrambled backwards, away from the grave, just as the girl reformed. Blazing upwards, she was wreathed in flames. She tried to move towards Sophia, but the flames tethered her and her hands could not reach past the cold iron fence surrounding the grave. She screamed in frustration as Sophia pushed herself up, and turned and ran.

Sophia's lungs were on fire. Her wrist throbbed with burning pain and her hand ached from clutching Mr Squiggles so tightly. She ran to the only person she thought might believe her.

Grandma Iris listened to her story, bathed her burns and put her to bed. Her great grandmother's bedroom smelt of lavender and slightly stale pot pourri. The warmth of the quilt, and the comfort of having Mr Squiggles pressed against her chest, helped to slow her thudding heart.

She drifted in and out of sleep for several hours. At one point she heard raised voices. Her mother was there, demanding answers, but Grandma Iris told her to be quiet. She could hear little snatches of their quieter conversation about a gang of girls from school—cyberbullying. Sophia was too scared to say no, Iris said. Not responsible for her actions. Iris wove a new story around Sophia as she slept.

The next morning, Iris drilled Sophia on the new version of events. She insisted that she must forget everything she had seen at the churchyard. When her parents arrived, Iris kissed her gently on the cheek and whispered in her ear. "In future, perhaps you'll listen to your old Grandma's tales?"

Selina Lock *is a mild mannered librarian from Leicester. In her alternative life in comics she edited twenty one issues of* The Girly Comic, The Girly Comic Book Volume 1 *and* The Girly Web Comic between 2002 and 2010. She has been involved in various collaborative comics, wrote a column for Borderline – The Comics Magazine, has recently written comics strips for Ink+PAPER #1 and Sugar Glider Stories #2, and has a story in the upcoming Alt Zombie anthology from Hersham Horror. She also helped organise the Caption comics convention between 2006-2011. She currently reviews books and graphic novels for the British Fantasy Society and is one half of Factor Fiction, alongside her partner Jay Eales. Her daily life is spent in service to the god Loki, who currently inhabits the body of a small, black, scruffy terrier. Website: factorfictionpress.co.uk.

THE GLASS CHAMBER
by Adam Lowe

She fell from the sky like a star, burning a hole in the forest, which plumed silver towers of smoke like great feelers among the clouds. It was these slow-writhing arms of smoke which drew the trogs to where she slumbered. They were short and thick like the ginger roots they dug up and ate, pale and grey like the worming things in their underground caverns, and hard as the flint they fashioned into tools and weapons. So when they found her, soft and light, encased in a casket of glass and crystal, her hair feathery as something from the sky should be, they were immediately enchanted. They martialled offerings of daffodils like golden blunderbusses, and garlanded her cairn. They raised her on a bier of birchwood and brought offerings from the forest: wild roses, crab apples, fresh meat, honey.

In time the animals were enchanted too. They came to her bier and stared into the windows of her chamber, wondering what manner of creature she was. Her trogs began to sing to her, in their own glutinous tongue of gutteral sounds and grunts, which only made the birds sing louder and the rain pour harder. But gradually this forest serenade had another, more languorous effect. Tubers of twisting black hair began weaving through the birchwood bier and snaked through the ground itself. Later, these reaching roots anchored themselves into trees and shrubs, spreading like a web through the forest. Soon they were tunnelling through flesh, binding animals into a weird web of life. The trogs, disturbed by this, managed to step over the hair-fronds as they spread, but soon came to recognise their goddess as the source of the affliction.

Indeed, the woman's hair had grown wild, tangling through the length of her crystal chamber, which rainbowed like a prism where the sun struck through the torn canopy. The trogs took up their flint weapons and their crab apples and began pelting the chamber, hoping to free the mess of hair and the young woman from whom it spewed. Though their weapons were flimsy in the face of the crystal and glass, they eventually shattered the chamber and watched as the hair sprung loose in great vines.

The trogs' destruction of the sarcophagus only served to speed up the twisting progress of the woman's hair, as it invaded soil and flesh and plant alike. Soon the forest was threaded with her hair, made into a web of it, that connected every being to every other being, and to her. The trogs had either fled or become trapped, wed to her scalp forever in the spaces where they were suspended between trees, tethered by her locks.

A knight came by the forest one summer evening, dressed from head to toe in armour. Spying what he thought was a strange type of moss or creeper, he disembarked from his horse and came to the edge of the forest, where the trees were caught up in the hair. He examined the hair and found it silky smooth to the touch, but noticed too that it coiled forward towards him as he stood there. He instantly stepped back, but when the hair met the glinting steel of his armour, it flailed, then recoiled, seeping back into the forest. It seemed the hair, which sought to connect to the life around it, was unable to meld with the inorganic suit of armour.

Deciding it was best to leave his fleshly horse behind, he strode into the forest, cutting through the thickets and vast networks of webbing locks, and saw how they repaired themself after cutting. Determined to discover what lay at the heart of the forest—what cause was the root of this hair—he continued, till he reached the bier with its shattered coffin and its deathly, slumbering inhabitant. When he drew near, he realised she was indeed a corpse, albeit perfectly preserved. She didn't breathe or move or answer to his touch or his call. But she did pulse with some forbidden life. It was as though the hair itself siphoned life from the surrounding forest, making of it a circulatory system for her cadaver.

As the knight stood over her, he marvelled at how truly beautiful she was. Her face was poised in silence, but seemed now possessed of a distant satisfaction, a creeping smile that hinted at rising contentment at the point of her death. Her body was perfect, too, with its gentle curves and smooth, porcelain skin. Just then the knight knew he couldn't resist her, this goddess of the forest. He pressed his body against her, wishing he wore no armour, and leaned in for a kiss. His lips met hers and instantly something charged between them. He didn't realise, but the lips seemed to pull him in, locking him in embrace with her, as the coils of her silken hair slithered up his suit of armour, making for the exposed pink of his face. Within moments the hair had latched to him, fixing him, and the kiss seemed to become a sucking, as if of the very air from inside him. Then he slumped lifeless, his face grey and pale, and tumbled to the forest floor. The cadaver, now blushed with colour, lifted from her repose, stretching pristine limbs, and opened a mouth full of butterflies. The trees around her quivered, the vines coiled and snaked and pulsed, and the earth itself seemed to breathe.

As she looked about her, noticed the new texture her thorny hair had taken and felt the clay damp of her skin, the goddess of the sky realised she was reborn, and growled the laugh of wolves.

Adam Lowe is an award-winning 'all-round madman of letters' (according to Tom Bradley). He is a publisher, author and journalist. Originally from Leeds, he now lives in Manchester. He has held a number of residencies, including at I Love West Leeds Festival and Zion Arts Centre, and has had attachments with West Yorkshire Playhouse and the Royal Exchange Theatre. He has had commissions from the Cultural Olympiad (part of the London 2012 programme), BBC Radio 4 and BBC Writersroom, Freedom Studios, Contact Theatre, Theatre-in-the-Mill, Stage @ Leeds, Night Light and Conor McKee Productions.

His limited edition novella, Troglodyte Rose, *was nominated for two Lambda Literary Awards in 2009. Meanwhile, Adam's latest poetry collection,* Precocious, *has been selected for a GCSE coursework module at the Grammar School at Leeds. Transgressive in nature, it deals with such issues as cybersex, female genital mutilation and wanking off in the frozen food aisle in ASDA.*

TO THE STARS THAT FOOLED YOU
by John Palisano

And from her blood came demons. Small puddles congealed and formed wax-like shapes. Alex saw little nubs stretch out, morphing into small arms and legs which moved on their own. At their tips, three prongs poked forward, wiggling and sensing the Earth's air for the very first time. A reheated, rotten smell blossomed, reminding Alex of the stench fuming from the bums on Brooklyn Avenue.

Alex stepped closer. *These things are what John had been after*, he thought. *These little monsters were what made up his Nancy and had driven him over the edge.* She'd be free now, Alex knew. She'd also been unable to be saved; John knew that there was no repairing her. The demons had eaten far too much of Nancy for her to ever recover. There was only quiet inside her. *There was only quiet.*

"What time are you coming back tonight?" Alex looked to his father, who busily stashed pens and a sketchbook inside his courier bag.

"Probably around eight," said his father, who didn't turn around. "Maybe sooner. Who knows? You going to be okay?"

Alex nodded. "Sure," he said. "I was going to go to the movies today."

"Movies? Who needs to go to the movies when you're living here at Hotel Chelsea?"

Alex sat down in a chair, and as he did, he could smell the musty odor of the ashtray on the table near him. His father was silhouetted against the window. The sun was too bright for Alex to see anything outside the window. "I don't know," he said. "I like going outside sometimes, too."

239

"Of course. I get that. But the movies aren't outside. They're inside. I used to love just sitting in Washington Square and people-watching."

"I'll probably pass through there," he said. "But that place is getting filled with druggies."

His father grunted and zipped his bag. "Well, I'm sure you'll find something to keep you busy." He hurried up to his son, curled an arm around his neck, and planted his lips on top of his head. "All right," he said. "See you tonight."

Alex waved and stared at the door after his father had closed it. His guts felt tied up in knots. His eyes watered. Things were never going to be the same. For some reason, he knew that. For every reason he was glad his father was gone. *He's vulnerable. If he stuck around today, he'd be in trouble. What's coming today is no good. What's coming today is the worst kind of trouble.*

There was Pop, walking out the door to go to work. He's always at work—never at home. That's why Mom left him and we all split up. They're living in Ocean City, New Jersey, her and my brother. I'm in the city with a father who's never around. I feel like an orphan. I feel alone and underground, like a part of me has already died.

I dream of the big trees and the chorus of chirping birds where I could ride my bike around the neighborhood, along the sidewalks and in the streets. The cul-de-sac is still perfectly safe.

Back in Ocean City, the worst trouble came from the older neighborhood kids. He'd just turned thirteen, but they were eighteen. *Not here, though. Not in this place that always smells of heat and motor oil and gas and crowds.* The streets were nowhere near as crowded as they would become later in the afternoon.

New York ran faster and faster all the time, it seemed. People didn't look up when they were hurrying along; they stared straight ahead at invisible pinpoints several blocks away. *None of them even see me hovering among them, going to school, going out in search of food, going downtown to the record stores to look through the endless bins of cardboard and vinyl.* Alex smelled the slightly burned pretzel smoke drifting across the street. It reminded him of the stories his father told him of how he first came to New York and attended the Institute

Of Art and how he'd go up on the rooftop with the girls and kiss them. Whenever Alex passed the school he always stopped, looked up and tried to picture his father as a young man in his leather jacket and long hair, up there with some hippie chick gazing out over the nighttime New York skyline.

Sometimes he wandered inside the guitar stores on music row and thought he might pick one up and give it a try. *One day.* He'd use all the knowledge of records and *Creem* and *Rolling Stone* so that it'd all add up.

He passed 7th and made it to 6th without stopping. He knew he didn't have far to go to make it over to the Village. His stomach rumbled but he forgot about it, even as he passed his favorite Italian place by Saint Mark's. *Maybe one day I'll bring someone there*, he thought. *Maybe when I'm older and I'm in college or have my own money. That'll be cool.*

He passed the Bottom Line club, and remembered it from a few years back when his father and uncle had set lounge chairs on top of their garage, drank beer, and listened to a live broadcast from the club featuring Bruce Springsteen. He liked that the band sang some of the oldies his mother liked, but played them louder. Up until then he'd really just liked Kiss and the Partridge Family. Bruce changed that, and opened a door toward other artists like Bob Dylan, Woody Guthrie, and Neil Young. Walking past the club he smiled, remembering that night.

He was off to discover more diamonds amongst the stacks of LPs. Bleeker Street was the gateway. Crossing through Washington Square Park, he saw an old man strum an acoustic guitar. He was sloppy, and could barely play. Alex stared at the man and imagined what he'd look like younger. He fantasized that maybe one day he'd stumble upon some forgotten legend playing alone in just such a way, and that he would be friends with him and, well, he just better be ready for when that day came, because if he wasn't ready he'd miss out.

And that wasn't the half of it. Those were the kinds of thoughts that always seemed to race through Alex's mind whenever he walked through the city. Thinking back to his childhood, he remembered how, growing up in the suburbs, he had been devoid of any such thoughts. Instead, he would think about building a ramp to jump with his bike, or how high he'd be able to climb a tree before it wouldn't be able to support his weight. But there was something magnetic and inspiring to him about New York: The electricity he often heard mentioned by his older friends surged through him. That was what living in the heart of New York City gave Alex.

A plume of sweet, dry, toxic diesel smoke enveloped him and he covered his mouth with his hand. The sharp smell stayed high in his nose for several minutes and made his temples ache. *Man,* he thought. *What kind of crap are we breathing in? Why don't we just get rid of all the cars and make this city walking only? That'd be really cool.* All the transportation moved underground, which it already was anyway. *Science fiction,* he thought, *but if enough people stuck together, it could happen.*

Rounding the corner he saw a familiar row of stores and coffee shops. *I can never remember what all the streets are called. Maybe I will after a few more months of living here.* Then he was struck by an image of his mother and brother standing with him in the same spot a year earlier, and her giving them both ten dollars. That was before they hated him, because he had chosen his father's side in the fight.

"You would turn your back on your mother," she'd said.

And his brother scowled from behind her, wouldn't step forward. Nodding. Yes. Alex was the traitor. Wrong words were exchanged and a great divide carved between them.

But you cheated, mommy. You took the policeman home and we both heard what you were doing in there with him. We're old enough now to know. And the look on Pop's face when he came home early and put down his shoulder bag and went upstairs and I wanted to stop him so he wouldn't be hurt but he had to know just what you were up to. I could have distracted him and showed him something outside so you could hear him and Georgie sweet Georgie the cop you called him could sneak out the back door where the dogs go out and do their business. Just like you had to do your business, right mommy? You had to do it! Something inside compelled you. An itch you had to scratch that pop couldn't give you—wouldn't give you.

242

And there Alex stood, looking for something in the music that might take him away and make him remember the good times and forget the awful things. He listened to promises, and believed the dream.

There were never the same people behind the counters at the record stores. It wasn't that bad because he could be anonymous.

He went right to the middle of the stacks and flipped, stopping if he recognized a name or saw an intriguing album cover, especially if he spotted pretty girls, although he tried not to stop too long at those. He didn't want anyone making fun of him, or catching him . He made it to the 'S' category and found a Springsteen record in a plastic sleeve. The cover looked to have been handmade on a copy machine. He withdrew it and couldn't believe what he saw written on it: *The Bottom Line 8/15/75*. The same one he'd listened to with his father. He'd be able to relive that night forever. It was thirty dollars. He didn't have anywhere near that, but he tucked the LPs under his arm. How would he be able to get it? He didn't bring the emergency MasterCard his father gave him, either, because he was too scared he'd lose it.

"Hey, Buddy? Any way you hold things for people?"

The fellow behind the counter looked at Alex for a second before checking the store for other customers. "Depends what you want held," he said. "Let me see what you've got." He nodded once.

Alex produced the bootleg and the fellow's left cheek twinged. Alex didn't think the guy would approve. He had a safety pin stuck in his leather jacket, which probably meant he was a fashion punk. The nametag sewn into his shirt said his name was Phil.

"Aw, come on. Really? You're into that guy, too? What's everyone see in him?" asked Phil the Punk. Alex didn't understand why he was still wearing his Getty gas station shirt if he worked in the record store. Maybe he had two jobs.

"He's cool. And I heard this on the radio with my dad."

"You think your dad's cool?"

Alex hesitated. "Yeah. I do. He's a painter. Does movie posters

243

and stuff."

"My Dad's an asshole." Phil looked away. "Why do you want me to hold it? Why don't you just buy it? Doesn't your dad give you dough?"

"Not since we moved out from Mom."

"Oh. Got it. How much do you have?"

"Ten bucks."

Phil flipped the bootleg around. "Says it's thirty bucks." He reached under the counter and stole a sip on a Coca Cola.

"I can give you a deposit."

Shaking his head, Phil said. "I can't. Sorry. We don't do that here." Alex felt crestfallen as Phil looked away. Without looking, he said. "Just give me the ten and take it." He slipped it inside a brown bag and faced Alex. He pointed a finger right at his nose and lowered his voice. "But don't hang around. I don't want Bob seeing you leave with this."

Alex slipped the money from his pocket as fast as he could, slipping it on the table. "Here."

Phil handed him the bootleg. "Enjoy. And go have some fun." He stood and shook his hand. As he did Alex noticed him putting the ten into his own pocket. "What?" he asked,

"Nothing."

"Damn right it's nothing," Phil said. "We got to do what we got to do, right? Cheap old Bob could afford to pay me a lot more anyway."

Alex felt simultaneously flush and pale. Was he stealing? If this Bob guy showed up, would he be caught and get in trouble?

"Okay," he said. "I appreciate it."

"Whatever." Phil turned away and Alex scurried out of the record store into the warm October air. His stomach hurt from both being hungry and nervous. He'd spent his last dollar on the record.

It was getting dark out much earlier and Alex really wanted to be done with everything he had to do before night fell. Not only that, but being able to beat his father home would be perfect. He pictured himself plopping the first side of the bootleg record on his little portable battery-operated player. His father would come home, open the door, and would hopefully enjoy the music once again. But first, he spotted a smallish box of LPs near the front door of a record store across the street. Someone had written 'FREE' in magic marker on a piece of cardboard and laid it on top of the records.

Kneeling in front of the box with the bootleg resting against him, Alex flipped through the discs. Most of them were educational, or sound effects, or in foreign languages. But near the back he discovered a Sinatra LP so worn that the black cover looked gray. Instinctively, Alex slipped the vinyl from the cardboard. There was no sleeve, but the vinyl seemed to be in decent shape. *Probably very playable*, he thought. He returned it to its cover and stood, looking around for a moment. He was sure there had to be some catch to it. After several seconds of no one chasing him away, or even looking twice his way, Alex walked away with his free record. He'd scored well and didn't want to push his luck. His head did hurt though, and he knew he needed food. Luckily for him, when he straightened his legs he felt the unmistakable poke of loose change in his pocket. He couldn't figure out why he'd gotten so lucky, but he bought a Reggie bar and a Coke and made it all the way home.

When Alex walked through the lobby he felt a chill in his gut. The baby hairs on his forearms stood up and his eyes watered. There was nothing he could see, and the room was empty. Regardless, he had to wipe tears from face. From the edges of the room, he imagined unseen things sizing him up. Something bad, he thought. Some kind of sticky darkness painted the room. Dangerous vibes stopped him cold.

Follow your gut. If something seems wrong, than it probably is. That was his father's advice he heard in his head.

But where else could I go?

He stepped closer to the front stairway. His stomach tightened and his ears warmed up. Another set of voices echoed downward.

"You can't possibly need more," someone said. "I've been

245

here four times in the past two days and it's just the two of you."
The new voice sounded hyper—angry. This was not a person Alex
wanted to know.

*Don't go up there. Stay away. Come back later. There's bad stuff
going down.*

Despite himself, Alex approached the top landing of the
stairs. The group spoke loudly. At first he couldn't place the accents,
but soon recognized one of the men as Russian. Alex slinked down
and Alex did his best to stay out of their line of sight

A second voice, this time, a high-pitched woman. "Don't say
that, Rocket. We lost a whole bit of it when Stevie came by. He took
a lot of it."

"Forget it, Nancy," Rocket said. "There's no way I'm going to
have either of you two bringing me down with you. See you later."

A man's voice, British, each word slow and slurred. "Shut up!
You're a wanker! You'll be back!" He nearly spit the last word.

The people sounded like they were on his floor. Just what he
was trying to avoid. Alex ascended the staircase. *Maybe if I hurry
they won't see me and I can . . .*

"Hey, kid! You're here just in time to meet your new
neighbors."

Alex couldn't believe his bad luck. Jack waved him closer. For
a second Alex wished he could turn around and run out of the Hotel
Chelsea, unseen.

"You're going to love these two."

"Really?"

"Yeah." He gestured to Alex. "This kid knows more about
music than I do for cryin' out loud."

Alex finally got to see who was speaking when a lanky
pale fellow with spiked black hair leaned out from a doorway. His
eyes were bloodshot, but kind. Cigarette smoke poured out of the
bedroom behind him.

"Hey Sid? Who's the kid?"

Sid looked back into the room then to Alex. "What's your
name, Mate?"

Alex told him, and gave him a good firm shake.

Sid pulled his hand back. "Ah man, come on. Imagine I'm going to need that now, aren't I?"

Clutching his albums close to his chest, all Alex could think of was lifting the lid on his record player and listening to his new music.

"What you got with you there? That what I think it is. Um. No. Probably not. Can't be."

Sid reached out and grabbed the records. He glanced over the Sinatra record, even turning it around to read the songs.

He studied the Springsteen bootleg for a few moments.

"What are you doing? Sid? What're you looking at?" Nancy asked.

"This is a strange record."

"Yup."

"Why don't you all come inside here? I'm lonely."

Something was wrong. Alex sensed it in Nancy's voice. She sounded like she'd been hurt or injured. Without even seeing her, Alex pictured her thin and tired face.

"This is some ancient music for a little guy to be listening to."

"I don't know," Alex said. "A good song's a good song. Don't matter who sings it."

"Sid?"

He looked at Alex a minute, seemed as though he were really pondering what he'd heard. "Maybe. But once in a while things are about a lot more than just the song."

Then it was Alex's turn to stare. Sid toyed with what looked like a dog collar around his neck, clamped shut with a small padlock.

What does that mean? Alex thought. *Is he like a dog? An animal that needs to be leashed? He doesn't look strong. He doesn't care if he gets hurt. Doesn't care if he bleeds. Likes pain. Enjoys bleeding.*

Alex nodded. "Yeah, I get it."

"Sid? Sid? *Sid?*"

His smiled slid from the center of his mouth to one corner, folding his face in a snarl. Can I borrow this? He showed Alex the

Sinatra LP.

"Okay." Alex didn't think he'd ever see it again.

Sid nodded and crept around.

"Sid?"

"We got some music to listen to."

Alex kept still. He didn't want to turn his back to them and Sid had gone inside his apartment without shutting the door.

"How are we going to listen to that? We don't even have a record player."

"Ah, whatever. We'll borrow one." Alex heard kissing sounds and groans. Before he got any more involved he rushed away to his room.

Blood dribbles from her mouth. A bloom of orange light descends inside the building. The Angel Gabriel calls, just like his mother used to warn him. *Angel Gabriel comes for everyone when it's your turn to go to the Promised Land.* Tonight he travels through the rooms and the halls following the scent of spilled whiskey and thinned bowels, of empty, hungry souls. Blood rolls across fingers. Sticky, watery, tainted yellow. Fingers that once caressed and made a heart open where it was once closed, the orange light pilots them to open her with the pocket knife.

She won't feel it. She can't feel anything, anyway. He hears the whispers. *It's not you. Nancy needs this. Start things over for her. Wish Baby.* Someone's little girl grown too fast like a bundle of ripe grapes too early in the season. *Be the sun that dries them and lets them fall. There will be unthinkable pain to come if you don't and you wouldn't want that, would you?*

The top of his thumb presses against her belly and he can't see the hilt of the knife underneath. He can't feel it anymore. He remembers how the fine baby hairs on her stomach felt—how clean and salty her skin tasted. This would be their last touch and he felt cold and detached. He looks in the mirror to check if he is crying because he can't tell—none of his nerves are working.

A stranger looks back at him from the mirror. The man has

black skin, dark as the underground. He blinks and the man looks like Jet. Behind Jet he can see Steve sitting on the bed strumming his white Les Paul. *That already happened. This already happened.* He looks down and she's crawled away from him under the sink. There's no one in the mirror except Sid. No one. He's sad. *Never more alone.*

"Don't want to leave a mess for you, Sid," she mumbles. "There's water in here. I can clean everything up. No big deal. Just let me sleep. I'm tired, Sid. He gave us some bad shit, is all."

He finds himself standing back several feet away and looking in on the bathroom, where his Baby, his Angel Girl, rests. The knife is on the ground and he checks his hand. It is clean and her blood is not there. He is clean. She is clean. He hears something behind him and sees a face in the hallway he recognizes but just can't place. The face is in darkness and shade. Is it the Italian? The Iranian? The Puerto Rican? Or is it the shade making their skin darker? Gabriel is leaving, his duty fulfilled.

Where's the boy?

Sid screams his name.

The Hotel Chelsea vibrated and Alex sat straight up, believing he heard someone yelling his name. *What the heck is that?* He looked around his room and expected to see his father. Then he remembered that his father said he wasn't coming home and asked if he'd be all right. He was going to spend the night at Judy's place. Judy—the new woman. She was prettier than his mother, and nowhere near as mean. Not yet, at least. His father told him that they all get old and mean eventually. *And what about Nancy?* He wanted to ask his father. *She's already old and mean. What does that mean?*

Someone was playing music loudly. He could barely tell what the song was it was so distorted, but he focused and figured it out.

Frank Sinatra. "My Way."

Am I going to get in trouble for this? I gave him that record. The last thing he wanted to do was to jeopardize them having a place to live. Not that he believed the Hotel Chelsea was perfect, but his father loved the Hotel.

He kept waiting for someone to yell to turn it down, but no one did. The song was almost over as Alex crept from his bed and inched towards his front door. Just as it ended Alex perked up and put his ear against the door.

The record player was so loud he could hear the needle dropping on the grooves. He waited for someone to holler and scold Sid. Instead, the song started again.

He stood from the door and went to the bathroom. It was almost noon and he couldn't believe he'd slept so late. Alex was supposed to meet his father—supposed to go to the studios and meet up for lunch. Later they were all supposed to go out for dinner. His mother was coming into the city to try an. "...figure a few things out." Of course, Alex was skeptical. The last thing he wanted to do was to head face-first back into the abusive, unkind life in Ocean City. Anything was better than that, even listening to someone blast Frank Sinatra records in the hallway.

Alex got in the shower and started getting clean. The song was so loud he was beginning to think it was playing inside his own head.

No. Not that. It's still coming from the outside. Go in and do what you have to do. He's trying to make you crazy on purpose so you will go outside in the hallway and they'll be there.

He pictured them standing there, covered in blood, covered in white, foamy, soap. They were trying to get clean. Wash away the pain with soap and gore. Bleed out and clean out. Bleed away and clean away. That was it. Yes. Yes. Yes. Their eyes were vacant. Their hearts colorless and albino, beating outside emaciated bodies. Sid hands him the records, a smear of blood-tainted mucous left behind from his hand. Alex doesn't want to touch it. *Because sometimes it's about more than just the music.* He could hear Sid in his head. Alex washed harder and quicker and tried to think if he could go out through the fire escape or one of the other ways. There was nothing he could think of. The Hotel Chelsea just wasn't built that way, not from where they were. Damn. *Maybe if I hurry up and get out of here fast enough they won't see me.*

The music stopped.

Sirens.

Finally someone had called the police. Alex heard voices. Footsteps filled the hallway. *What had taken them so long?* New York certainly wasn't like Ocean City, where if you called the police they were there in their squad cars within a few minutes. Maybe that's what everyone meant when they said living in the city was hard and cold. He wanted very badly to run away out into the street, and get on the subway, and to see his father. He'd tell him that they couldn't live there any more, that things had changed, and that bad people had come to lay their hats with them. Not a place for a young boy, nope. Not even a place for most normal people. Yes, he was normal. He wasn't like them and he was fine with that. And so was his father. And so what?

Two knocks.

Was it his door? Was it the one next door?

Alex didn't want to answer. He hopped on his bed, and wrapped the blankets over himself. They probably had heard him in the shower. They probably heard that he was in there. Damn it! He was still wet. There was no knock. Alex grabbed his clothes, which he'd laid out on the foot of his bed, and put them on as fast as he could. Then he got right back into bed, right back under the covers, right back underneath.

What are they going to do? Come in here? This is my fault. I shouldn't have ever let him have that record. I think I spurred him into doing something. It was me that inspired all this. And something bad's happened. Something terrible.

Bam!

The knock nearly sent him flying from his bed it was so loud. He wished his father was with him and hadn't abandoned him by going to work. If only he hadn't been alone through all this.

"Alex?" The voice was familiar. "You home?" His father. "I forgot my keys." Could it really be his father after all? Could it really have been just the right person. "Alex?" his father sounded less patient, and nervous.

He didn't want to answer, afraid that it might be an impostor.

251

It seemed too good to be true. How could his father know he was in trouble? How would he have known while he was a t work?

Then he heard the key jangling and there was some mumbling. "Okay, okay, thanks." The door opened and he saw his father being let in by the building's superintendent.

Stopping for a moment, his father regarded Alex. "You okay?"

Alex didn't see the Superintendent, but heard him.. "Kid's scared. Look at him."

"Okay, okay," said his father. "Thanks. Let me talk to him."

"Alex?" he said. "I saw something on the news. There's been some bad stuff this morning. We need to go." His father rushed to him and hugged him. "I'm so glad you're okay."

He couldn't say anything back for several minutes. As they walked out from their apartment and down the stairs, he saw the policeman ganging around Sid's room. For a moment he got a glimpse inside. It looked as he'd remembered it, although there was no cigarette smoke. Someone took a picture and he saw blood on the rug. Black, branch—shaped pools of inky spilled chocolate syrup. It was out in the hallway, too. He couldn't help remembering that he'd been standing there only yesterday, in the same spot, where he'd given Sid his free Frank Sinatra record. And now, in a blink, everything had changed. Everything went still. Everything went black, and Alex and his father never looked back.

John Palisano's journey to horror fiction is a strange one. For a while he toured with with rock bands, while writing songs, poetry and fiction. His first fiction publication was at Emerson College, where a short film was produced from an early foray into scriptwriting. After college he moved to Los Angeles, where he took an internship with Ridley Scott. He learned much, and worked on many big budget films, as well as producing a couple of low-budget films himself. But he found the demands of filmmaking tiring and instead began writing fiction. He discovered that placing his stories with professional magazines was more difficult than financing films, but he continued to write anyway. Many years later, he now faces the impending release of his novel Nerves *from Bad Moon Books, which is due out in the winter of 2012. In the meantime, he has lots of short stories appearing soon, and several movie projects, too.*

Out Now:
Women Writing the Weird
Edited by Deb Hoag

WEIRD

1.   Eldritch: suggesting the operation of supernatural influences; "an eldritch screech"; "the three weird sisters"; "stumps . . . had uncanny shapes as of monstrous creatures" —John Galsworthy; "an unearthly light"; "he could hear the unearthly scream of some curlew piercing the din" —Henry Kingsley

2.   Wyrd: fate personified; any one of the three Weird Sisters

3.   Strikingly odd or unusual; "some trick of the moonlight; some weird effect of shadow" —Bram Stoker

WEIRD FICTION

1.   Stories that delight, surprise, that hang about the dusky edges of 'mainstream' fiction with characters, settings, plots that abandon the normal and mundane and explore new ideas, themes and ways of being. —Deb Hoag

RRP: £14.99 ($28.95).

featuring

Nancy A. Collins, Eugie Foster, Janice Lee, Rachel Kendall, Candy Caradoc, Mysty Unger, Roberta Lawson, Sara Genge, Gina Ranalli, Deb Hoag, C. M. Vernon, Aliette de Bodard, Caroline M. Yoachim, Flavia Testa, Aimee C. Amodio, Ann Hagman Cardinal, Rachel Turner, Wendy Jane Muzlanova, Katie Coyle, Helen Burke, Janis Butler Holm, J.S. Breukelaar, Carol Novack, Tantra Bensko, Nancy DiMauro, and Moira McPartlin.

Out Now:
Bite Me, Robot Boy
Edited by Adam Lowe

Bite Me, Robot Boy is a seminal new anthology of poetry and fiction that showcases what Dog Horn Publishing does best: writing that takes risks, crosses boundaries and challenges expectations. From Oz Hardwick's hard-hitting experimental poetry, to Robert Lamb's colourful pulpy science fiction, this is an anthology of incandescent writing from some of the world's best emerging talent.

Featuring
S.R. Dantzler, Oz Hardwick, Maximilian T. Hawker, Emma Hopkins, A.J. Kirby, Stephanie Elizabeth Knipe, Robert Lamb, Poppy Farr, Wendy Jane Muzlanova, Cris O'Connor, Mark Wagstaff, Fiona Ritchie Walker and KC Wilder.

Out Now:
Cabala
Edited by Adam Lowe

From gothic fairytale to humorous pop-culture satire, five of the North's top writers showcase the diversity of British talent that exists outside the country's capital and put their strange, funny, mythical landscapes firmly on the literary map.

Over the course of ten weeks, Adam Lowe worked with five budding writers as part of the Dog Horn Masterclass series. This anthology collects together the best work produced both as a result of the masterclasses and beyond.

Featuring
Jodie Daber, Richard Evans, Jacqueline Houghton, Rachel Kendall and A.J. Kirby

Out Now:
Nitrospective
Andrew Hook

Japanese school children grow giant frogs, a superhero grapples with her secret identity, onions foretell global disasters and an undercover agent is ambivalent as to which side he works for and why. Relationships form and crumble with the slightest of nudges. World catastrophe is imminent; alien invasion blase. These twenty slipstream stories from acclaimed author Andrew Hook examine identity and our fragile existence, skid skewed realities and scratch the surface of our world, revealing another—not altogether dissimilar—layer beneath.

Nitrospective is Andrew Hook's fourth collection of short fiction.

RRP: £12.99 ($22.95).

Acclaim for the Author

"Andrew Hook is a wonderfully original writer" —Graham Joyce

"His stories range from the darkly apocalyptic to the hopefully visionary, some brilliant and none less than satisfactory"
—*The Harrow*

"Refreshingly original, uncompromisingly provocative, and daringly intelligent" —*The Future Fire*

ND - #0155 - 270225 - C0 - 229/152/15 - PB - 9781907133343 - Gloss Lamination